12/2017

THE
BREATHLESS

THE
BREATHLESS

TARA GOEDJEN

DELACORTE PRESS

Text copyright © 2017 by Tara Goedjen
Jacket art copyright © 2017 by Arcangel and Shutterstock

Visit us on the Web! randomhouseteens.com

Educators and librarians, for a variety of teaching tools, visit us at RHTeachersLibrarians.com

Library of Congress Cataloging-in-Publication Data
Names: Goedjen, Tara, author.
Title: The breathless / Tara Goedjen.
Description: First edition. | New York : Delacorte Press, [2017] |
Summary: Sixteen-year-old Mae Cole is determined to uncover who is responsible for her sister's mysterious death, but Mae's search takes a terrifying turn when she starts to dig up long-buried secrets about her family's dark past.
Identifiers: LCCN 2016040460 | ISBN 978-1-5247-1476-5 (hc) |
ISBN 978-1-5247-1477-2 (glb) | ISBN 978-1-5247-1478-9 (el) |
ISBN 978-1-5247-7068-6 (intl. tr. pbk.)
Subjects: | CYAC: Death—Fiction. | Secrets—Fiction.
Classification: LCC PZ7.1.G62 Br 2017 | DDC [Fic]—dc23

The text of this book is set in 12-point Janson Text.
Interior design by Jaclyn Whalen

Printed in the United States of America
10 9 8 7 6 5 4 3 2 1
First Edition

Random House Children's Books supports the First Amendment and celebrates the right to read.

For my mom

I looked with timorous joy towards a stately house:
I saw a blackened ruin.

—CHARLOTTE BRONTË, *Jane Eyre*

We die with the dying:
See, they depart, and we go with them.
We are born with the dead:
See, they return, and bring us with them.

—T. S. ELIOT, *Four Quartets*

PROLOGUE

IT ISN'T A NIGHT FOR raising. It isn't night yet at all. It's a hazy gray afternoon, with the promise of rain. A layer of fog covers Blue Gate and the woods that surround it, but we can see inside the windows.

Here a family gathers at the kitchen table near a girl with hair that gleams. Her green eyes have a hint of gold, and she is a pretty thing. The kind of girl everyone points to and says: something big is going to happen to her one day.

Today is her sixteenth birthday. In two years she'll be dead, but she doesn't know that. What she knows is a secret. It's shiny and tempting, glistening like the girl's blond hair. But she doesn't tell anyone—not yet.

Her father carries in the red velvet cake with pink candles. Somehow he has never figured out that his girls don't like pink. Like all fathers, there are so many things he doesn't know. He just wants to see his trio of daughters as perfect, he wants to believe they are happy and normal and safe. But who is ever safe?

His oldest girl blows out the candles, and then after her stomach is full of sweetness, she tugs on her quiet sister's hand. "Come with me."

"All right," the quiet sister says. She is good at saying yes, and this will get her into trouble later. Thirteen and small for her age, she trails Ro upstairs like a shadow.

"Listen," Ro says, "there's more to our family than you've ever imagined." She does this, makes grand statements—when she speaks, everything seems bigger. The younger sister wants to be exactly like her when she grows up. "The stories are real," Ro says. "I'll show you."

She pulls her sister into her bedroom with a body sculpted from swimming, her white tank top revealing strong tan shoulders. She grins, a bright smile that makes people feel special and loved. The younger sister looks at these things and thinks, *How will I ever be like her?*

"There it is. I found it in the house." Ro's voice is filled with awe. Sitting on her desk is a book. It is old and green and thicker than the Bible. "Go ahead," Ro says, "open it." But the younger sister remembers their grandfather's words, and her body goes stiff.

"Don't be scared," Ro whispers, her sugary breath at the girl's ear. "Trust me, okay? I want us to share this."

So they sit down on the bed together and look at one page, just one. The very last page of the book. It has a thumbprint in the bottom corner, and staring at that smudge makes the younger sister's world go dark.

Neither girl realizes that life is both good and bad, dark and light—the way it has been since the beginning of time. Neither of them can see the shadows swirling around them, hovering close, because all shadows are drawn to the light. She is a bright one—this older sister, this sixteen-year-old girl who melts everyone she touches. But a single flame is not enough to hold back the world's darkness.

Like we told you, she will be dead soon. So it happens. Though when a light goes out, it can be raised again. You just need a book that is like a box of matches.

CHAPTER 1

STEAM SETTLED OVER THE BATHROOM mirror. In the candlelight, Mae traced a name on the glass. The more she stared at it, the sicker she felt. When she couldn't take it anymore, she stepped out of the pile of wet clothes at her feet and eased into the hot bath. A flush shot through her body, all the way to her toes, and she watched the paint streaks running from her hands in faint trails of color.

Mae thought of her sister and shut her eyes, trying to block out everything else. Small waves sloshed against the cracked sides of the tub, and she turned on the faucet so it was dripping, making ripples. There was a slight lift underneath her, that feeling of being raised by the water. She'd read once that you could rid yourself of pain by pretending you were floating outside your body. Or you could breathe into it, make yourself feel the edges of the pain, try to find the end of it.

Inhale, exhale. Inhale. Mae dunked her head and held herself down, needing to know what her sister had felt.

5

She opened her eyes under the water and looked at the dark ceiling, at her hair floating out in wavy strands. Then over at the foggy mirror, the melting white candles by the sink, the rusting tub. That waterline above her— the surface so close with the promise of air. Her lungs were burning, but she forced herself to stay under, staring at the line of water like a horizon, her chest hot and tight. Ro was found on the shore, the tide at her legs. Her head bloody, with no other sign of struggle. Ro dead and everyone blaming Cage Shaw.

When her lungs were about to burst, Mae finally shot up for air, gulping it in. It was hard to drown yourself, maybe impossible, unless there was something or someone holding you down.

She took in deep breaths as water coursed over her eyes. It was like being outside earlier that day, when she'd tried to capture the rainstorm on canvas. Painting was the one thing that helped her forget. Now that it was summer and school was out, she couldn't rely on the noise and bodies of the other kids to crowd out the dark thoughts, so she painted instead, kept her hands moving. If she had more friends it might help, but she didn't want to answer questions about Ro, or go to parties with Elle and drink until she forgot. So today she'd set up her easel on the porch while the rain had poured from the sky, loud enough to water down her thoughts into colors.

The other way to get rid of pain was to shove it behind a door in your mind and hope it didn't leak out. Mae had assigned a door for all the memories that hurt. Black was the color of Ro's door. Her mother's was pale yellow. A red door held back her dad's anger. And her granddad's was white, the color of the milk and brandy she took to him when he couldn't sleep and couldn't find the words to ask for it. All the doors had faded to the back of her mind—all except for Ro's.

The black door usually kept the memories from seeping through, which was a good thing. You could wish a thousand times that something hadn't happened, but you couldn't undo it. You couldn't feel sorry for yourself either, because then you'd just rot, starting with your heart. Mae wasn't going to rot. She would paint until her fingers fell off before she did that. She'd keep the doors shut tight.

She held out her hands. Her fingertips were starting to wrinkle, but at least the paint was gone. The bathwater was warm against her skin, her knees were sticking up like two little islands in the flickering candlelight. A breeze was coming from the bathroom window, leaking through the cracked glass pane, and outside everything was dripping. Her lids went heavier and heavier. Things would get better; maybe all it took was time. . . .

A noise startled her upright.

Mae gasped because the bath was cold, like ice. The room was dark now. Every candle had burned down to a pool of wax. She must have fallen asleep. It was so cold in the water, colder than the air.

A faint glow of moonlight was coming from the window, and the rain had stopped. All the fog was gone from the mirror but somehow *Roxanne* was still there, in thin smears across the glass. The name looked strange now; it didn't look like her handwriting at all.

Mae got out and wrapped a towel around herself, drying off over the uneven tiles. In the mirror was a shadow: long hair, dark eyes. She was going to smile more this year—she was going to try harder, like Ro would have wanted.

As she got dressed, she heard someone singing in the hallway. Maybe Elle was still awake? She yanked her shirt over her wet hair and then pulled on her sister's red sweatshirt, thin with a zip up the front, the one she hadn't washed since it happened. She breathed in the scent—cloves and mint—then stepped out of the bathroom.

Elle's room was quiet and dark, and so was Sonny's. Mae heard the sound again, now more of a whisper. Probably just Elle talking on the phone, but something felt off. Her heart started thudding as she moved deeper into the shadows, passing the long railing that overlooked the foyer and the old chandelier that trembled with her steps.

The humming—it seemed more like humming than whispering—grew louder the farther she walked over the cold floorboards. Prickles raced across her skin when she got to the end of the hallway. The noise was coming from Ro's room.

Mae's heart quickened. She leaned toward the door, listening.

Nothing. There was nothing, because no one went into this room anymore. But she had heard . . . *what?* There was only silence now on the other side of the wood.

She wasn't supposed to go in—her dad's rule. She touched the brass handle, and then opened the door and fumbled for the light switch.

Overhead, the bulb flared bright and burned out. She blinked in the dark, her fist tightening around the handle.

"Who's there?"

Moonlight was shining through the curtained window, casting shadows.

"Elle?" she whispered. Then, because she couldn't help herself: "Ro?"

She wasn't getting enough air; she really might faint. The room was dark, empty. She had expected to see her twin, or even her granddad, but there was no one. Just the shapes of furniture no longer used. Piles of clothes that hadn't been worn in almost a year, books that hadn't been opened.

Then she whirled. A soft tapping noise was coming from the wardrobe. In the murky haze she could see its door was ajar.

Mae forced herself to step all the way into the bedroom. The tapping was louder—it sounded like her granddad's cane striking wood, *tap thud, tap thud, tap*. It was coming from the side of the wardrobe, behind its open door.

She took a step closer, willing her heart to stop beating so hard. In front of the wardrobe she hesitated, and then she pulled the door back.

Ro's jewelry box was on the ground, overturned. Its gears were whirring and stopping, whirring and stopping.

Mae stared at it, relief making her legs go watery. On top of the lid, the delicate ballerina twitched, hitting the floor over and over. One of its ceramic legs had broken off, but the rest of it was intact, its arms clasped together like a halo as it shuddered.

Her dad wanted this room kept exactly how it was—he needed it that way. She scooped up the jewelry that had spilled: dangly feather earrings, threaded shell bracelets, a gold locket, the sand dollars Ro had kept for good luck. Her sister's wide bangles were scattered across the floor, and she gathered them up one by one, then found a ring by the bookshelf.

Strange—a ring she'd never seen before. She picked it up and held it in the moonlight. It was a gold band studded with tear-shaped rubies. It looked like an antique. The black door in her mind creaked open, and it came to her. This was the ring Ro had been wearing that last day. Elle must have rescued it, stored it away in the jewelry box.

Mae turned it over in her hand and then slid it onto her finger. It was too big, so she took it off, slipped it into the jewelry box, and put the box back on the wardrobe.

As she turned to leave, the curtains billowed out. A breeze swept through the room, and Ro's sketches on the wall fluttered. Mae tensed on instinct and then almost laughed aloud. The old windows in the house opened outward and sometimes rattled loose in the wind. Some animal, probably a squirrel, had gotten in and tipped the jewelry box off the wardrobe.

She closed the latch and turned to go again, but as she

stepped around the edge of the mattress she kicked something sharp. It skidded across the floor and under the bed. Another piece of jewelry? She crouched down to grab it and froze, her hand outstretched.

Lying beneath the bed was a leather book.

Mae stared at it a moment and then pulled it out, a knot tightening in her stomach. Just as she started to open it, a floorboard creaked in the hallway. She shoved the small book into her sweatshirt pocket and hurried out of the room, closing the door behind her as softly as she could. One side of her sweatshirt was heavy now, dragged down by the weight in her pocket. She'd made it halfway through the hallway and had almost reached her own room when—

"Mae?"

She spun around, startled. Her dad was standing in the dark with a glass in his hand. "Thought I was the only one awake."

"Me too," she said, her voice coming out strained. But he hadn't seen her in Ro's bedroom—he wouldn't be this calm.

Sonny held up his drink. "Nightcap." He was in jeans and a T-shirt, like he hadn't gone to sleep yet and wasn't planning to. He turned, and Mae thought that was the end of it, but he waved her on. "Come downstairs."

"I—" Mae started, but her dad cut her off.

"Come on, you need a glass of milk," he said. "It'll help you sleep."

She nodded. It was clear she had no choice but to

have the milk, but she didn't know what to expect. Sonny mostly kept to himself; a conversation alone with him was new territory.

Mae followed him down the curving staircase, the book heavy in her pocket, as if aching to be read. He flipped on the light in the kitchen and she blinked at the brightness. It hit the windows and the French doors that opened into the overrun garden. Light streamed over the stone cherub by the roses and the pink lantanas and trickled onto the high green hedge. Everything was still glistening from the rain.

Sonny grabbed a saucepan and poured milk into it. "Trick is," he said, "can't heat it up too long or it makes that sticky layer on top."

"That's the milk skin," Mae murmured. "It's from the protein, Dad."

He shot her a look and then switched off the stove, his long ponytail swaying across his back. He always told them to use his first name, though he never said why. Maybe that was less painful, since there was no one to call Mom.

"Try it." He tipped the milk into a mug and set it on the table next to his glass of whiskey. His chair groaned as he lowered himself into it. "When I was a kid, your grandpa would heat up milk when I was scared and couldn't sleep."

"He did?" Mae stilled—it felt like if she moved, her dad would stop talking. Sonny never talked about when he was young. He never talked much to anyone, though neither did she. "What else did he do?" she pressed.

He held his whiskey, seemed to think a moment. "I'd get nightmares. Blue Gate seemed so old, even back then. Your grandpa would read me stories about magic. Said it could protect me." His face broke into a smile, the way it hadn't in a long time.

Mae's hands flexed—she wanted to draw him like this. She edged into the seat beside him, cupped her palms around the warm milk. "And then what happened?"

He swirled the whiskey, the scent sharp and heady. "And then I grew up, Mae, and I told him he was full of shit."

She winced. Her granddad didn't stand a chance against Sonny. He took a sip of his drink and looked at her. "I found the back door open today."

"Oh." Her heart dropped; the milk was just a trap. He'd only sat her down for another lecture. Why had she thought this was somehow different? "I'll make sure it's locked next time." It shouldn't have been open; both she and Elle were so careful.

Sonny let out a sigh, scratched at his hair. "You girls think I'm too hard on you."

He didn't know the half of it. Didn't know how she tiptoed around the house, waiting for him to turn like when the sky darkens with a sudden storm.

"I only want to keep you safe," he said.

"I know." She tilted the mug to drink so she wouldn't have to say anything more. Elle knew how to push until he snapped, and sometimes she knew right where to stop, but Mae didn't like that in-between ground where anything she said could be taken the wrong way. Instead, whenever she felt like yelling at him, she shoved all her anger through the bright red door in her mind and slammed it shut.

"I think he might come back one of these days," Sonny went on, "and when he does, I'll be ready."

Mae coughed, choking on the milk. She knew exactly who he was talking about. She set her mug down hard, but her dad didn't seem to notice. "How do you . . ." She cleared her throat. "Why do you think he did it?"

Sonny shrugged, his eyes going dark. "He was always dwelling on her."

She straightened in her seat, grasped her mug tighter. Arguing with him wouldn't help, and neither would talking about Ro. Every time she said Ro's name it was like she'd hit him, and Sonny didn't like getting hit.

"Dad . . ." She forced herself to speak. "Whatever happened, it's not your fault."

It's not anyone's fault, she wanted to add, but she didn't know that for sure. No one did. Not yet. She shoved her hands into her pockets, felt the edge of the book she'd taken.

"You're a good kid, Mae," he said, but he didn't look at her, just swirled his glass of whiskey. "You know, with fishing, there's a lot of time to think, sometimes too much. It can pull you down in the bad thoughts, if you're not careful."

That must be why he'd quit. Why he hadn't worked

since Ro died. She took a sip of the milk, held it on her tongue. She didn't know how to make him feel better, so she said what she'd been wanting to hear. "It's going to be okay."

He shook his head, his shoulders tight. "I just don't know, Mae." She caught the sharp scent of his drink as he lifted the glass. "Maybe one day you'll understand what it's like to be a father."

"No," she said. "I don't think I'll ever understand what it's like to be a father."

Sonny looked at her and for a moment it seemed he might smile again, like she'd said the right thing. Instead he sighed. "You should be asleep." He stood, drained his whiskey. "I'm headed that way myself."

At the doorway he stopped, and she saw that his pistol was tucked into the back of his jeans—he'd been carrying it around since it happened. Her stomach twisted.

"I count myself lucky to be your dad, Mae Eliza." He was turned from her, already walking off, so she could hardly hear him. "Must have done something right, huh?"

Her eyes watered and she felt a knot in her throat. She didn't know whether she was happy he'd said it or sad because she'd never live up to Ro. Ro had been his favorite and with her gone, he was just going through the motions.

Mae stayed at the table, listening to the floorboards creak as he went upstairs. She was tired of worrying about him, tired of not being able to say her sister's name aloud, and she didn't know how much longer they could last without answers.

She waited until she heard his door close and then pulled the book from her pocket. In the light of the empty kitchen its leather looked greenish and old. It was small, the size of her hands held together side to side, but it was thick and tied shut with a ribbon. The back cover was missing, torn off completely, but the front cover was etched with two dark coffins.

It was her sister's green book. The one Ro had found in the house and swore was a secret, the first and only time she'd shown Mae.

And here it was again.

Mae weighed it in her palms. It felt heavy, its leather almost warm. A gritty resolve settled in her stomach, and for the first time in nearly a year she didn't feel so aimless—she knew what she had to do. When she stood to turn off the light, she could feel Ro beside her, whispering with her red velvet breath, *Open it, Mae, open it.*

CHAPTER 2

CAGE WOKE WITH A LOUD gasp like he was drowning. Whiteness was everywhere—sea foam. He blinked. It was a ceiling, the old kind with those white popcorn bubbles. He tried to sit up, but his arm snagged on something and his head felt like it'd been hit with a tire iron.

He got a flash of memory, saw his motorcycle upside down in a steep ravine with thick kudzu at the bottom. He'd been stuck in it—tangled in green leaves, their vines pulling at him, and . . . nothing else came to him. Except a fight with Ro. As soon as the thought snaked through his mind it left, like a sheet pulled over his memory. And now he was in a bed, but not his own.

Another sharp stab at his arm, and he looked down to find a needle in his vein. His eyes followed the tube up to a bag of fluids hanging from a silver hook. He turned his head and nearly pitched to the side with dizziness as a searing light tore through his vision. Beside the window was a curtain, splitting the room in half, and she was standing at the door.

Thank the good Lord. Maybe she could fill him in, tell him what the hell he was doing in a hospital.

"Ro?"

She stepped toward him. "You're awake."

The voice was all wrong. It was tinny, shrill. His stomach tensed like he might get sick, and he blinked and saw an older woman, wearing white and holding a clipboard.

"We were hoping you'd wake."

Cage yanked the IV out to sit up and get a good look at her.

"Gentle," the woman said, pushing a button. The cot whirred to an upright position, and she eased the IV needle from his grasp.

"What happened?" His throat was scratchy, like he hadn't used it in a while.

"I was hoping you could tell me."

The woman sure did a lot of hoping. She handed him a paper cup full of water and he gulped it down.

"Thanks," he said, but his mouth still felt dry. It reminded him of what his mother used to say when he asked for candy in the store and they didn't have any money. *People in hell want ice water, but they don't get it, do they?* He could remember his mother—clear as day, even when he wanted to forget her—but the motorcycle accident . . . He was drawing a blank. The not-knowing of it scared him, and the water churned in his empty stomach. He clenched his jaw so it wouldn't come up.

"Your head, how does it feel?"

"Like it's still attached." Actually, it hurt everywhere, but he wasn't about to tell her that. "What happened?" he asked again.

The nurse or the doctor or whoever she was got him another cup of water. "Well, you stumbled into the hospital yelling and screaming, fit to wake the dead." She shook her head and a strand of blond hair fell from her bun. "No wallet, no phone, and nothing you said was making any sense. We sedated you and then you were out like a light."

"I—I don't remember."

"That's okay, we'll get you all fixed up." The professional tone was back in her voice, but she couldn't hide the worry on her face from him. He and worry were old friends.

"What's your name?" the nurse-doctor asked. "Let's start with that."

His heart went fast in his chest like it was fighting to get out. If he'd crashed the bike, if he'd hit another car and damaged something . . . He couldn't afford to be in trouble again.

"I don't remember." A lie, but until he knew what he'd done he was keeping quiet.

"You don't remember," she repeated, suspicion on her face now. He shook his head, and she scribbled something on her clipboard. "How old are you?"

Probably didn't matter if he told her. "Seventeen," he said.

"And where are you from?"

He shrugged. "I move around a lot." He could tell her about Ohio, where he was born, or New Orleans, where his mom had moved him when he was a kid, or Gulf Shores, where he'd gone to live with his uncle last year, or Blue Gate, that decaying pile of bricks on Mobile Bay, where he'd spent all his time with Ro this summer.

"Do you have a history of drug use?"

Of course she'd ask. "Nothing to write home about."

"Tell me this," she said. "What's the last thing you remember?"

"I don't know," he said, feeling a pang of frustration. He needed to get out of here, figure out what he'd done. Call Blue Gate, meet up with Ro. Her father would let them borrow the truck to find his motorcycle. Sonny didn't like him, but the man never said no to his daughter.

The nurse touched his shoulder, as if she'd been talking for a while and he'd missed it. "What hurts?" she asked, her face creased with worry again. He knew that look well—it was his mother's look. She even had the same dyed-blond hair, the same wrinkles.

"My chest." He skipped the part about how his skull felt like it'd been caught in a trap and then sunk to the bottom of the ocean. The hospital gown was stiff, cheap cotton, and he lifted it up. A large purple bruise had spread across his ribs. It was the worst he'd had yet, even counting the fight in New Orleans.

"You've probably been in an accident," the nurse told him, as if he was too disoriented to have figured that out by now. "The doctor will want to run some more tests."

He let his eyes close. "I don't feel too good," he said. If she thought he was sleeping, maybe she'd leave. He kept still while he heard her writing notes, bustling about the bed.

"Just sit tight," she finally said. "I'll be back in a minute with some forms."

Cage waited until he heard the door click shut. Then he threw his legs over the side of the cot and stood, swaying. He poked his head around the curtain.

Another bed. The man in it was in a deep sleep or a coma, with wires and cords hooked to him. His cheekbones stuck out like he hadn't eaten for years, and his eyelids were bruised, poor bastard. Fresh yellow flowers and get-well cards were next to his bed, and a suitcase was on the chair beside him.

Cage crossed the room and rummaged through the suitcase, found a T-shirt and some oversized jeans with change in the pockets, a pair of redneck boots. He pulled the thin gown off to trade it for the clothes. A bolt of pain ran through him, and he bit down on his lip to keep from yelling. Whatever he'd done to himself, he'd done it good, that was for sure. At least his mother could be proud of him for something.

At the bottom of the suitcase was a wallet. He paused and then checked the door and the cot. Guy didn't look like he'd be waking anytime soon. Cage flicked it open and grabbed the cash.

"Sorry," he whispered. He found the license, memorized the address to pay him back when he could, and then strode to the window. They were on the second floor, a pretty short drop to the lower-level awning. He tried to open the window, but it was stuck, painted shut, so he took a deep breath and pushed hard, lifting through the swell of pain in his ribs. With another shove it slid up.

Cage sucked in the warm outside air—that fresh, hot smell of freedom—then thrust his head through the opening. He couldn't see anyone on the lawn below. A shred of luck.

He felt weak, but he managed to cling to the windowsill and lower himself down. He dropped onto the awning and it held steady. The nearby windows had their curtains closed, more luck. He jumped to the ground, his knees hitting the grass.

A sharp thudding was in his head—he could feel his heartbeat in his skull as he straightened. The paved walkway was empty, and the lettering on the building said LINCOLN MEMORIAL HOSPITAL. He was east of where he'd expected to be, almost like he'd been going home. He wished he still had his phone; he wanted to look at a map.

Beyond the hospital parking lot was the highway. He started forward and then heard someone shout.

"Sir?"

He kept going.

"Sir!" Footsteps now, right behind him, and he whirled.

"I'm going to have to ask you to come with—"

His fist collided with the man's face. The security guard crumpled to the ground.

"Sorry," Cage said, and then turned and ran toward the highway, caught his breath curbside. When there was an opening in the traffic, he shot across the road. His stolen boots pounded over the pavement and he almost slid, hopping up onto the sidewalk on the other side. The gas station had an old pay phone and he went for it.

He dialed the only number he knew by heart, but her cell phone just rang and rang. There was hardly ever reception at Blue Gate; it was too far out and he didn't know the home line. He hung up, tried again, and then slammed the phone into the receiver a few times. An old woman pumping gas flinched like she was scared of him.

Cage looked at the rise of the hospital across the street. The day was hot as hell. He wiped his hand across his forehead and it came back wet. Just sweat—no blood. Another shred of luck. He'd never get a ride if it looked like he was bleeding to death.

He glanced at the line of semi trucks idling in the lot and knew what to do. Calm down, act casual. He strolled toward them as easily as he could with boots too small and pants too big. Probably a dead man's clothes. But the clothes were clean, that was good. And fairly expensive, which was even better. These things counted when you needed a favor. People didn't like to get too close to the poor. They'd donate money, maybe, but let a poor person into their car? You'd be dreaming.

"Hey, sir. Can I get a lift?"

The trucker didn't even ask where he was going. Didn't

even glance his way. Cage was used to that, though. The downcast eyes, no one trusting him. This trucker was no different, because he walked right on by and heaved himself into his cab.

One, two, three, four. Cage walked down the lot, counting his steps so he wouldn't get angry. The next trucker he saw was taking a piss, singing loudly while he splattered the pavement. Cage passed a woman trucker and kept going, not liking his chances. *He* wouldn't pick him up if he were a woman.

He got near the end of the row. At the very last truck he heard the creak of hinges. Someone was climbing into the cab. The lettering on it had been painted over, but it had Alabama plates.

Cage walked around the grille to the driver's side. "Excuse me?"

The creaking stopped. The trucker poked his head around the door. "Yeah?"

"Headed toward Gulf Shores, by chance?"

"Yeah," the man said, his eyes narrowing under his hat like he could see where this was going and didn't like it.

"Can I get a ride, sir?" Cage tried not to sound desperate. Desperate never got people anywhere.

"Asked for my fair share of rides when I was your age," the man said. There came a long moment of silence and then: "Sometimes you get lucky, sometimes not." He hauled himself into his seat and slammed the door shut.

Cage's hands went to fists. He'd have to try the pay phone again or put his thumb out on the highway. With his luck he'd probably get arrested, and he'd made a promise to Ro about that.

The engine growled to life and he backed away. He heard a shout and turned.

"Gulf Shores'll take you ages on foot," the trucker called out the window. "You want a ride or not?"

Cage could have kissed him. He hustled over and swung open the door, the stench of oil and exhaust thick in the heat. "Thanks," he said, and held out some of the cash.

The trucker waved it off. "One thing, I don't talk much. I like the quiet."

Cage nodded. That was good, because he had a lot to think about. "Fine by me."

As they pulled onto the highway there was a new thudding against the inside of his head like something was trying to get out. He'd probably be all right with some painkillers, some water. He was thirsty in a bad way. Should've used the cash he'd lifted to buy a Gatorade.

He shut his eyes, and the faintest memory came of Ro. *This is bigger than both of us, Cage.* The nervousness was back in his gut. He didn't like not knowing how bad they'd fought, not being able to remember. Like he'd gone and gotten blackout drunk. He leaned forward, put his head in his hands. The trucker switched on the radio.

After they crossed the Alabama border it started to pour. Cage stuck his head out the window and let the rain sting his face. When water began to splash inside, he rolled the window up, told himself Ro'd be fine. She was always fine, that was her magic. She'd forgive him for whatever had happened. He wiped the rain off his face and looked out at the highway—they weren't too far now.

The air-conditioning ruffled the photographs tucked into the crevices around the truck's dashboard. A picture fell to the floor and Cage leaned over to pick it up. It was a photo of a woman, and he set it back near the radio, careful as he could.

"She got sick," the trucker said, taking off his hat.

Cage nodded, but he didn't want to think about sick people. He stared out the window, the pain in his skull making him hot and dizzy. He rubbed at his eyes. The beat of the windshield wipers scraping the blur of water erased and re-formed the road ahead and he felt he was fading in and out with the movement of the blades.

"Been around here before?"

Cage jolted upright and realized he'd almost fallen asleep. "No, sir." He didn't know why he lied, but he did.

"Never liked these parts much," the trucker said.

The woods hemmed in the road, and the rain slanted. They were getting into Blue Bay now, that small, secluded town just off the Gulf of Mexico. When the highway grew narrow, he knew the gravel road to the house was close. *This is bigger than both of us, Cage.* His heart started careening, and he counted to ten. "Just here," he said, the timber gate in sight, those rows of trees hiding the house away.

The trucker looked him over. "You don't belong here, son. I can tell. No offense."

"Just here," Cage repeated, and the noise of the air brakes was loud as the truck stopped on the empty road.

"Thanks for your help," he said. He swung his door open and jumped down from the cab. The man waved and the truck jerked forward, gaining speed, its red taillights growing faint before blinking out completely.

And then he was alone, almost. All around him, the sound of rain tapping the leaves. Maybe the unease he felt was a warning. But even if he and Ro had fought before he'd left, she'd still want to see him. He'd tell her about the crash, and she'd be glad he was okay. Ro didn't hold grudges.

Ahead was the driveway with the broken gate. The sign next to it had once said BLUE GATE but was mostly worn away. He'd never heard of houses having names before he met her. Her family came from old money, but they'd lost it a long time ago. Someone burnt through it out of revenge, Ro said. All they had left was this place, run-down and overgrown with weeds.

His boots crunched over gravel as he started forward. Two long rows of oak and crepe myrtle reached out on either side of the drive. It curved enough that you couldn't see the house, not from here. He kept his eyes straight ahead, the sky gray with drizzle. In his mind, he saw his motorcycle hitting the guardrail, remembered flipping, the sharp slide into the kudzu, all that green. He'd been alone when he'd crashed—he remembered that now. Thank Christ she hadn't been with him.

He sped up his stride. His heart felt lighter just thinking about her. But halfway down the drive the back of his neck went cold, as though someone was watching him. Staring between his shoulder blades.

CHAPTER 3

BLUE GATE, 1859

GRADY'S HANDS ARE COVERED IN blood as he drags his brother out of the gate. A dark smear runs over the dirt.

"Jacob? Jacob!"

His little brother's face is smashed near his left eye from the horse's hoof and his shirt is torn. Grady puts his hand on Jacob's chest—no heartbeat. He lurches back, his palm warm with blood.

"No," Grady says, his voice shaking. "No, you're okay." But his brother might be dead and Grady can hardly breathe. This can't be happening. "You'll be fine, you hear me?"

He looks toward the house. His father isn't home, he's still visiting a patient and won't be back until tomorrow. There's no time to wait for him—he has to do something! But what? *What?* And then a chill shoots down his back and it comes to him. A half breath later he's carrying his brother as he runs, Jacob's head bobbing against his shoulder. There's only one place to go. Grady swallows down the dread in his stomach and keeps running toward the woods.

"Help!" he yells. "Please help us!"

He still knows the direction of the cabin, knows it from the way his hair prickles at the nape of his neck. He charges forward, weaving around trees and dodging branches, his brother heavy in his arms. Grady runs deeper into the woods, frantically searching for the old cabin. Here the trees are closer together and the sun is blocked from sight, but he keeps going, despite his father's warning. This is for Jacob. Anything for Jacob.

"You'll be okay," Grady says, his breathing ragged. He can't look down because he's afraid of what he'll see—the bruising, the wide gash across Jacob's pale brow. Thinking about it makes adrenaline shoot through him, and he runs faster. *There!* There, ahead. This has to be it. He's sure of it.

As soon as he veers onto the overgrown path he feels sick to his stomach. He doesn't belong here; he can feel darkness eating at him with every footstep. *I have to*, he thinks.

And then the cabin is in front of him and there's no turning back. It's covered in shadow from the trees, and behind it the shed and well are being choked by vines. An ax is wedged into a log, but otherwise there's no sign of life. Grady tries to ignore his terror and heads for the cabin door, still carrying Jacob. The old woman's got to be here—he doesn't know what he'll do if she isn't.

"Help!" he shouts again. "I need help!"

A bad feeling rushes over him and he turns. Behind him is a boy about his age, with the palest skin Grady has ever seen. He's holding the ax and staring at him with dark eyes.

"My . . . my brother," Grady fumbles. "My brother, he's hurt. I need the . . ." He won't say *witch*. "Pearl," he says instead. "Isn't her name Pearl?"

The boy doesn't answer, just shifts the ax higher in his hands. Grady's about to yell for the old woman when someone grabs his elbow. He startles—there's a girl by his side.

How? He didn't see her coming, didn't hear her either. She's standing next to him in a slip of a dress, a yellowish color that must have been white once, and there's a faded red scarf wrapped around her hair and a red apron around her waist. She has to be the boy's sister—she has that same pale, pale skin.

"Lay him down," the girl says, pointing toward the cabin. Somehow the door opens before Grady can touch it and he stumbles into the dark room. Baskets are dangling from the ceiling and cuts of meat are hanging at the back. He takes another step and a sour smell hits him. In the dim light he can make out a cot near the fireplace, a shape huddled under blankets.

"Don't mind Miss Etta," the girl says. "Just put him on the table here." At the sound of her voice Grady finds himself leaning over, laying Jacob's body on the stretch of wood. His breath catches when he sees his brother's face where the horse got him. It's too late for a doctor, he knows that now without a doubt. He turns back toward the girl and she holds up a hand.

"I might can help," she says. "No promises."

"Now leave." The boy's standing in the doorway, the ax still in his hands, his dark eyes trained on Grady. He gestures with the blade. "Go. Come back in the morning." He smiles strangely. "Or don't."

Grady looks down at Jacob. His chest isn't moving; he isn't breathing. Should he really leave him alone here? And where is the old woman?

"Come back at dawn," the girl whispers, somehow at his side again when she wasn't before. "Nothing you can do now. Nothing but wait and see." It could be his imagination, but she seems to steal a glance at the cot before pushing him toward the door. "Go now."

This is what happened last time, when he came here so long ago. Last time they shut him out too. But last time it had worked. One more look at the girl—at her dark eyes with a glint of amber—and then his feet are moving.

He lurches outside and the boy is in front of him again with the ax and nothing is making sense. The trees seem taller all of a sudden, and the wind is swirling, making the leaves rustle around him, and the ground at his feet is covered in gashes—someone has drawn lines in the dirt, deep lines that run all the way up to the door. He blinks and the girl is at his side too and his heart starts to race. He knows there's some magic at play; it's more than just quickness.

"I can't leave him," Grady says. Something's digging

into his spine and he yanks his book from his back pocket and then notices his hands are shaking. "I'll wait all night if I have to, but you can't make me go."

"Can't we?" the girl asks, and her brother laughs.

Grady forces himself to ignore them. He sits down with his back against the wall of the cabin, then opens his book and starts to sketch so they can't see how scared he is. First he draws the well, swarmed with green vines. Next, the baskets full of green cuttings hanging near the shed. And the chimney, with smoke trailing up even though it's hot.

"It's getting dark," the girl tells him. "You shouldn't be here anymore."

Grady clenches the book. "I'm staying," he says. All of a sudden it's like his breath is smothered, and he feels her before he sees her. The witch. His head turns of its own accord and then the old woman is stepping out from the trees. Her hair is white, her eyes dark, her features delicate like the girl's.

"M-Miss Pearl?" he stutters. She looks just the same as before, as if he's only seen her yesterday and not ten years ago. "I'm—"

"I know who you are and why you come." The witch's voice is low and hushed. "I remember Rose, but you're not here for her, are you? You're here for someone else."

His heart aches when he thinks of what happened. "My brother. Can you help him?"

The witch looks to the sky like it's speaking to her, then turns back to Grady. "Let the night take you far and the morning bring you near," she says. "And don't miss the morning. Never miss the morning."

He doesn't want to go, but he has to do as she tells him. He remembers that from the last time he was here. *Jacob*, he thinks, *I'm doing this for him.* His little brother, who can never leave the animals alone. Grady's heart feels bruised, like the horse kicked him too, and all he can think of is Jacob, alone on that table in the cabin.

"You'll heal him?" he asks Pearl.

Her eyes say *Maybe, maybe not.* "It's my daughter who spoke to you first," she says. "Ask Hanna."

"Hanna," he repeats, and looks at her. Grady takes in the girl's dark amber eyes, the strands of her even darker hair that half cover them. Her pale skin, the veins showing through. She's not much older than him, he decides, yet his brother's life is in her hands. This girl is his only chance to save Jacob. This girl he shouldn't be talking to, this daughter of a witch.

"Come back in the morning," Hanna says, "and then you'll see."

Grady nods, and this is how it begins: with his desperation. Right now he has no idea what will come to pass, because the future is a door that only opens when it's ready. At this moment Grady believes his intentions are good, yet it's only pain that's coming—not just here and now, but rippling years and years later—and even if he did know, even if we could warn him, it's already too late.

CHAPTER 4

IT FELT WARM TO THE touch again, almost like it was alive. Mae lay back on her bed, the zipper of the sweatshirt cold against her neck, the book in her hands. The ache of missing Ro swelled up inside her, just like it had last night, but this time she was ready. Now her fingers tingled, and she felt a rush of adrenaline as she untied the ribbon. The thick book fell open and its earthy scent hit her like a thing long buried.

What she noticed first was an epigraph in perfect calligraphy.

Before me things created were none, save things eternal, and eternal I endure.

It sounded old-fashioned, the wording as antiquated as the handwriting. Across from it was the inside cover, yellowed with age. Spidery black ink ran halfway to the bottom. It was a list of names, crowned by a single word: *Initiates.*

Initiates of what? But she'd expected something like this, a reason for Ro's secrecy.

Underneath the odd heading was the name *Grady Deacon Cole II*, followed by a date: *July 1859*. Grady had been the first child born at Blue Gate; Mae remembered hearing that from Ro. She'd said terrible things about him . . . or maybe that was his father. Ro had liked to scare her, and she'd also liked bending the truth, so Mae didn't know how much to believe.

Another name was written directly beside Grady's— something with an *H*? The letters had been scratched out so many times the page had torn, but the cursive on the line below was legible: *Emily Rose Cole*. After that was another Cole she didn't recognize, and then her granddad's name, *Grady Deacon Cole VI*. Printed neatly on the next line were three words that made her eyes water.

ROXANNE ELIZABETH COLE

Mae stared at her sister's name and then at the one above. They were written in the same handwriting— her granddad's before his stroke. Her heart skipped as she realized what it meant. Ro had lied when she said she found the book. It had belonged to their granddad first; he'd given it to her.

Mae stared at the page for a half second longer and then shoved the book and ribbon into her bag on the way out of her room. She quickly took the back steps to the attic, switching on the light to see. Here the corners were sharp and the steps uneven, as if this second stairwell had been made in a hurry. Blue Gate had been added to piece by piece over the years, and some pieces made little sense, just like their family.

At the top of the staircase a flickering line of gold was coming from underneath the door. A lamp was on, which meant he was here. She started to knock, but the door was already swinging open like it sometimes did.

"Granddad?"

He was sitting in his chair in the suit that he always wore, though no one ever came to visit. His back was to her as he stared out the window. A stack of books was beside him, his worn Bible on top.

"Can I show you something?"

He stayed motionless, his whole body stiff. Mae sucked in a breath, fighting the edge of panic, but then his hand moved. He was fine; the doctor had even said he was looking better and that she shouldn't worry so much.

She wanted to shove the green book at him, ask him all the questions that were brimming inside her. He could explain why Ro had it, why she'd only taken it out when she thought no one was looking. The more she knew about her sister's life, the closer she'd be to figuring out what had happened.

Her granddad still hadn't turned, which meant he was thinking. She shut the door behind her, loud enough for him to hear, and stepped deeper into the room.

This part of the attic had a slanted ceiling, a single bed, a desk, and rows of bookcases on every wall except a newer plywood one that led to a storage space. It was cool enough up here, since it was insulated, and the fans and old air-conditioning unit made it livable. Near the bed, her granddad had spread out his picture collection on a narrow table—they were the first eyes he saw in the morning and the last he saw at night. Antique frames trapped the faces of every Cole who'd lived in the house. Sonny didn't want his picture added to them, said it looked too much like a memorial and he wasn't dead yet. But Mae loved old things; she liked visiting cemeteries, and she liked these black-and-whites too.

A nearby frame smacked flat on the table—she must have grazed it with her bag. It was lying next to a daguerreotype of the first Grady Deacon Cole, with his ash-colored hair and pale eyes. Beside him was Rose Louisa Cole, dark-haired and thin, the one the doctors tried bloodletting on when she got sick.

Mae picked up the fallen picture and righted it. It was an image of their firstborn child, Grady Deacon Cole II. Mae had always thought he was good-looking from his portrait in the hallway, with his blond hair and blue eyes. But this picture was muted and dark, his eyes full of secrets. It reminded her of Ro—all those hushed whispers about the things the Coles used to do. Right now Grady's gaze was on her, like he knew what she'd found.

"Granddad?"

He still hadn't faced her, so he was either deep in thought or deep in sleep. Mae walked over to the window.

Her granddad insisted on keeping his bedroom up here; he liked looking out the highest windows of the house. They were four stories high, if you counted the raised basement to protect against flooding. From here she could see the stretch of trees and a glimpse of Mobile Bay. Her fists clenched when she thought of the beach, and she looked down at her hands, willing them to relax. Her fingertips were dark with something—dirt? soot? When she brushed it off on her shorts, her granddad finally turned to her.

The afternoon light from the window fell on his face, and his skin seemed to glow. He looked almost ghostly, with his white hair and pale blue eyes. He smiled at her and squeezed her hand, and then she knew he was ready to talk.

"I found this last night." Mae pulled the green book from the canvas bag at her hip. "It belonged to you once, right? Then to Ro."

She wanted to ask more questions, but the look on his face made her stop. He started breathing funny—a gasping noise was coming from his throat like he was choking. His sweaty hand batted at her wrist. His writing pad. He wanted his writing pad.

"It's here on the desk," she said, her voice coming out too high-pitched. He fumbled with the pen and then clamped his arthritic fingers around it and bore down on the paper. He held out the notepad with his shaky scrawl.

DID YOU USE IT?

Her cheeks started to warm. She'd read the beginning of the book, but *used* it? What did that mean, anyway? His eyes searched her face, and her granddad looked more and more frantic the longer she took to answer.

"I didn't do anything with it." That was the truth.

He bent his head to scribble some more and then stared at the green book again. There was a loud thud as the pen dropped from his fingers and rolled across the wooden floor. His mouth was opening and closing and he was straining to speak.

"Granddad, look at me," Mae said, hiding her panic. "Now smile." It was a test the doctor had given her. Smiling on command meant he wasn't having another stroke.

But he was shaking his head, and his lips were moving, only nothing was coming out. Mae threw the book down and grabbed his hands, pressing them tight so he'd listen. "Please," she said.

At last he seemed to hear her. Slowly, slowly, the edges of his mouth lifted in a smile that didn't meet his eyes.

He was okay, he was just upset. It wasn't a stroke, except now her own heart felt pinched. Her granddad was rarely like this—he was usually easygoing, trying to cheer everyone up with his little notes.

She let go of his hands, and his gaze flicked to the book beside her.

"I know it's meant to be a secret," she said. He tapped at his writing pad again, but she just wanted him to stop thinking about it. "Let's forget it. I'll put it away. I won't bring it up again."

His eyes darted between her and the book, and after a moment he nodded. She watched him for a minute, waiting for his breath to steady, and then made a point of finding a good spot. Standing on her tiptoes, she slid the book onto the highest shelf, where he couldn't see it.

When Mae turned back, he was sitting on his bed. His face wasn't so pale, and his eyes were dry now. She leaned against the bedpost. "Ready for dinner?" Her question sounded hollow to her own ears, the lightness forced. She wasn't surprised when he shook his head.

"I'll bring you up some supper later," she said. "And I . . ." She stopped, though she wanted to say *I won't mention the book again. Ever.*

He settled back against the pillows. His white eyebrows shaded his lids, and his face was slack, exhausted. She'd risked making him sick again, triggering another stroke.

Mae glanced toward the shelf. The green book was too far up to see. Good. She pretended to tidy her granddad's room until she saw the slow rise and fall of his ribs, his face relaxed now, his eyes shut. Then she walked quietly to the shelf. On her tiptoes, she pulled out the book and shoved it into her bag, ignoring the stab of guilt that cut through her. She made sure he was still sleeping and then shut the attic door and ran down the narrow steps, sneaking in behind Elle in the kitchen. She sat at the dinner table and double-checked that the canvas bag was latched.

"Trying to set us on fire?"

Mae looked up to see her twin towering over her. Heat from the old stove drifted out as Elle batted away tendrils of smoke. After everything that had happened, she'd forgotten to take the lasagna out.

"You look terrible," Elle said. It was the same thing she always said whenever Mae wore the red sweatshirt. "You okay?"

She wasn't, actually, but she couldn't explain why without mentioning the book. "Just thinking."

Elle did a little twirl, her black dress and auburn hair fanning out in unison. "Well, think about coming out with me later," she said, nudging Mae's shoulder.

People didn't really talk through words—it was all in the gestures, in the eyes. And Elle's eyes were forceful, like the brightness of her hair. Everything about her was a force, especially the way she stomped around Blue Gate, pulling back curtains, cleaning away the dust, pretending things weren't falling apart.

"You know who invited us to a party tonight? Lance Childers. He's back from his exchange," Elle went on. She was grinning as if nothing had happened, like she wasn't bothered by the fact that Lance had been the one to find Ro's body last year.

"Let me guess," Elle said. "You'd rather stay home in your sweatshirt and paint."

"Something like that." Mae set her bag on the chair beside her. She'd start reading again later, find out what the book had meant to Ro and why it had upset her grand-dad so much.

Elle yanked on her sleeve and whispered, "*Seniors* will be there," before she turned and shouted, "Food's getting cold, Dad!"

Mae glanced past the kitchen table to the archway. Sonny was hunched over his desk in the next room, his back curved like a slab of stone. If she ever tried to paint him, he'd look the same in every portrait: hardened and barren, almost like the backdrop of a desert. "Give me a minute," he said.

"I'm hungry and it's never a minute," Elle snapped, heading toward him.

Mae could sense her sister was after a rise, which meant she had some time. Her fingers itched to hold the book again, and she slid it out of her bag, hiding it under the table. Her heart skipped a beat as she fumbled to untie the ribbon, stealing another look at her dad's back and Elle's flashing hair as they yelled at each other in the alcove.

The ribbon fell away and Mae opened the book, squint-ing at the writing. After the odd epigraph the ink grew thick, spanning the paper edge to edge. She skimmed a couple of pages and kept going. The book was written in various handwritings, as if all of its owners had made en-tries in it over the years. Her fingers started tingling as she turned the pages, faster and faster. Maybe Ro had written

in it too. Maybe she'd left some clue about wl
to her death.

Mae clutched the cover tighter. This was
she'd been waiting for. Something to go on beside.
dad telling them that the police were doing eve
they could. Finding the book in her sister's room
been a good thing, even though looking at it felt wro
like she was spying on Ro, invading the space she som
how still filled.

Mae glanced over at Elle and her dad in the alcove
and then flipped to the end. On the last page was a dark
thumbprint in the bottom corner. This was what Ro had
tried to show her before. This was what she'd turned
away from, the smell of red velvet cake thick in the air.

Mae's mouth tasted sickly sweet as she stumbled over
the strange heading—*A Ritual for a Raising*—and the even
stranger words that followed. They were written in sloppy
cursive, almost like the writer had been in a hurry.

> *Please follow carefully:*
> *Harbor love in your heart,*
> *while in your hand*
> *hold the loved one's belongings.*
> *Then begin the offerings.*
>
> *For death feeds life*
> *as blood feeds the ritual,*
> *and little creatures show the way.*
> *A cat for nine*

The page ended there. It seemed unfinished, like there should be more, but there wasn't anything else, and the back cover was missing completely. She reread the heading again—*A Ritual for a Raising*—and still had no idea what it meant. Why had Ro wanted to show her this so long ago? Why had she never mentioned it again, keeping it to herself instead? It was like a riddle Mae couldn't quite grasp, and the dark thumbprint made her feel dizzy—there was something odd about it. The entire book was odd, but it had been Ro's, and she'd been devoted to it. She went back a page, trying to make sense of things. Before the raising ritual was a list, labeled *Signs of the Raised*—the writing underneath it nonsensical—and on the page before that was the heading *Putting to Rest the Raised*, which was followed by some sort of prayer.

"What's that?"

Mae flipped the cover shut so fast she felt the sting of a paper cut. A bright bead of blood oozed out of her finger as she slipped the book into her bag.

"Textbook. Summer reading," she said.

Elle made a gagging face and headed to the counter, then took a bite of the burned lasagna straight from the pan. Her eyes went to the alcove. "Dad," she called. "Soooonny. It's officially cold now. Congratulations."

Sonny slid back the chair at his desk, and the newspaper clippings around him fluttered as he stood. "Lord-we-thank-you-for-this-food-Amen," he said, looming over the kitchen table before sitting down. "Where's your grandpa?"

Mae felt queasy. She thought she'd shoved his panic behind the white door in her head, but now it was all she could think of. "Resting," she said. "I'll bring him up a plate later."

Sonny nodded and then looked back and forth between them. "If you girls are going out again tonight, you tell me—"

"Where, who with, and when we'll be home," Elle finished, taking a big sip of orange juice. She'd put on too much red lipstick and it left a ring on the glass. "We know already."

"So you *know* not to be going out alone." It was his new rule, ever since last year. He glared at her, his long hair messy under his cap, his ponytail in a knot.

"I'm not," Elle said. "Mae's coming. Aren't you, Mae?"

"Mm-hmm." Mae gulped down her glass of water and clenched her bag strap, nervous about her lying face. Her dad narrowed his brown eyes at her but didn't say anything.

"Well, that's settled." Elle began serving up her plate first. "You know what? I was thinking about my bed-and-breakfast idea—"

"Not this again," he said, and Mae pulled a pencil from her bag and started drawing on her napkin with her left hand while she ate with her right. She was halfway done with her food by the time Sonny picked up his fork.

"We distinguish ourselves with the menu," Elle said. "Make it traditional Southern fare, have stories about Blue Gate on the place mats. Doesn't that sound good?"

"Don't matter what it sounds like," Sonny said. "We're selling."

Mae gripped her pencil tighter. He'd been talking about moving all year, and she was dreading it. "It's really not a bad idea," she said, and Elle threw her a grateful look. "Might get some money flowing in if it's done right."

Sonny slammed the table near Mae's plate. "I told you it doesn't matter," he said.

"But Blue Gate's perfect for it." Elle waved her fork in the air, pointing at the bay windows that opened over the field and the surrounding woods. "It's huge, and it's practically a historic landmark. People like that sort of thing."

"Mae, quit drawing," Sonny snapped. "We're having supper together."

Mae dropped her pencil onto the table, glad Elle was still talking. The sketch of an eye stared back at her from her napkin.

"I'll clean up the house in the next few weeks before school starts and you'll see what I mean," Elle said, nodding to herself, convinced she was right. "It's about time we cleared some of this old stuff out anyway."

Their dad's shoulders tensed and Mae held her breath, but he only looked away. He would either stay quiet like this or he'd lose it. In the past year she'd seen dishes shatter against the wall; she'd seen him spend all day firing his rifle in the yard, or empty a fifth of whiskey in a single afternoon. Gone was the dad who used to take them out on the sailboat as kids, letting them reel in every fish he caught.

"A bed and breakfast would give you something to do," Elle went on. "It's called work."

"I've got things to do," Sonny grunted. "I'm heading over to the wharf."

A flicker of hope hit Mae's chest. "You're going fishing?"

"Nope. I've got a lead."

Mae stared down at her plate until it blurred. She knew exactly who used to work at the wharf, and her dad didn't need to be going there with a gun. "Did someone see him?"

"Maybe," he said. "Plenty of pieces of shit around these days. Hard to tell them apart."

She wanted to know what had happened to Ro as much as he did, but Sonny would skip judge and jury. "Are you looking into anyone else?"

"Can we just stop talking about it?" Elle asked, her voice rising. "I'm sorry I brought it up. All I meant was that the house needs cleaning."

A knock came from the front door. Mae grabbed her bag and got to her feet, glad for an excuse to leave the table. Her dad called out behind her to check who was there, but she already knew. The old chandelier clinked overhead as she opened the heavy door.

"Took you long enough," Fern said, her chubby arms folded across her T-shirt.

"Could say the same about you." Mae stepped aside and swung the door open wider for the eight-year-old.

Fern's mom worked the night shift as a nurse and slept during the day, so she was free to roam. "The rain keep you away? Your stomach usually brings you over earlier."

"It's my legs that bring me over, Mae," Fern said, ducking past her. "And it stinks in here," she added, skipping down the hall until she was swallowed up by shadows.

Mae closed the door behind her and locked it. Then— finally alone—she couldn't help herself. She felt in her bag for the book, its spongy leather cover.

Prickles flashed down her spine as Ro's stories of their family came flooding back. How they'd done cruel, cruel things. Mae felt a rush of vertigo—maybe because the foyer was so high, shooting above her like the very sky itself, or maybe because of the portraits that she could never escape in the house. Rows and rows of old paintings hung along the staircase and through the hall. The Coles were staring down at her, all those pale blue eyes that seemed to say *We know what you have, what you're hiding*.

The best portraits could talk to you without words. They could tell you exactly what they thought of you, send a hex through their gazes.

"Mae?" her sister called, startling her.

She shoved the book away and followed the sound of Elle's voice to the kitchen. Fern was at the table, her legs swinging from her seat, and Sonny had escaped to the alcove, the open archway between them.

"If I eat my greens, will I be as tall as you when I'm six-teen?" Fern asked Elle. "I'm already just about taller than

Mae." She blew air through her lips. "How come you're twins but you don't look the same? She's got dirty-blond hair and you're a ginger."

"I like my hair," Elle said.

"We're fraternal twins," Mae added absently, trying not to think of the book until she was alone.

"What's that mean?"

"What did I tell you before when you asked?"

Fern shrugged, a smirk on her face. She knew Mae would explain anyway, and Mae knew she was right. Facts were easy to talk about. It was personal stuff that was harder. Like *What do you think happened to Ro? And How do you feel about her being gone?* She shoved those questions behind the black door in her mind and double-bolted it.

"It's when two separate eggs are fertilized by different sperm, so we're not identical."

"Why, thanks for that, Mae," Elle said, stacking the last of the dishes in the sink. "I'm glad I'm not still eating."

"Anyway," Fern went on, "Lance told me neither of you are as pretty as your sister."

Elle turned the faucet off. "Did he say we were pretty?"

"Tell your cousin not to talk about her," Mae said, defensiveness rising.

"Lance don't listen to me," Fern said. "He don't listen to nobody. And he's always talking about Ro, now that he's back." Fern was chewing on one of her curls, which had somehow ended up in her mouth with the lasagna. "You know what else he said?"

"What?" Elle asked.

"I can't tell you." Fern ran her finger and thumb along her lips, zipping them. "It's a secret."

Mae wanted her to come clean, but acting interested was what she was after. Fern liked games, just like Ro had. Her sister once drenched herself with fake blood on the porch and scared them into thinking she was dying, and she'd also pretended to choke at a restaurant, bowing to her open-mouthed audience when she was done. Every trick was usually morbid, and all of them ended with her laughter.

"What sort of secret, Fern?" Elle asked, playing right into her hands. Then she turned, her face bunched up as smoke seeped out from the alcove. "Not inside!" she yelled.

Sonny had lit a cigarette and was sifting through the newspaper clippings on his desk, circling a page with red pen. When he saw them looking at him, he swooped forward and shoved the clippings under his arm. A photograph flitted down behind him as he stood.

"Gotta go," he said. "Meeting the boys."

"Take this child home on your way," Elle told him.

"I'm not a child," Fern said. "I'm eight."

Mae's curiosity got the better of her, and her mouth opened before she could stop it. "What secret?"

Fern put her finger to her lips with a "Shh," and Elle rolled her eyes and marched into the foyer, heading up-stairs.

"If you're coming, come on." Sonny left the kitchen with Fern following behind, leaving Mae alone. When the front door slammed shut, she glanced at the empty hallway and then picked up the photo that had fallen to the floor. It was lying facedown, Ro's handwriting scrawled on the back.

R.C. & C.S.

She turned it onto its glossy side, and one look was enough to send her running to the door, barging out to the porch and into the drizzling rain, her Cons slipping on the steps. But the sandy driveway was empty; wet tire tracks disappeared down the road. Her dad's faded blue truck, with his hunting gear and gun rack, was gone. There was only the old fountain with the twin gargoyles and the two beech trees ringed with rocks. One big tree for her mother, a younger one for Ro.

Her throat seized, and she looked down at her hands. Her fingertips were dark again with something black, ash or grease maybe. She wiped them on her shorts and thought about calling Sonny, warning him not to do anything he'd regret, but his cell phone wouldn't have reception, and he wouldn't listen to her anyway.

Sliding the picture into her pocket, she felt the new bottle of paint she'd been meaning to put away, and then something soft and bendy. She pulled it out. It was her granddad's writing pad—she must have accidentally picked it up earlier. The only words on the page were shakily written.

Must know

And then, below that, another word in capital letters.

DANGEROUS

Mae took in a sharp breath and balled the top sheet in her fist. She felt trembly, like a chord that had been plucked. *Dangerous.* She almost choked on it. *Dangerous.* It was an anxious word, slammed her right in the ribs. If her granddad could still speak, maybe he would have told her more about the book—about why it was so important to Ro—but she couldn't risk asking him now.

Mae turned around and looked up—high, high, high along the cracked wall of the house. All the way to the attic window, where she could just make out a face through the glass. *Granddad?*

He was peering down at her, watching. She shivered, suddenly feeling cold.

Strange. For a moment he'd looked like someone else. Someone much, much younger.

CHAPTER 5

THE PAIN BETWEEN CAGE'S TEMPLES flared, and he shut his eyes against it. When he opened them, his vision was blurry. After a moment it slowly sharpened, so that the house he was facing seemed to rise out of the trees themselves. Its high mansard roof slanted among the leaves, and its painted brick that looked more bluish than white spilled into the woods.

He faltered, his boots heavy on the gravel all of a sudden. He stared up at Blue Gate, trying to see into her bedroom, and then glimpsed someone at one of the upper windows. It was a huge house, the kind that couldn't be taken in with just one glance. If a house could be lanky, this one was. On the outside, it was too tall, had too many pillars on the wraparound porch, and its spire was crooked. Inside, the rooms were strangely shaped, full of unexpected corners from the attic to the basement. Ro loved it, but to him Blue Gate had always felt . . . off. His mother would say he was being superstitious like his dad, but he couldn't help how he felt. Something was wrong with the place, even if he couldn't say what it was.

Cage had been around tales of such things from his summer job at the wharf. Nautical stars and fleurs-de-lis carved into masts for luck, and ships that were said to be haunted. Thing was, people secretly believed in the stories they whispered, even if they sounded ridiculous in daylight. Ro was a believer, but in a playful way, like she was holding back a wink. There was nothing to like about her house or the book she'd inherited—coincidences that struck too close for comfort—but she'd promised to overlook his past, which was more than he ever expected. So he ignored her book, didn't tell her not to play around with it, that in parts of New Orleans they took that sort of thing seriously. He said not one word, and in truth it reminded him of his mother, so he was happy not to bring it up. Ro's grandfather wanted it kept a secret anyway; she wasn't supposed to tell anyone about it, not even her sisters.

But he and Ro told each other everything—that was the other promise. He'd have to own up to his motorcycle accident, even though he'd bragged about being good with a bike.

The shadow at the window was gone now, and he started forward again. It wasn't dusk yet, but the porch light was on, and that burning bulb seemed like a beacon. A lighthouse in the woods.

Cage strode down the gravel drive. The rain had stopped, but his stolen clothes were still wet and his skull was throbbing. If he'd been in the hospital overnight, Ro might be worried. They'd been fighting before he'd rode off, that much he knew, but she still would have expected him to call. His mother never gave much good advice, but she said to always apologize to a girl if she was angry. Even if you weren't sure why. So he'd apologize. He'd knock on the door and Ro would answer. He'd say he was sorry, and she'd make things okay—she always did; that was part of her magic. She'd help him find his bike, or what was left of it, and then he'd drive to the docks in Gulf Shores for work. Simple.

He walked past a pair of beech trees in the yard and the crumbling fountain and then took the porch steps two at a time. The rocking chairs were empty and so was the porch swing—its chain was broken and it hung crooked. The red paint on the door was fading, peeling away. Could take a brush to it if Sonny would let him.

He knocked once and then waited. No answer, so he rapped the iron knocker and then felt something soft weave around his ankles. A small black cat, one of the strays Ro looked after. He leaned down and put his hand next to it, let it nuzzle against him.

Footsteps came from inside the house, and the cat darted into the bushes. Cage straightened, but no one opened the door. He knocked again, louder this time, and then waited what seemed like forever. The door opened just a crack, the metal chain still latched.

Ro's younger sister stared at him, her brown eyes wide, that half-curly hair of hers long and loose and no makeup on. She was the kind of girl who didn't know she was pretty and didn't care either. Not like Ro, who knew but didn't hold it against you.

"Hey, can you get Ro for me?"

Without saying a word, Mae slammed the door in his face.

His head was starting to throb again, and this wasn't helping. He wanted a hot shower, some food, and a gallon of water—his thirst was sucking his very soul dry—but mostly he just wanted Ro. And now he was stuck out here with the door locked. Ro must be angry with him for sure, had even told her sister about their fight.

He knocked again. *Come on, Mae.* He swore he heard breathing on the other side. Mae had always been a bit off the beaten path. Wild-animal shy and nothing like Ro.

"You still there?" he said. "Mind letting me in?"

When he was about to turn away, maybe throw a pebble at Ro's window the old-fashioned way, the door opened again. Her sister was staring at him, the chain still latched.

"You know why I'm here," Cage said.

Her lips parted, but she didn't speak. She looked confused, almost stunned. The look of someone who'd taken an elbow to the head. That dazed stare, then the rapid blinking, like she was surprised to find herself standing in front of him.

She started to say something and then stopped. Mae was only a couple of years younger, but Ro was the one who ran the house and always had. Maybe their fight had been worse than he realized. Could be she didn't want to see him or had finally dropped him for Lance.

"Where . . . where have you been?" Mae asked.

Good, at least she was speaking to him now. Another bolt of pain shot through his skull, and he breathed out hard and ran his hand over his hair. His scalp felt tender—maybe he was bleeding.

"Look," Cage said. "I crashed my motorcycle. Can you please get Ro?"

"You want Ro?" Mae's voice was barely a whisper. She looked confused. "But . . ."

He waited, trying his best to let her finish. Mae had trailed off, and now she was tilting her head to the side as if she couldn't quite remember who he was.

"But . . . you can't," she said.

Her sidestepping was frustrating the hell out of him. "She might've told you I *can't*," he said, trying to keep the bite from his voice, "but I *need* to talk to her."

"I don't understand." Mae's chest rose and fell under her thin sweatshirt. Her breath was jagged, like she might hyperventilate. It reminded him of his mother, after the smoking got to her lungs.

"Let me in for a second." His hand went to his head again—he needed to remember, explain himself. "Please, Mae." He tried to swallow, but his throat was too dry.

After a long moment Mae slid the latch, and the door swung open a bit more. She stood there, blocking the entrance, even though there was nothing to her—she was all sinew, and timid as anything. He thought about pushing

57

her aside and hollering for Ro, but instead he let out a breath, wiped his boots on the mat.

"I'm trying here, real hard," he said. Mae was still gaping at him. He glanced over her shoulder and caught a face in the shadows. But no, it was just all those portraits on the walls. "I know she's home," he told her. "I saw her at the window."

She put her hands up to her mouth and blinked like she was holding in tears.

"Look," he said. "Look, don't worry. I'm not mad." She took a step back, and he saw his entrance and went for it, lunging through the doorway. The foyer reeked, it needed air. "She upstairs?"

Mae's hands fell away from her face, and she was doing that weird breathing again.

"Talk to me."

"I— She—"

A banging noise behind them. Cage turned to see the other sister barging into the foyer. Elle was taller than Mae and looked a little like Ro, if you took Ro's face and stretched it out.

"Listen—" he started.

"Get away from her," Elle snarled. She lifted something, and his chest knew what it was before his eyes did.

She was holding a rifle. His heart was going *thud thud thud thud* and he was vaguely aware of Mae beside him. "Call the cops, Mae," Elle said.

Why the *cops*? "Hey, I know your sister and me got in a fight, but—"

58

"Stop." Elle cut him off. "Keep your hands up and shut your mouth."

"Elle!" Mae snapped out of whatever daze she'd been in and finally moved. "Put it down!"

If Elle hadn't had the gun, Cage might have laughed, but she was serious, her face tense with anger. "Turn around," she said, the rifle aimed at his chest. "Slowly."

He didn't want to turn around. Elle wasn't going to shoot, but the thought of putting his back to the barrel made him feel sick. He stayed facing her, his muscles frozen up. It was hard to think with a gun pointed at him. As many fights as he'd been in, he'd only ever had one aimed at him once, and that had been at his mother's place. "This is a misunderstanding."

"Shut up," Elle said, and then came the unmistakable click. She'd cocked the gun.

"He doesn't know—" Mae started, but her sister let out a sharp laugh, the rifle still on him.

"Is this supposed to be some sort of joke?" Elle's voice had risen a notch. "Do you think this is funny?" Her bangs were matted with sweat.

"I'm not laughing," Cage said. It was all happening too fast, and he wasn't sure what to do. Run? Yell for Ro? He stood in place, every muscle in his body taut.

"Elle, he doesn't know," Mae repeated, louder this time.

He glanced at her and then back at the gun. "Know what?"

Elle kept the barrel aimed. "Mae, pick up the phone and call the cops like I told you."

For shit's sake. Only in Alabama. Only in Alabama would a sixteen-year-old girl be shoving a rifle in his face. The floor seemed to tilt and he was sweating and he felt his control slipping away. *Stay calm, stay calm.* But something didn't make sense, and doubt had begun to crawl into his stomach. A little snake of doubt, and it was twisting and turning in his gut.

"Ro is—"

"Mae, don't talk to him." Elle cut her off. "And *you* keep your hands up."

The snake in Cage's stomach sank fangs. He was scared now, and the gun wasn't half of it. "Where is she?"

"You know where she is!" Elle yelled, stepping toward him. "You did it, and then you took off and hid." The rifle bobbed up at his face. "You think you can just come back here after all this time? Act like it never happened?"

The floor tilted again, fast, and he felt he might lose it completely. "What? What are you . . . ?" He was trying to form words but his head was pounding. "Did *what*?"

"You coward. Own up to it."

"I'm not," he said, even though all he wanted to do was get out of this stinking house. "Mae, what's she talking about?"

"Ro's gone," Mae told him. "You ran, so we thought—"

"What do you mean, *gone*?" His chest heaved when he said it.

"Ro's dead." Mae was still talking, but he couldn't hear anything more, because he was stuck on *dead*. Kept hearing it over and over. *Dead. Dead. Dead.* But she couldn't be. No, not Ro. Not her. He was desperate now; he felt like he was in a dream, a nightmare.

"We know it was you," Elle said.

The rifle was shaking. Her look said she hated him, and his head was a drum and his heartbeat was in his ears and everything around him was fading, going gray. *Dead dead dead dead.*

His vision blurred—the barrel was closer now. Elle's voice in his ear: "You'll regret coming back."

Something was wrong. It was a trick, it wasn't real. He thought of that thing of hers, that thing that shouldn't exist, that shouldn't be possible. "Is this about the book?" He tripped on the words, tried to think straight, to breathe. "Has she—"

"Just stop talking!"

His eyes were on the stairs now. He'd call Elle's bluff and run up to Ro's room. She was in her room and everything was all right and the girl he loved was alive.

"Please put it down," Mae begged her sister. "Please. We need to talk to him."

"No," Elle said, and she was crying now. "He did it, I know he did."

And then everything happened fast—Mae was shouting for him to leave and stepping toward her sister and he was turning away from them and that horrible echo, *dead dead dead dead*, and the next thing he heard was the roar of the gun and his heart stopped in his chest.

CHAPTER 6

ELLE'S MOUTH WAS MOVING AND Mae tried to listen, except the words were muffled. Her sister grabbed her elbow, hard, and then nearly tripped over the rifle. She was talking, but it sounded like she was underwater. "Are you hurt?" Elle's voice was getting louder, it was surfacing. "You shouldn't have grabbed at it," she said, full volume now. "You're hurt, Mae. You're in shock."

She *was* shocked, because of Cage. He'd been right here, at the door, and for a minute she'd expected Ro by his side.

"Oh my God, it's everywhere!" Elle was patting her down with hard slaps that stung.

"I'm okay," Mae said, "I'm okay." But her legs didn't want to move. The blast of the gun had gone atomic in her head, like her body had turned to ash. It felt as if all the little pieces were floating down into a pile, gathering back together. "You didn't hit me."

"But the blood." Elle's face paled—she was looking past her now—and Mae followed her gaze to the wall.

The house was bleeding. Thick, dark red droplets were spattered across the door. Her stomach clenched, and she stepped forward to touch it, to know for sure.

"I got you, I did," Elle was saying behind her, shrill and fast. "I'll call an ambulance."

"Wait." Mae stared at the splotch of red on her fingertip as she brought it toward her lips. She breathed in, and just as she was about to taste it, Elle grabbed her wrist. "It's not—"

"Blood?" Elle was touching it now too.

Mae looked down and saw the shreds in her sweatshirt pocket, the spatter. The bullet must have grazed the plastic bottle she'd had inside. Pompeian Red was the color; she'd liked its name—a nod to Mount Vesuvius, volcanic, molten—when she'd saved up enough to buy it.

"You didn't shoot anyone, Elle." The bottle had exploded. On the walls and door was acrylic resin, powdered cinnabar. All that red reminded her of something—

"If you're not shot, then . . ." Elle was getting worked up again. "Cage. We have to call the cops." She turned, and Mae knew to grab her before she picked up the phone.

"Do you really think—"

"Dad does. And if he sees him?" Elle reached for the phone, but Mae clutched her tight, needing time to think. Cage had been asking the wrong questions. He'd acted like he didn't know Ro was dead, even though he'd been on the boat with her that day. Just now, when he'd knocked on the door—it was like time had spun backward.

Elle's eyes narrowed. "I can't trust your judgment with him," she said.

Mae felt the sting of her words but tried not to show it. "You know what Dad will do if he finds out Cage was here." She could see Elle start to give, just a fraction, and she took it. "You don't want that, and neither do I."

Elle's neck was going splotchy, turning the color of her hair. Her sister knew as well as she did that a call to the cops would go straight to Childers, that he'd let their dad do whatever he wanted, and then there'd be blood on the door instead of paint.

"You could have hit me or Cage just then," Mae said, tamping down a sudden rush of anger. "It was lucky you missed. But you know Dad won't."

"I didn't mean to shoot at you." Elle's neck was even more flushed now.

"Promise you won't say anything. Not yet, at least." Mae squeezed her sister's hand, wanting to get through to her. Their family never said things like *I love you* or *Thank you*. They just squeezed hands. Elle shook her off and then turned and walked out of the foyer.

"Elle!"

She didn't answer, and Mae's heart clenched tight. It was good Elle hadn't picked up the phone, but she was used to getting her way, and Mae had no idea what she would do.

The bullet had left a single hole in the wall. As she

stared at it, she felt as if she'd overlooked something important about Cage, like trying to take a picture through a foggy lens. She needed to go find him, but first she had to get Elle on her side.

She heard heavy footsteps as her sister stomped back into the foyer, carrying a bucket and a rag. Mae felt a rush of gratitude and nearly pulled her into a hug.

"I owe you," she said, but Elle didn't speak, just grabbed the rag and tore it in half, and then they both started scrubbing the paint on the walls. The silence was loaded the way it always was post-fight, and Mae cleaned quickly, wondering if it was a mistake not to turn Cage in. He hadn't believed them about Ro; he'd acted like he thought they were lying, which meant he'd search all of Blue Gate for her—she knew he would, because that was what she would do. Covering that much ground would take a while. He'd still be out there.

Mae kept cleaning as Elle walked out of the foyer again, returning with a picture frame and a hammer. Without saying a word, her sister pounded a nail above the bullet hole, and then hung the frame. It was a black-and-white of Blue Gate, back when it was first built.

"Where'd you find that?" Mae asked, desperate for her to start talking again. The sooner she did that, the sooner she'd know if she'd convinced Elle to stay quiet.

"There's boxes of them," Elle said. "They all smell like mold. The whole house smells, and I can't stand all the mess anymore." She pointed at the wall. "And I really can't stand *this* mess, Mae."

Mae knew she didn't mean the paint or the bullet hole. She meant Cage. She meant Ro.

"I'm going to figure it out—" She sounded more confident than she felt. Maybe Elle was right about not trusting her when it came to Cage—maybe she did have a soft spot for him. That worried her, but Sonny with a gun worried her more.

"What if Granddad had seen him?" Elle asked. Her eyebrows were pressed tight, matching the way she held her shoulders. She was all elbows and curves and teeth. Everything about her was ready to fight, to pull another trigger. For all the times Mae got frustrated with Elle, she admired her too. "Did you think about that?" her sister went on.

"Of course I thought of him." Their granddad was another reason why there couldn't be sirens again, not unless they were sure. She knew what would happen if his blood pressure went up too high and she couldn't calm him. "I have a plan," she said. "Let me—"

Footsteps sounded on the porch and they both whirled. The door flung open and their dad stepped inside the house, wiping his boots on the mat without looking up. "I've got Childers waiting in the car. Just swung by to pick up some drinks." He paused, staring at them. A soiled paper bag was in his fist. "What's wrong with you two?"

Mae looked down at her hands. "Why do things always have to be wrong?" she said, because she didn't want to lie to him.

He stamped his boots off some more. "Gonna hurry up and fill me in?"

Elle sighed and Mae's jaw went tight. "Oh, I was cleaning up the foyer for the B and B, sir," Elle said, glaring at Mae, "and one of your guns went off. That's all."

Mae said a silent prayer of thanks, but Sonny stepped forward. "That's *all*?" He glanced back and forth between the two of them and slammed the door behind him. He paused, staring at something. Then he reached up and touched a drop of paint, smearing it across the wall.

"I don't have time for this." He turned, his brown eyes finding Mae. "And I don't much care for liars." His voice got harder when he said it, as if he somehow knew, and her heart went double time.

"It was an accident," she said.

Sonny seemed like he wanted to yell, but he held it in, his chest swelling. "Don't you *ever*," he whispered to them, "touch my rifle again. Unless you need it." He dropped the paper bag by the door and took off his cap, scratching at his head. "And there is no goddamn B and B," he said to Elle, striding off toward the kitchen.

Elle crossed her arms and shot a withering look at Mae. "Great, now he's angry. This is your fault."

He was angry because of the gun going off, not because of Cage, but Mae didn't argue with her. A moment later they heard Sonny's boots treading the floorboards as he came back into the foyer, a twelve-pack in his hand. He grabbed the rifle, and Mae felt her insides knot up. Cage was still out there.

"Don't you want to leave that here? It's not deer season," she said. "And it's almost dark."

He checked the safety and then opened the door. "There's always a season, and we got lights."

"Wait!" Elle called out, and Mae nudged her. If Elle told him about Cage, they'd hunt him down right now—he couldn't have gone far, and Childers had dogs, horses too. Mae reached out for her again, but Elle stepped away. "Dad," she said, louder now.

Sonny turned, his body framed in the doorway, filling it. He seemed distracted, like she'd pulled him from a thought.

"Did you find out anything at the wharf?" Elle asked, and Mae held in her breath.

His scowl came back. "Shaw's uncle said the same thing he always does."

"Which is?" Elle pressed.

"Nothing much. The uncle was doing him a favor by giving him work, trying to help him out. Says he hasn't seen him." Sonny sucked air through his teeth, shook his head.

"What's in the bag?" Elle nodded at the paper sack he'd tossed to the floor, and Mae wished she'd stop talking so he'd leave.

"Cottonmouth," Sonny said. "Damned near stepped on it. Childers didn't want his dog eating it." He kicked it toward her, and Elle crinkled her nose. "Throw it out, will you? I gotta go. The boys are waiting."

The door slammed behind him, and they heard it lock from the other side. It was his way of reminding them that he was in charge, that he was keeping the house safe.

Mae let out a sigh and then adjusted the picture frame to make sure the bullet hole was covered. "Just give me some time, okay?"

"If I ever see Cage Shaw again," Elle said, "you won't like it." She shoved past her and went upstairs. "And take care of the snake!" she yelled.

Mae's throat felt tight when she swallowed, but she knew why Elle was mad. Seeing Cage made it seem like everything with Ro was happening all over again. She stared after her sister, wanting to smooth things over, but she didn't have much time.

She hurried to where she'd left her bag and picked it up, slinging it over her shoulder. The weight of the green book in the canvas rested against her hip, and the pocket-knife her dad had given her for her birthday poked out from the top flap. Reading the book could wait, and so could apologizing to Elle. Her sister's silence would only hold so long—in the meantime there was something she needed to do.

She opened the front door, surprised to see Childers's shiny black truck still in the driveway, Sonny arranging the spotlights and the rest of the hunting gear in the flatbed. Her dad's closest friend was behind the wheel, wearing camo instead of his usual cop uniform and letting his dog lick from his beer can. When he spotted her, he raised his drink in a greeting.

Then she saw Lance, for the first time in nearly a year, and her heart skidded in her chest. He was sitting next to his dad, leaning over in his seat, his baseball cap pulled low. Now that he was back, she'd have to figure out a way to get him alone, talk to him about Ro.

Mae waved toward the truck as she strode past, keeping her step quick over the wet gravel. She called out to Sonny that she was going for a walk and then picked up her pace. Even with the late summer days it'd be dark soon. If Cage was still at Blue Gate, she needed to find him before they did.

Just as she hit the woods, she glanced back. The black truck was driving off, going in the other direction, but in its side mirror she swore she saw Lance looking at her, his hat shading his face. She'd never been able to figure him out—he'd never let her get close enough—but Ro had always liked him. After a long moment, he lifted his hand in a wave.

CHAPTER 7

THERE WAS BLOOD ON HIM, but it wasn't his. He crouched down in the woods and held up his splattered shirt, took a hard look at it. If he went to check if anyone was hurt, Elle would shoot at him again. He'd gotten her wrong— she'd pulled the trigger after all. It could be she wanted to scare him, or maybe she was a shit shot, but whatever it was, he wouldn't try her twice.

Cage glanced over at the back of the house, scanned the tall hedge. He kept expecting to hear sirens, see someone barreling out of the back gate, but he didn't.

He stared down at the red spatter on his shirt and then reeled—they'd told him Ro was dead. There were spots in his vision, bright white spots like he might pass out. He forced himself to take deep breaths. He couldn't lose it, not here. *One, two, three.*

He sank lower into the shadows, into the cover of wet undergrowth. His breath was going fast, and his throat was so dry he couldn't swallow. Her sisters had told him she was dead, but that couldn't be right. His hands clenched, and he dug them into the ground, mud splaying through his fingers. A flash of memory and he saw his tire hitting the guardrail. His bike sliding into the kudzu, tangling in it. Blood running down his face and getting in his eyes, a sense of dread. And before that, they'd had a fight. She'd been shouting at him.

A bolt of pain flared and his skull felt like it might split open. They'd told him she was dead, that he'd done it. He needed to figure out what was going on. Get clear of Blue Gate, go to his uncle's house in Gulf Shores, try calling her cell again.

His gaze fell to the red stains on his shirt. He wasn't in pain, not from a bullet—the ache he had was in his head. The longer he stared at his shirt, the more he was sure it wasn't what it looked like, it wasn't blood. Maybe this thing with Ro wasn't everything it seemed to be either. It was one of her games, and she was about to come out of the house in stitches because she'd got him good. It was only a prank. She'd pretended to have a seizure once in a hardware store, just to see what her dad would do, but this was worse, more calculating. And there'd been something off about Mae a minute ago—he could've sworn she was lying to him about Ro. Their family was different from most, and he'd never trusted her dad. If Sonny wanted him out of Ro's life, then this would be the way to do it. Cage gritted his teeth and stared up at the house again. The sky was slowly darkening.

Think, Cage, think. He scanned the trees and did a double take. Someone was in the distance. Someone with blond hair standing in the woods, looking his way.

Ro?

Adrenaline surged through him and he got to his feet quick. It had to be her; of course it was. He found the strength in his legs again and was sprinting, weaving around the trees, sticking to higher ground. He wanted to yell out her name, but he couldn't risk it.

When he got closer, he saw she was in a long white T-shirt, the kind she wore over her swimsuit. She turned and took off running too, deeper into the woods. It was getting darker now, coming on night and hard to see. But she wanted him to follow her. She was leading him away from the house so they could talk.

He ran as fast as he could over rough ground, dodging holes and fallen logs, ducking under low branches. He went hard to keep pace with her, and even then she'd slip out of sight, only to reappear farther ahead, farther than he thought she'd be. He kept going, almost laughing with hysteria and relief. No one was following him, and Ro was just ahead. She was alive, and when she led him to a quiet spot she'd explain everything.

He passed a wide oak tree and saw the blur of her shirt in the gathering dark. They were coming up on the old cabins now. She shot past the clay foundations and crumbling walls, the old well. When the cabins were behind him, he came to a split in the trail.

He stood for a moment at this fork. The muddy track

ahead was overgrown with brambles and saplings and barely visible. Shielding his eyes with his forearm, he barreled through the sharp tangle of branches and up a small hill.

Then, through a gap in the trees, it was before him: the barn's roof, its unadorned walls. It was a massive storage shed, really, with a huge rolling door wide enough for the sailboat and trailer to fit through.

The side door was swinging shut—she'd gone inside. He rushed after her, the rusty knob loose in his hands as he turned it, barging in.

The dust hit him first. It made him cough—deep, hacking coughs that cut at his lungs. Then he straightened. He thought she'd be standing there with a big grin on her face. Instead there was just the shape of the boat, draped in a white cover like it'd been put to sleep.

"Ro?"

She didn't answer. There weren't any windows in the barn, but the skylight on the high ceiling leaked in the last of the light. He started to smile—she'd step out at any moment, and God he wanted to see her.

"Ro, come on."

She liked to scare people, that was her thing. Leaping out of a dark room and making someone scream, and then laughing about it. He hated when she did that, though it was sort of cute.

"You make me run after you," he said, "and now you're hiding?"

He found a flashlight by the boat trailer and turned it on, dragged the beam over the barn walls. Ro's pranks were her only downside. That and the book, but at least the jokes made him laugh sometimes. Like her game with the statue in the back garden. She'd go over to the one-eyed cherub and pull something from a silver box she'd buried underneath its feet. *Oh, look!* she'd say. *Another present from the gift cherub. Hold out your hand.* It was childish, but Ro was still charming in a way no one else could be. A piece of Chiclets gum, that was what he'd gotten first. The second time was a sand dollar for good luck. Then a fortune, already ripped from the cookie. *A long-hidden opportunity lies ahead if you are not timid.*

Thing was, he'd never been timid. "Ro!" he called into the barn. His voice echoed back at him, and he walked around the boat to see if she was on the other end, near the chairs and small fridge where she kept snacks and drinks. He and Ro were the only people who used the place, really. It was her hideaway, when she wasn't on the water. Sonny sometimes took the boat out too, but he'd let Ro have the barn.

"Come on out," Cage said, beginning to lose patience. "We need to talk."

Piles of old furniture were against the far wall, covered with tarps, and a workbench was in the corner, a row of tools hanging above it. Half the barn had an exposed second floor, also used for storage, but he couldn't see anyone up there. No ladder in sight either. Then a shadow moved beside the fridge and he turned. He pointed the flashlight, saw nothing but the wall.

"I crashed my motorcycle," he said. "Head's killing me. It's been a shit day."

She didn't answer. Was she waiting for him to say he was sorry about the fight? He wanted to tell her in person, face to face.

When he walked closer to the kitchen area, he noticed that the fridge was coated in dust, the plug curled on the floor beside it. Pinned up over the bar were a few dusty pictures, some frames on the counter. Cage scanned them quickly, hoping she'd get bored and just come out. He saw a photo of Ro with her grandfather and Sonny, all holding up speckled trout, big ones with black dots across their fins. The next photo was Ro with her sisters, both twins looking away from the camera—Mae with a smudge of paint on her cheek, Elle with too much lipstick—while Ro grinned into the lens. He searched for the picture of the two of them at the dock, but it was gone.

The whole wall in front of him was dusty. It looked like a sandstorm had swept through the barn, but they'd only just been here the other day. Maybe the door had been left open.

"Ro?"

The silence was starting to get to him. Worry was in his stomach, coiling in his gut. She wasn't answering him, and it wasn't just the wall—*everything* in sight was covered in dust, like no one had been in the barn for a long time. It didn't make sense, and Christ, his head ached. He found an old bottle of Sprite on the floor and drank it warm—it was flat, but he didn't care. When he set the empty bottle down, he heard a clattering noise behind him.

He turned with the flashlight. A picture frame had fallen, toppled to its side on the plywood bar. He went over and picked it up, wiped away the dust with his thumb. It was a shot of her—her wide smile with that little gap between her front teeth. Her grin had gotten him the first time he saw her. She'd been playing a trick on that day too.

"Ro," he said into the barn. "Please come out. Tell me what's going on."

She had to be here—he'd followed her in. When he looked at the streak his thumb had left on the glass, it hit him. He glanced down at his borrowed boots and lifted one. A half-moon scuff mark was in the dust covering the floor. He saw the trail of footsteps behind him—his own footsteps—and he tracked them, walking around the boat until it was at his back, the barn door ahead of him now.

When he raised the beam of the flashlight, his fist closed over the frame.

There was only one set of footprints on the dusty cement floor. Only one, and they were his. A searing ache tore through his head. Another bolt of pain and his knees hit concrete as the world went black.

The boat pitches and salt water sprays his arm. Cage opens his eyes to the bay, the sail full as the boat cuts through the water. The sun's beating down on the deck and glinting off the metal fasteners, and he's thirsty like he hasn't had a sip of water for years.

There's a can of Coke on the table, and he shakes the last of it into his mouth. Nothing but a few sweet drops. He pulls out a map from under a stained coffee mug. Something seems off, but he's not sure what. The map ruffles in the wind and the can tips over and there's a loud peal of laughter. "Cage!"

"Ro?" On the other end of the deck he finds her. She's sitting on a cushion and smiling at him, her blond hair shining and the scent of coconut oil on her skin. Beside her are a couple of sandwiches on a plate with the crusts cut off the way he likes.

"What kept you so long?" she asks, taking a drag of her cigarette. It's slender and smells of cloves. Funny thing is, she usually never smokes around him. She knows how he feels about it, but he's not going to tell her what to do.

She pushes her sunglasses back like a tiara and he's hit with the shocking green of her eyes. "You get distracted over there, sailor?"

"Ro," he says, feeling strange for some reason. "Where . . . ?"

She laughs again. "You and your maps. You ought to just go in my general direction and you'd do all right."

"Maps," he says. He feels off-balance, feverish. "Did I fall asleep?"

"Am I supposed to never take my eyes off you?" She smiles and rests her head back on the cushion, the locket at her throat flashing. "I'll admit it's tempting." She exhales, and smoke curls into the sky and then disappears. He remembers having a terrible dream, can't shake the bad feeling it left.

"You're quiet," Ro says.

His fingers run along the warm curve of her shoulder. For the first time in his life he feels lucky—he's felt this way ever since meeting her. Only one more year and then no more school. She might marry him if he gets up the courage to ask. They could wait till she finishes college, even. Her dad won't like it, but if he works hard enough at the wharf, saves enough money, Sonny might warm to the idea. Cage will do whatever it takes.

Ro grabs his hand and trails her fingers over the scars on his knuckles. Then she pulls him down next to her and leans into him, all oil and legs and her red bikini top loose. He holds his breath as she unties her top, lets it fall.

Her eyes find his. "There's something you need to know." The smile leaves her face and he tries not to worry. Is this about Lance again?

"Tell me, then." He wraps his hands around her waist, pulls her close. "I'm listening." And he is—he's taut just waiting for her to speak.

She moves her lips to his ear. "Cage," she whispers. "*Caaaaaaaaaaaaaaaaaa . . .*"

But then her voice trails off and the clouds whirl overhead and all of a sudden there's nothing under his feet. He's falling back, feels his skull smack against wood, and then he hits cold water, no time to breathe in. He sinks down, down, and blood is streaming, he doesn't know where it's coming from. Air, he needs air.

He tries to swim upward, but his legs won't obey and he can't feel his arms. He's desperate for air, but he can't move, he can't. He hears shouting from somewhere and panic surges in his chest, he needs to breathe, it hurts, he can't move and he's going to die, he knows it. His body spins toward the wavering sun above and a cloud passes overhead and the water darkens and Christ he wants air, his lungs are screaming, he needs to breathe, he needs air, and he opens his mouth and gulps down water in painful bursts.

CHAPTER 8

THE COVERS WERE TANGLED AROUND Mae's legs, and her T-shirt was damp with sweat. Her bedroom smelled foul, thick and clotting, and she sat up, coughing to get a breath, and then stumbled to the window and opened it. She leaned on the sill, trying to let in air, feeling disoriented and still half asleep. She'd read once that the body paralyzes itself while dreaming, and she felt that way now, she could barely move. There was something important she had to do, but her head was cloudy and she couldn't focus.

Morning sunlight blazed off the antique mirror next to her bed as she rubbed at her eyes. Her room looked older than it did at night, with its warped floorboards and cracks in the walls. The ceiling was also cracked, and painted a light blue with white clouds that were flaking at the edges.

A dream tugged at her memory, but the sun was bleaching it away. The bedside lamp was on—its bulb was hot,

81

she must have fallen asleep without switching it off. When she saw the green book shoved under her pillow, her stomach twisted and it all came rushing back. Yesterday had been both bad and good. Bad because she'd searched for Cage around Blue Gate but hadn't found him—she'd lost her chance to talk to him about Ro. Worse, she'd let him *get away*, Elle had reminded her, which made her feel sick. After staying out until dark looking for him, she'd come back to the house and opened the green book, to see if it had any answers. And it did.

Because before she'd died, Ro had written in it. And *that* was the good thing, the hope Mae was clinging to. She bet that somewhere between the first page and the shredded pages at the back Ro had written something important. Maybe even incriminating. She needed to read more now, but there was still that smell—so sharp and violent it made her eyes water. When she couldn't stand it anymore, she threw the book into her bag and pulled on a clean T-shirt and jeans, grabbing her Cons on the way out.

In the hallway the smell was stronger, and she coughed as it filled her lungs. What was it? She followed the smell past her dad's room and down the hallway, the stench the heaviest at the end. She found herself staring at Ro's door again, at its brass handle, and felt like running away. But she only had to open the door, that was all. Just open it.

She glanced over her shoulder to check that she was alone, then swung the door open and peered inside. For a moment she half expected to see the jewelry box on the floor again. But everything was in place: the bed was still made, the sketches were hanging neatly on the wall near the bookshelf, and the wardrobe was shut, the way she'd left it.

The room seemed normal, except for the smell, which wasn't in the air so much as it was clinging to everything around her—the furniture, the bedding, the curtains. Gasping now, Mae ran to the window and threw it open. When she turned back, she saw it. A black thread running down the wall and across the floor. It was a steady line of ants, trailing from the windowsill all the way to Ro's bed.

Mae steeled herself and crossed the room, kneeling to look underneath the bed. It was shadowy and dark, and in the corner a single black eye stared back at her. She jerked her head up, slamming it on the metal frame so hard it stung.

An image came together in her mind. It was a bird, only a bird. She crouched back down and she was right. A red-winged blackbird lay with its wings spread and its claws turned up.

The trail of ants leading to the bright spot on its wing made her want to cry. It must have flown into the room two nights ago, when she'd discovered the window un-latched, Ro's jewelry scattered across the floor. Mae got up, found an empty shoe box in the wardrobe, and then forced herself back toward the bed. She picked up the bird, feeling its lightness, its soft feathers, and gently set it into the box.

A banging noise came from the hallway, followed by a shuffle of footsteps. She took one last look at Ro's room before rushing out. Her granddad's cane was thudding down the hall now, tap *tap*, tap *tap*, getting closer to the stairs. She headed after him, putting the shoe box in her room to deal with later. She reached his side just as he turned her way, about to take the first step down the stairs, his Bible tucked under an elbow and his cane in his other hand. His white hair was combed flat, wet around his big ears, and he was wearing his suit, even in this heat.

"I was just," Mae started, catching her breath, "going down too."

Her granddad smiled at her with sad eyes. He didn't put up his usual playful fight about being helped down the staircase, which was too slippery for him, the old walnut worn slick with footfalls. He seemed calmer this morning, but he wouldn't have forgotten about the green book. He thought it was still on the top shelf of his bookcase, and she needed to keep it that way. She'd find a place to read alone later—somewhere out of sight.

As she guided him down the steps, the portraits on the walls glared at her, especially the seventeen-year-old steeped in shadows: Grady Cole II, his oily blue eyes following her like he wasn't fooled at all. She'd never been good at lying, but she could usually slip under the radar and go unnoticed. It'd been especially easy with Ro a magnet for any eyes and Elle so loud, fighting for attention. Being quiet meant she could hear more things, see things she might miss otherwise.

Mae clung to her granddad's forearm as he took the curving staircase. His clawlike hands were too stiff to make fishing lures, but he could still grip his cane, jot his little notes to her. Her eyes watered and she shoved his lack of speech behind the pale white door in her mind, along with his stroke, his cane, his fixation on the Bible. All those things meant he might be dying, and she didn't know if she could take it. Sometimes she wished she could go back to being a kid, when it seemed that everyone would live forever. When Mae was very young, Ro told her that their mother had never even lived on earth—*she's an angel in heaven, watching over us and keeping us safe forever.* But Mae knew now that no one could keep you safe.

"Almost there," she said on the last step. They crossed the foyer and her granddad's cane tapped all the way to the kitchen, where Elle was piling dishes in the sink.

"I made breakfast, since you slept in," Elle told her, bullhorning her voice like she always did around their granddad. For some reason Elle equated aphasia with being deaf, even though Mae had explained it to her. One was a language disorder caused by trauma to the brain—in this case a stroke—and the other involved eardrums.

"Hi, Granddad," Elle said, loud and slow. "Please help yourself!"

Mae glanced at the table and raised her eyebrows. Four bowls of flaky cereal were drowning in milk next to a carton of fake orange juice. "And you want to start a bed and breakfast."

"It's called being busy," Elle said, flicking dishwater at her.

Mae ducked, and then took a seat as her granddad

began eating, her mind slipping back to the green book and what she'd read so far. She couldn't think of it without remembering Ro's sixteenth birthday, how her eyes had shut tight until Ro finally gave up on showing her the book. And now she wanted to finish it.

But it would take time. The book was thick, the lettering cramped, trailing from edge to edge or cascading in circular shapes. Besides the raising ritual, there were other spells: some for curses, some for love, so many she hadn't been able to get through them yet. There were also lists of old-fashioned remedies and what seemed to be haphazard sketches. Notes were scribbled in margins, strange sayings and codes like *Chana 4 chana* and *RC =AC, J = E, H = GCI* and *Good Deeds for Good.*

Throughout the book the handwriting changed several times, sometimes on a single page, though none was Ro's. And then, just before sleep had caught up with her last night, she found it. Part of a page had been folded over, and when Mae smoothed it out, she discovered her sister's writing underneath like a treasure. Even now, she could still see Ro's sharp slashes over the hand-pressed page:

> *Initiated on sixteenth. Vow of silence.*
> *Another attempt unsuccessful.*
> *—RC.*

It was too brief, too cryptic. Mae thought about Ro and her games—that was what this had to be. The writing didn't sound like Ro. It was stilted, a mimicry of all the other pages in the book, as though she'd been trying to lay down her own riddle in ink. Even so, seeing her sister's handwriting warmed her, like standing next to a fire when you hadn't realized how cold you were. Now she was even more determined to read the rest, to find out what else was there from Ro and piece it all together.

"Where's mine?" Fern's high-pitched voice interrupted Mae's thoughts. The girl was standing at the kitchen counter, her blond curls tangled over her Invisible Man T-shirt, the same one she'd been wearing yesterday, and she was digging at her nose.

"Use a tissue," Elle said.

"What for?" Fern screwed up her face and Mae laughed. Fern didn't care what others thought. Even at eight, she had one of those old, wizened looks like the fruit sculptures they made in art class as kids: a cooked apple head with golden curls on top.

"Who let you in, anyway?" Elle asked.

Fern claimed a cereal bowl. "Your dad, of course."

Other voices were coming from the foyer, and a moment later Fern's uncle appeared in the kitchen, so tall he had to duck through the doorway. Childers was wearing a camouflage shirt over his police uniform, and Mae stiffened.

"You ought to go with us. It's on your land," Childers was saying to Sonny. He turned to Mae's granddad. "Morning, sir."

"Go where?" Elle called out. Her voice was muffled because she was bent over, twirling her auburn hair into a bun.

Mae gripped her water glass. Elle was eyeing Childers now, and the collar of his uniform that was poking out, and Mae silently started to chant: *Don't tell, don't tell, don't tell.*

"I was talking about gator season," Childers said. "You gotta catch 'em at night," he told Fern, "with big lights and harpoons."

"I already know that, Uncle Chill-chill," Fern said, and he gave one of her curls a tug and turned back to Sonny.

"So you game?"

"Ain't gators I'm looking for," Sonny said, opening the newspaper he was carrying. His cap shaded his face; it looked like he hadn't slept in a while.

"What are you looking for, then?" Elle asked. She glanced between him and Childers, and Mae stayed rigid in her seat. Surely Elle wouldn't say anything.

"Hey there, old Grandpa Cole," Fern said, yanking on his cuff as she took another bite of cereal.

He stopped slurping his breakfast to pull a cluster of pink lantanas out of his shirt pocket for her. Then he scrawled something on his notepad that made Fern laugh. Mae usually loved his flowers, his little notes, but right now she felt queasy, like she might get sick. If Elle told Childers and her dad about Cage, it would all be over.

Fern leaned in, her blond hair tickling across Mae's ear. "Your face looks weird," she whispered. "Lance says that when people look weird it either means one of two things." Her breath smelled like stale milk. "*One*, that they are, or *two* . . ." Fern paused intensely for a moment, like a preacher in a church. "Or *twooo*," she drawled, "that they're hiding something. Are you hiding something?"

Mae felt her neck flush. "The world is full of secrets," she said, trying to sound casual as she kept her eyes on Elle. But luckily, her sister seemed to be lost in her own thoughts now, checking her reflection on her phone, and Sonny was already headed into the alcove, Childers trailing him.

"What you got in there?" Fern asked. "It looks ancient."

Mae whirled, grabbing her canvas bag from the girl's hands. "One day everything will be ancient," she said, her fingers fumbling to close the latch.

Fern punched her arm. "Not me. I won't ever get old. You know what Lance says?"

"What do I say?" Lance's voice echoed in the foyer, and Mae turned.

He was leaning up against the kitchen doorway, looking carefree and nothing like he used to. Mae tried to keep the shock from her face. After Ro died, Lance had gone away for a study-abroad year and now he was back, looking like a completely new person. His shoulders were broader, it was obvious he'd been working out, and his curly brown hair was shorter, but it was more than that. It was the way he held himself.

"Never you mind," Fern called out to him.

"Hi, Lance," Elle said, a smile on her face as she stared his way. She'd mentioned Lance's "junior year transformation" when she came home from the party last night, but Mae hadn't believed it until now. He wasn't just stronger, he was also tan, like he'd been out in the sun all summer. He'd traded his usual black band T-shirt and scowl for a white button-up and an amused grin, and his quiet awkwardness had somehow turned into charm. As Mae stared at him she figured out what was bothering her: this Lance reminded her of how Ro used to act. Waves of confidence were radiating from him, the kind you couldn't fake.

"I thought you were waiting in the truck?" Fern asked.

"Too hot outside," Lance said. "Hot in here too," he added, and winked, his hazel eyes on Mae. She managed a smile and then studied her granddad's bowl of cereal. It had turned into a lumpy puddle of milk, and she searched for pictures in the floating strands of wheat, hoping Lance would look away. She'd never liked attention, and this new Lance was making her uncomfortable, even though he'd been their neighbor for so long. "Isn't it, Mayday?" he asked.

She felt an ache in her chest. That had been Ro's nickname for her. "Tends to be, this time of year," she said.

He nodded slowly, like her answer was profound. "Anyone up for horseback riding today?" He smiled, flashing dimples. Fern was busy plucking her lantanas, scattering pink petals across the table, and Mae knew Elle was

90

torn—she was scared of horses—but the stricken look on her face meant she wanted to go.

"What, no takers? Who's up for a swim, then?"

Lance's eyes didn't stray from Mae's as Fern shouted, "Me! Me-me-me!"

Maybe he'd stop staring at her if she gave him an answer. "Later," Mae said at the same time her sister said yes.

Lance turned to Elle and grinned. "I want to do everything I couldn't last year. That means warm water, horses, fishing, you name it. L.A. was fun, but it's no A.L."

His joke was terrible, but Mae laughed, surprised by it. The Lance she remembered hadn't made jokes, though she'd never really gotten to know him. Like her, Lance had kept to himself at school, stopping by the house when he could. He never came to see her or Elle—he came for Ro, just like everyone else had. He got up to fish before school like Ro did, went hunting with Sonny and Childers when Ro did, and he always read the same books, worshipped the same horror films and slasher movies. He was the first to stalk her in the school hallways, before all the others, girls and guys alike, and he was the one to find her body on the shore. It hurt knowing that he was there first, when it should have been her, or Elle, or their dad.

Her granddad's chair screeched across the floorboards and Mae hauled up her bag before Fern got at it again. She took the opportunity to leave by helping him through the kitchen, tap *tap*, tap *tap*, while Lance looked on. His hands were in his pockets, jingling his keys, and his curly hair was halfway covering his hazel eyes.

"Good to see you, Mae," he said as she passed, smiling wide enough to flash his dimples again.

"Welcome back." She was so unsettled by the change in him that she was glad when her granddad's cane finally tapped its way into the foyer. "Want to go outside?" she asked.

He squeezed her hand, which meant *Thank you* and *Yes* and *That's a good girl*, and she felt a fresh wave of guilt for stealing the green book from him. But it had to be done. If it had answers about Ro, she needed to find them.

Mae waited as he sat down in one of the rocking chairs, safe in the shade of the porch. He'd stay there all morning, reading his Bible and petting the black and calico strays that hung around. Those little cats were the reason her granddad kept a bag of kibble in his pocket; the cats would scratch if you tried to take them inside.

"I'm going for a walk," Mae told him. He waved brightly and she was off, knowing exactly where she could read alone. Her bag bobbed against her hip as she strode into the woods. It was a good day to be outside, but Ro would say that it always was. *Quit shutting yourself in your room with your paints. Get out into the world.* Everything had been easy for Ro; she hadn't been afraid of anything new in life—and maybe that was the key.

Mae was now deep in the woods. It was cooler here, the sunlight dappling across the ground. When she glanced over her shoulder, there was only a sliver of the bluish house and its tall hedge through the trees. Her granddad's white hair was a tiny splotch, a floating orb next to one of the pillars on the porch.

Instead of veering onto the track toward the beach, she walked farther into the woods, hurrying now. Sometimes it seemed as if the land kept going and going, and being in the middle of the woods like this felt like she was falling back in time to when there wasn't even a house, when all of it was just trees and swampland and dark blue water.

The turnoff to the Childers place was close enough to smell their stables, that damp scent of manure and hay, but Mae kept straight, skirting patches of mud from the recent rain. After another mile she glimpsed the distant spikes of the wrought-iron gate. The cemetery was a sprawling, shadowy place—the perfect spot to read undisturbed. Trees bordered its fence and rose between headstones and old statues. On the far side was a narrow dirt access road that eventually led to the highway.

Just when she was close enough to see that the cemetery was empty, a deer darted out of the woods in front of her. Mae jumped back, startled. It was a small thing, not much older than a fawn, and as it leaped into a thicket, little dots of red splashed across the grass near her feet. The blood was a shock to see, the way it always was, and without thinking she changed course, following the stippled ground. A drop here on a leaf, another drop there in the mud.

Mae veered around a thick copse of trees, her hair catching on a low branch, tangling up in it. The deer was just ahead, limping away. Blood was oozing from its hind leg, like it'd been shot. She kept after it, weaving through trunks and past a creek that had formed from all the rain.

A small green clearing was ahead, covered in kudzu. Those vines were invasive—they could crop up anywhere—but to swarm like this took at least a year or two. Strange she'd never seen this place before.

When she got to the edge of the kudzu, she stopped. The deer stood knee-deep in vines that had swelled across the ground and crept over the bushes, cloaking them in green too. Stems and tendrils had sprawled across the trunks of the stubbier trees, swallowing them completely, halted only by the larger trees and the little creek. Just beyond was a small cement dome—an old hut of some kind. The deer lay down in front of it and watched her with its head tilted.

Mae felt bad for the creature. She'd never liked going hunting with her dad and Ro—aiming a gun felt wrong to her, like she knew it would tear through her own heart if she pulled the trigger—but Sonny had taught her the etiquette of hunting, how you never leave an injured animal to die alone.

She lunged into the kudzu, moving toward the deer to find out what was wrong. The ground under her feet was uneven, and when she tried to step around a small green bulge she fell. Her bag hit the ground and the book tumbled out. As she reached for it, she saw what she'd tripped over and gasped.

A gravestone.

The kudzu-covered bulge was a gravestone. Her stomach went cold. Why was a grave marker out here, beyond the cemetery gates? She stared past it and her heart lurched. The sea of kudzu flowing toward the dome was full of small mounds.

She was surrounded by headstones—she was in an old graveyard.

She looked at the marker she'd fallen beside, and a tingle ran down her neck. Ignoring the vines underneath her hands and knees, Mae crawled forward, and then she pulled leaves off the closest grave and the smaller bulge next to it. The gravestone was old, its stone pockmarked. Etched across it was what looked like a horizontal figure eight. The symbol for infinity? Beneath it was a date, 1860, and underneath the date were letters, but they were weathered and hard to read.

"'I laid me down and slept; I awaked,'" Mae whispered, running her fingers across the stone, "'for you raised . . .'" She stopped, she couldn't make out the rest.

"I *awaked*," she said again. It was a loud word, a word that meant a change, that meant *Open your eyes*. It seemed a cruel thing to write on a gravestone. And why wasn't there a name on it? She turned to the little slab next to it, pulled away the tangle of vines.

This grave was smaller but had the same date: 1860. Then came an *L* and a *U*—

Even in the warm sun, a chill shot down her spine and she glanced up. The deer was watching her, standing now with its white tail twitching, one of its hind legs raised.

She needed to help it if she could. She quickly scooped up the green book from the ground. It had landed in the vines, and she brushed the dirt from its spine, pulled out the stems between its pages. As she flicked away a stray leaf, she froze.

There was a row of cursive, each line identical to the next. *I love Hanna, I love Hanna, I love Hanna, I love Hanna, I love Hanna, I love Hanna,* the same three words written all the way down the page. It seemed strange and obsessive, childish, but it was the last line that caught her attention. At the end of the page was this: *Hanna told me her secret name.* And then, beside that line, the thing that made her go still.

One symbol: a figure eight. Someone had run their pen over it again and again.

Mae looked at the grave, at the exact same symbol etched across its stone. Her heart was going fast in her chest and it was hard to breathe.

Just a coincidence, that was what Elle would say. Her dad would find a rational explanation, like maybe the page had been dog-eared, or the spine crooked, naturally falling open on that spot, but she didn't want to be out here anymore, not among these graves—she felt like an intruder. She closed her eyes, and then she didn't feel like an intruder at all; instead she felt like she'd been lured here, like someone had played a trick on her. That thought sent her scrambling to her feet. She shoved the green book into her bag; she'd check on the deer and leave this place.

But when she turned toward the domed structure, the animal was gone.

A patch of darkness fell across the kudzu. Overhead a cloud blanketed the sun and the air went suddenly cold, as if it might rain any moment.

Then she saw the leaves trembling near the dome. Someone was standing in its shade. When he stepped out of the cover of vines, her hands tightened around her bag.

There he was, not ten paces away, his shirt muddy, his jeans torn. His darker skin made his eyes stand out all the more—those blue eyes that were watching her.

"Take me to her," Cage said, his voice carrying over the silence. "Now."

CHAPTER 9

BLUE GATE, 1859

THE WITCH DOESN'T KNOW THAT Grady's watching. The trees shield him from her gaze, but he's close enough to hear her breathing and see the strands of her long white hair. Pearl kneels down in the mud and claws at it, bringing up what look like tiny animal bones. She stoops over again near the cabin and draws sharp lines across the ground with the edge of a bone. She stands, whispering something, and then whirls, her dark eyes finding Grady's. His stomach tenses and he resists the impulse to back away.

"Where your eyes go, your hand will follow," Pearl says to him. She's looking at him like he's bait. Like he's nothing more than a palmful of animal bones. Her son steps out from behind the shed, the ax in his hand.

"Do you like what we do?" Pearl asks. The pit of Grady's stomach goes heavy. No matter how kind Hanna is, her mother is something else. She's not the devil worshipper his father claims, but she's still someone to fear. Someone who can harness untouchable things like breath, like the beating of a heart.

"Give me your hand," Pearl says. She's holding a knife now. Mud is on her dress, mud is caked on her fingers. Her white hair swirls around her even though the air is still. Grady feels a shiver deep inside. This is why his father made him swear never to come here.

"Give me your hand," she says again, and her blade gleams in the light. Then there's another voice, a softer one.

"Mother," Hanna calls. She's stepping through the cabin's doorway. Her hair is tied back with the red scarf, and she's wearing the same slip and long apron she always does, and the laces on her boots are missing. Grady has never seen anyone who makes him stare like her. "I did the work, so it's me he owes," Hanna tells her. "Put that away."

"We were only talking," Pearl says, but the knife disappears into her pocket.

Hanna turns to him. "Ready?" she asks, and Grady nods, his head clearing with a rush. *What just happened?*

"Come on." Hanna points and he gratefully follows her inside the cabin. The smell of raw meat hits him as he ducks into the gloom and then pulls the book from his back pocket. It's his journal with the leather cover. The reason he's here.

"Where should we start today?" she asks.

"You choose." He gives her the dip pen he brought and sits down beside her at the table. Teaching her is payment for saving his brother, but it's an easy trade. He likes sitting next to her in the candlelight. He likes how her dark hair brushes across his arm sometimes, how the cabin smells of meat and smoke. And spices too, just like Hanna. Garlic in hanging baskets, gingerroot ground in the mortar and pestle on the small table.

After a while Hanna's pen stops and he reads what she's stuck on. "'T-h-i-n-*g*.'" He stresses the last letter. *Anything*, he thinks; this is what he would do for her.

"I know," Hanna says, but she rewrites the word anyway. She holds the pen too tight; she never wants to let it go.

"Now read it back to me," Grady tells her.

"To use for any-thing." Hanna skims her finger along the top of the page as she reads her careful letters. She has learned fast, and he's been learning too. Everything she writes he memorizes, just like he's memorized the shape of her face so he can see it when he closes his eyes.

"As a gen-e-ral pre-ven-tion and pro-tec-tion," she says, reading out the next line. She pauses and looks at him. "I'm going to add the ingredients to it. We need to hurry. The sun's almost down."

He nods and then his eyes go to her lips and his heart goes *tap tap tap* like the pen against the page.

"Quit it." She has stopped writing now, and he can't help it—he leans in and kisses her cheek, so fast he's not sure he did it at all.

She pulls back and tilts her head at him. He wants to kiss her again but he doesn't know what she's thinking, so he waits. Her eyes have two glints of light in them from the candle. Makes it look like her pupils are glowing. Makes her look magic, and there's no denying what she can do. Grady saw his brother dead, and then he saw him alive. That next morning, after leaving him with Hanna, Grady came back to the cabin and there was Jacob, his messy blond hair sticking up in a hundred different directions and a grin on his face. He had a bandage around his eye where the horse had kicked him and that was all. Whatever Hanna and Pearl did to him had worked to get his heart pumping again. It was more than just healing, it had to be. But Hanna says she won't write that remedy down in the book. She's worried most people can't be trusted with it.

"Grady," she finally says. The pen goes *clunk* on the table. She leans forward and kisses him and his stomach drops and then the world drops away until her lips finally leave his.

"Night's coming. Almost time for you to go, Grady Cole," Hanna whispers. "Your folks will wonder where you are."

His father's with a patient, and he knows exactly where his mother is: in bed with another headache. Grady pulls off his hat and rubs at his hair, not wanting to leave. His heart is quick in his chest and he can't stop himself from touching Hanna's cheek. Her skin is soft and warm—just how he feels inside when he looks at her. "Another lesson tomorrow?"

"I want to," she says. "But—"

"But what?"

Her jaw bears down like it does when she's thinking. "Maybe we shouldn't . . . ," she starts, and he holds his breath. "Grady, you don't know me. You don't know my family—"

"I do," he cuts in. It's true he doesn't know much about her family: one day they just appeared, built their cabin at the edge of Blue Gate's property, and soon word spread about their remedies, their magic. Pearl and her son remain a mystery; they even speak to each other in a language he doesn't recognize. But he knows Hanna—he knows how he feels about her, at least. Every lesson has made him fall more in love, and he wishes telling his father he wants to marry her wasn't so hard. Now Hanna looks away, at anything but him. Her gaze is on the fireplace, the strings of sage hanging to dry. "Hanna?"

"That's not even my real name," she says. He's shocked, but if she's got secrets, she can share them when she wants. Her shoulders are tense now, her dark eyes searching his own.

"Tell me what I should call you, then." He gently tilts her chin toward him. The red scarf in her hair is framing her face and she has that smell he loves on her, sweat and spices and ink.

"I can't," she says. She takes his hand and turns it up. "I'll show you instead." With her fingertip, she traces a symbol onto his palm. "It's my other name," she says. "One is ordinary and one is magic."

He's confused but won't let it bother him. "Could be easier just to call you Hanna," he teases. She laughs like he wanted her to, and it's the best thing he's heard all day. Maybe he could stay longer and they could do another lesson? Take out the ink, open the book again. He wants a reason to sit next to her, to be with her, but her eyes are going to the doorway.

"Night's coming," she says. "Go now, Grady." She thrusts the book and two small jars into his hands. "Take this, it'll help your mother's headaches. And this one's for Jacob."

Hanna saved Jacob just like Pearl saved his mother all those years ago. She was dying in childbirth and his father said there was nothing he could do, so Grady ran into the woods, found his way to the witch's house. His family is alive thanks to Pearl, and now thanks to Hanna too.

He feels bold enough to kiss her cheek again, which earns him another laugh before he rushes out the door. It's dusk, but he can see enough to find the trail through the trees. He glances back at the warm light the cabin makes and keeps going. He's almost to Blue Gate when he hears a whistle.

"Grady!"

His little brother's sitting on the corral's fence, waving at him. The bandage is still wrapped over his eye, and there's a blossom of a bruise on his neck.

"Finally!" Jacob calls out. He hops down from the fence and jogs over. His hair's sloppy like usual, and he's got a young bird in his shirt pocket, probably another one he's saved. "You went to the witch's house again, didn't you?" he asks, and Grady wants to lie but can't.

"Don't say anything," he tells Jacob. "It's our secret, all right?"

Jacob grins, and Grady smiles back at him. What happened with the horse is their secret too, and so far Jacob's kept it. He knows what their father would do if the truth was out. Grady ruffles his brother's sweaty hair and then smells pipe smoke.

No, no, no. He slowly turns, already knowing what he'll see. Standing just beyond the corral is their father. He's close enough to have heard everything.

"What's wrong?" Jacob asks, and Grady is afraid to answer. He wishes, in this very moment, that he could go back in time, could hurry a little faster. He wishes he could have predicted that his father would come home early. But most of all, he wishes his father was a different man. A man who greeted him instead of holding out a lantern and glaring with those pale blue eyes. Whatever he's thinking makes his face look cold and dark.

Grady's heart is beating fast, but it's not the heart of a creature caught, its death certain—no, this is a louder thing, a booming thing: this is the sound of a creature *alive*, and we hear it all the way from where we watch in the shadows. We hear it now, this insistence in his chest, this battering against his ribs, and we hear it a hundred years later, because there will always be this moment with Grady, right now and here, before the darkness swallows him whole.

CHAPTER 10

IT WAS A TRAP. HAD to be. Cage leaned against the cemetery's iron fence, hiding where it was darkest. No way Mae would show tonight. If what she said was true, Ro was dead and they thought he'd done it. *This is bigger than both of us, Cage.* That small memory of Ro shouting at him, that's what scared him the most. *Just back off!* Because if he'd lost his temper . . .

But he would never hit her. Never.

And her sister would never show tonight. She was probably calling the police right now. It'd be an ambush, with that big hulk of a man—Childers, that was his name. Asking Mae to come here had been a mistake, but he wanted to know for sure.

A footfall sounded and Cage turned toward the dark path, his fists tight. He'd go down fighting.

Another footstep and then Mae was ducking out from the trail. He scanned the woods behind her, but as far as he could tell, she'd come alone. A shred of luck.

She stood in front of him in the moonlight. Pine needles at her feet, Ro's thin red sweatshirt hanging over her torn jeans. Her hair was tangled-looking, long and thick, like there was more of it than her.

He was about to speak, but she put a finger to her lips and then pointed at the gate, toward the caretaker's hut, the reason they'd waited for dark. Cage nodded and went to the fence, heard her following with light steps. When he held his palms up to hoist her over, she looked at him with wary eyes. Then she reached into her pocket and pulled out a knife. Tried to flick open the blade, but it didn't work, so she just pointed the hilt at him.

"Don't try anything." The knife was trembling. It was the worst threat he'd ever seen.

"I'm trying to help you over."

"I'm just saying, don't try anything."

"You're not gonna pull out a rifle next, are you?" He was mostly joking, but she didn't see the humor, and then he thought of Ro and pain racked his chest. Mae's gaze stayed on him as she slipped the knife into her pocket and stepped onto his palms.

It was like she weighed nothing at all. He lifted her up and she grabbed the highest part of the fence, climbed to the top and hovered, half clinging, half standing, before she jumped to the other side. Not bad; graceful, even. He followed her over, feeling slow. His jaw bore down as he made it across, his head still feeling heavy from the accident.

When he straightened, he caught her watching him

with a frown on her face, like she was trying to decide something. At least the knife wasn't still out, though bringing a weapon showed she had sense. After a long minute when neither of them moved, she held a finger to her lips again and then gestured for him to follow her.

There were headstones all around them, statues scattered among the clipped grass. Pain tore through his head, and he tried not to think about why they were here. *One, two, three,* he counted, keeping himself calm.

Mae took off along a path that crossed through the graves, and he followed. Along the way she stopped at the statue of an angel, with wings so large they were blocking the path. Moss had grown between its fingers, outstretched and beckoning. The statue reminded him of a figurehead, a mermaid on the prow of a boat. He'd seen one like that while working at the wharf . . . but none of that mattered anymore. Not if Ro was here, in this place. He had to know for sure.

"This way," Mae whispered, nodding toward the back of the cemetery.

He kept following her. Having her here with him made it easier to imagine Ro. If her sister was here, then Ro would appear soon too. She'd shout out his name, say it was all a joke. Her worst, most god-awful prank of all. Mae would turn to him and admit she'd been put up to it. Ro was manipulative, but she always let you know you were being manipulated, which made the difference. It made it okay— somehow you wanted to do what she asked no matter what.

His shin scraped against a headstone and he glanced up, getting his bearings. He'd wandered off the path. Mae was far ahead now; he could see her messenger bag at her hip, the strap pulled tight across her chest. She moved quick and quiet, as if used to walking around at night, and he picked up his pace.

The moon was half full and the sky was cloudless, easy enough to see by. Around them the earth was sunken and wet and dipped in small valleys. Cherubs and curled serpents were perched on gravestones; unmarked crosses from the Civil War jutted up next to pauper stones. Then came the newer graves of polished granite. Cage's heart revved and he braced himself.

Mae stopped at the back fence. A tree was in the corner, dead and bent. It was blackened by lightning and its branches hung over a pair of graves.

Cage took another step and then he saw it: her name, etched onto the headstone beside her mother's. His chest seized and he couldn't breathe. He collapsed onto the ground with his back to the rows and rows of graves—the two rectangular blocks of granite and the tree in front of him. Mae stayed beside him. Standing so still she could have been another statue.

"I'm here," he whispered, his knees going wet in the grass.

Nothing.

"You're here."

Nothing.

He wanted to feel her—her presence, her touch, anything—but all he felt was sharp heartache, pain that was filling him so much there wasn't room for anything else. No room to breathe, to think. He looked away from the gravestone, took in a deep gulp of air, another.

He sensed movement beside him and quickly turned. On the trunk of the bent tree was an eye, staring at him. He thought of Ro's book, of the things she'd told him. But when he reached out to touch the eye, he felt only a rough knob, a scab of bark. For shit's sake. It was just the moon with its tricky light.

He stepped back from the tree to read the name on the grave again. ROXANNE ELIZABETH COLE.

"I'm sorry," he said.

He heard nothing in return, but Mae was stock-still, like she was terrified. He imagined Ro standing beside him—telling him to remember what he'd done.

He needed to keep his hands busy, keep moving. Earlier he'd found a candle and some matches in the barn, and now he pulled them from the pocket of his jeans.

The match flared when he struck it, and its light fell over her name. ROXANNE ELIZABETH COLE. BELOVED DAUGHTER AND SISTER. REST IN PEACE. It couldn't be her grave. Ro would have laughed at something that dull. *Rest in peace.* The rest of the engraving was covered by weeds, and he held his fists tight until he could get the words out.

"You saw them?" he finally said.

Mae's voice was hushed, tight. "Saw what?"

"You saw them bury her."

She nodded. Her eyes were wet and her face laid it all bare and then it hit him with a force. Ro in the ground. No more grin, no more pranks, no more swimming, no more laughter. Ro in a coffin. All her light shut under the dirt. It wasn't supposed to be like this. He'd do anything. Please, she couldn't be dead, she couldn't—

"Stop. Stop!" The yell snapped loud into the night, and hands were on his shoulders, pulling him back. He struggled and then realized it was Mae; she was breathing heavy. His knuckles were bloody, and the trunk of the dead tree looked as though it'd been mauled. He'd been hitting it.

One, two, three, four. Christ, stay calm, don't think about her. *Five, six, seven.* Start over. *One, two, three, four.*

"Hear that?" Mae whispered.

The sound of a twig snapping, something shuffling through the undergrowth. She was right—something was out there. And he was in here, crouched over Ro's grave. And they thought he did it.

"Get down." Mae was tugging at his shirt, and then his legs sprang into action. He ducked down with her, hiding behind the bent tree. Flat on their bellies, her bag between them.

They waited—tensed and listening. He didn't know how long they lay there, the damp ground soaking through their shirts. His knuckles stung; he'd shredded them up pretty bad. His arm was at a funny angle, falling asleep. Pinpricks in his right elbow, moving up to his neck. The woods seemed quiet now, but he stayed down, making sure. After a while he dared to talk. "It was probably just—"

"A deer or something," Mae finished, her voice soft. She sat up, but slow, cautious. Her brown eyes found his. "I want to know what happened that day."

"You and me both." He leaned back against the tree, his hand beside her grave. "I'd never do this," he said. "Don't care what they say."

She took a breath and the moonlight caught her hair just the right way and for a minute it looked like Ro's hair. He imagined how it used to feel in his hands, the scent good enough to breathe in deep.

Mae was quiet. Her gaze was flicking back and forth between Ro's headstone and their mother's. "You know my middle name's Eliza, for my mom," she said, nodding toward the grave next to Ro's. "Ro was the one who brought us up." She smiled, but it looked like she was trying not to cry. "I used to feel sorry for myself, not having a mom. But you know the quickest way to get over something?" She touched her throat like it was hard for her to speak. "Having something worse happen."

The other way was to have something good happen— like meeting Ro. But he didn't say that.

Mae watched him, her eyes dark in the night. Her hair was in her face, and she held her shoulders tucked in, like the sadness was all the way in her bones, and then he felt bad for making her come here. It would've been hard for her to meet him, but she'd done it anyway.

"My middle name is Lucky," he said, not sure why he was telling her. But maybe the talking would help. "I know, it's an awful name." He shrugged, and all of a sudden it hurt to swallow. "Thing is, I felt the opposite my whole life. Until the day I met her."

He wanted to talk about Ro, so he kept going. "When I met her, I thought, *wow*. What'd I do to deserve this? I thought, my luck's finally turned." His whole body felt bruised inside when he looked at the grave. "And now here we are."

"Lucky," Mae said. "Why'd your mom name you that?"

"Must have been her sense of humor."

Mae opened her mouth and then closed it with a little sigh. He thought of talking about the first time he'd met them in Gulf Shores, how Ro pretended to drown to see what he'd do. Or about the night she made a bonfire and how the barn nearly went up while she roasted the perfect marshmallow. Or the time she left a trail of riddles to his birthday present—a pair of mittens that sent them both laughing because it was sweltering and because she'd knitted what looked like an extra thumb. All of those moments rushed over him, and yet he couldn't remember the one day he needed to.

"Tell me something," he said to Mae. It'd been bothering him since yesterday when he'd shown up at Blue Gate. "How come you asked where I'd been?"

"What do you mean?"

"Back at your house. You said everyone thought I did it, because I ran. And Elle said something about me hiding out all this time."

She bit her lip, like she wasn't sure what to say. "Where were you?" she asked.

"I told you, I crashed my bike. Must have been . . ." He wanted to say *right after it happened*, but he didn't know for sure. "I woke up—" He skipped the details, didn't need to tell her everything. "I woke up and hitched a ride to your house."

"But—"

"The last thing I remember is taking the boat out with her," he said. "I must have been out a couple of days, or . . ."

Mae shook her head, her eyes wide, and confusion shot through him. "What? Tell me."

"You've been gone almost a year, Cage."

No. No, that wasn't right. *Think. Think, Cage.* He'd gone sailing with Ro a couple of days ago and they'd had a fight, and then he must have ridden off and crashed. He'd wound up in the hospital, had stumbled in from the street, like the nurse told him. Out cold for a few days at the most. Not a year. No way he'd been in there for a year.

Mae shook her head. "I don't know where you've been. If you've been hiding, or—"

"I wasn't hiding," he broke in. The anger came sudden and swift and he could feel it pulsing through him.

She looked at him, wary. "Everyone else thinks you were."

"And what do you think?" he said, his hands going to fists as he waited for her to answer. He didn't know why, but it felt like whatever came out of her mouth next could mean everything.

"I don't know yet." The way she said it, like a sigh, made all the fight leak from him. "But you were gone a year," she told him, her eyes still on his. "How do you think she has a gravestone already? That took time."

His throat felt hot. Why couldn't he remember? The guy in his room, the other patient. He'd been hooked up on life support, seemed he'd been there awhile. So maybe it was possible? Whatever happened . . . he wouldn't have hurt her.

Cage ran a hand through his hair—it felt longer than he usually kept it. The bruise across his chest was aching, everything was. He couldn't think straight. The way he saw it, he only had two options. Get away from Blue Gate before daylight, make sure no one recognized him. The other choice was harder, but it was the right one.

"I'll turn myself in. Tell them everything I know."

Mae went quiet for a minute. He wasn't sure she'd even heard him. "You told me you didn't do it," she finally said.

"Mae, I'd never touch her." But he couldn't remember, could he? All he remembered was them taking out the sailboat. And Ro shouting at him. *Just back off!* He glanced down at his raw knuckles and then something else came. Just like that, like a light switch flicking on in his head, he remembered the ring. Christ, had he really done it?

"I wanted to . . ." He couldn't say it out loud, not now. "I had a ring for her."

Mae turned to him. Looked as shocked as his uncle had been when he'd told him his plan. *You're seventeen*, his uncle said. He'd been pulling in a net of live bait. *You got all the time in the world.*

But the world hadn't given them shit, and now Mae was eyeing him and he didn't want her asking questions that might piss him off, so he kept talking. "It was my grandmother's," he said. "It was nice, real nice." Best thing he owned, and he wanted to give it to Ro. "Only . . ."

Only he wished he remembered more. What if he'd asked and she told him no? His temper, it was something he had to breathe through, it was always there, waiting for him to slip up.

"Only you don't remember," Mae said, and paused. She looked like she took her time with words, really turned them over before she spoke. "You're telling me you don't remember what happened that day. That you don't remember—an entire year." She shook her head. "And you want to give yourself up?"

He wanted to do the right thing. His jaw clenched tight, and he started counting in his head to keep calm.

Mae lifted her hair from her neck, coiled it into a knot. She was staring at Ro's grave like maybe it had answers. "Doesn't seem smart," she said after a minute. "Not when they're saying all those things about you. Not when they think you did it and you can't remember."

"What do you care, anyway?" His voice was sharp, but he couldn't hold it back. Here she was, helping him, only person in the world helping him, and he was practically shouting at her.

"I—" Mae started, and then shut her mouth.

They both went quiet, and an old poem wormed its way into his head. One Ro used to recite, every time they docked. *Home is the sailor, home from sea.* Here he was, back at Blue Gate. Only this time he'd come alone. *Home is the sailor, home from sea. And the hunter home from the hill.*

"Why are you helping me?" he said.

Mae brought her knees up to her chest and shivered. Her jeans were smeared with mud from lying on the ground.

"I'm not. I came here to ask you what happened." She spoke so softly he had to strain to hear. "And even if you don't remember, I don't think you did it."

It didn't sound like she believed what she said. It sounded like she was trying to convince herself. But she was here—she'd met him after dark like she'd promised, and that meant something.

"She loved you, and you loved her," she said.

It wasn't that simple. He'd seen a lot of shitty things done by people who loved each other. He needed to remember what happened. He needed to know for sure. If it was his fault—if he'd done something, lost his temper, hit her—then he deserved to suffer. But what if someone else had done it?

Sitting here all night in the mud and the moonlight wasn't going to help. He stood and held out his hand.

Mae didn't take it, just scrambled to her feet. They made their way to the gate in silence. She was quick to climb over and then he was up after her, dropping to the ground, a dull ache still in his head.

Out here in the woods, past the wrought-iron fence, the trees loomed tall and dark. He didn't know what to do. If there were records of his stay at the hospital, then he could prove to the cops that he hadn't just been hiding out for a year. But what if he'd only been in there for a day or two like he thought? Going to the police, especially with his record, was unwise. If he said he didn't remember what happened, they'd lock him up. But if he didn't hand himself over, they'd keep looking for him. He couldn't go to his uncle's house in Gulf Shores—wouldn't shame him like that, not after everything his uncle had done for him. Couldn't go to his mother's in New Orleans either. The worst thing would be the look on her face, like she'd known all along he'd get in trouble again.

Mae was humming now, really faintly, and the tune reminded him of Ro and then he didn't want to listen anymore.

"I should leave," he said. "Try to remember what happened. Come back when I do." He could go work in Mexico for a while. Or Alaska. Lots of folks hid in Alaska.

Mae didn't say anything. Only stared up at the moon,

just above the tips of the trees. Then she stopped humming, her lips tight, her brown eyes like his uncle's—hard to read.

"If you don't remember, don't come back until you do," she said. She stood there facing him. Her eyes were watering and the grief hit him too and he clenched his jaw, he couldn't lose it here in front of her. He needed a better plan than just running away, but he owed her a goodbye first. She'd helped him so far, hadn't told anyone he was here. She had no reason to help him either, none at all.

He cleared his throat. His mouth felt dry, gritty. "I never told you," he said, just wanting to get through it, "that I'm sorry. About what happened when we first met. I shouldn't have—"

"Don't," Mae said. "Don't apologize for that. Not now." Then she turned, started walking away. A few seconds later she started to run. She was heading back toward Blue Gate, where she belonged, and Ro was gone and she wasn't coming back.

Cage sank to the ground. The earth felt hard and damp and he thought of her grave and wished the motorcycle had killed him. He'd trade places with her. He'd trade if she'd let him.

Count, Cage. He could hear her now, see that playful smile. Her words came back to him, her little sayings. *Start with one, because it's better than nothing.* He was woozy— the trees spun around him and his head was aching. *Try harder. Get to your feet and lift your chin. Stand up and veni vidi vici your life.* He took a step and nearly fell over something. On the ground was Mae's bag. She'd forgotten it.

He'd take it to her, leave it on the porch where she'd find it. Then he'd get to the highway, hitch a ride before dawn to any place that wasn't here. He reached down and slung the bag onto his shoulder. It was heavier than he expected. The flap was open, and as he was tucking it back, about to latch it, he stopped.

He recognized it straightaway. That tattooed green leather with the back cover missing. A pair of coffins on the front. It was Ro's book. He'd never wanted anything to do with it before—he could hear his mother even now, teasing him. But here was the book, which meant . . . the scratch of some memory came.

He touched the shriveled leather and felt the ground drop away. The sky rushed down on him and his vision went black, he couldn't see a thing, and then it smelled like smoke. Fire and smoke and wood—the air sharp and thick and he couldn't breathe, not one breath, and he pitched over in a coughing fit, his chest heaving so hard he saw stars. Blinking, the ground swimming in front of him now. But he could see again. His lungs filled with a deep breath.

When he finally straightened, she was there. He was either dead or she was alive—and she was in front of him.

"Ro?"

She reached toward him. He stared at her wet arm, her blond mess of hair, soaking wet.

Cage.

Her eyes held his gaze. Then she smiled, but her teeth were bloody. She'd bitten through her lower lip.

He blacked out.

He's checking his uncle's nets in Gulf Shores and hoping the girl will turn up again when he sees someone else on the beach instead. This girl's in a red bikini and she's lying on a towel over wet sand. She's about his age, seventeen, or maybe a little older, and she's stunning—the type who'd never go for him. He stands on the deck with his arm up blocking the sun, the water between them.

She's on her stomach, reading, the towel bunched underneath her. Her hair's shiny, so bright it's hard to look at. She licks her fingertips before she turns the page and he wants to be that book.

A small wave rocks into the side of the boat. He's still watching her, can't help it. He wishes he was out on the beach instead of working, but he needs the money and at least there's the view. After a while the girl stands and shakes out her long hair. He hopes she's the type who likes to fish or hike, camp outdoors, except who's he kidding? Still, he can't take his eyes off her.

When it seems she might look in his direction, he turns. He's making up ways to introduce himself, now wishing he paid more attention in English class. He could ask her what she's reading, ask whether she prefers the ocean to the mountains, or if she knows how to read the stars, or just anything, like where does she live? But he'll miss his chance. He already took his break today, and by the time he finishes work she'll be gone. Probably wouldn't talk to a guy like him anyway.

He doesn't want to let his uncle down, so he goes back to work, double time now to make up for all the staring he just did. *Like a fool*, his mother would say. He spent the morning daydreaming about another girl and here he is again, his head floating on fantasies. Good way to mess up and lose his job like everyone thinks he will. The rope is rough in his hands and that salty smell of fish is strong enough to choke on. He focuses on the sun burning his neck, the sweat running down his back. He tells himself looking at the beach is off-limits, at least until he finishes. When he's hauling in the last net, the shout comes and he glances up.

She's in the water, waving her arms, so he drops the net and stumbles for the life preserver. She's alone in the waves, far from shore like she got caught in a current, and she's fighting the water and losing. The preserver falls short when he throws it and he curses. He scans the beach but there's no one in sight so he dives in, bracing at the burst of cold as he swims toward her, that red swimsuit like a warning.

When he's close enough to shout, he tells her it's okay. That he won't leave her. He's thinking, *Don't pull us down*, he's saying that as he reaches for her, *Don't pull us under*. She looks at him with eyes full of tears and coughs up water and then he's got an arm around her ribs.

"Just relax," he tells her. The waves aren't too strong and he thinks he could float her, drag her to the pier that way. He flips her onto her back, keeping hold of her as he treads water. "I won't let you go."

She coughs again, doesn't speak. He kicks hard toward the dock, his hand underneath her, guiding her. She's got her eyes shut, probably scared or in shock, he's not sure. Her skin is soft, like she belongs in the water, and he can't believe he's touching her.

They make it to the pier and then she wraps her arms around him—she's in his arms as she whispers her thanks and turns to grab the ledge.

He pulls himself up after her. She's on her knees now, dripping and coughing and laughing—he can't believe that she's laughing, and for a minute he's angry.

"What's your name, sailor?" she asks, and coughs again, but now she's smiling at him as though they might be sharing a joke.

"Cage." Before he can say more she puts a cold hand over his lips.

"You saved my life," she tells him. "That makes me bound to you forever." She smiles again and then says, "Seven for a secret, swear you won't tell." Her eyes are green with bits of gold that match the locket she's wearing. "Eight for a wish and nine for a kiss." She snaps her fingers and he can't stop looking at her. "Ten for a bird, you must not miss."

And he stares at her because he's not sure what to say and because she's not like any girl he's ever met before, not if she talks like this. The tide is lapping against the dock and the sun is hot over them and he doesn't want to leave her side.

"Life is good, isn't it?" she says, and she leans back on her elbows as if she's not going anywhere either. She laughs again. "Isn't that right, Cage? *Caaaaaaaaaaaaa . . .*"

CHAPTER 11

MAE HAD WOKEN UP AT dawn with Hanna on her mind. The girl with the secret name made her curious. Still half asleep, she'd gone to the collection of old boxes in the pantry under the stairs and pulled them into the dining room. Somewhere among the decades of albums packed away, she knew she'd find Hanna and the Cole who'd loved her, who'd written about her in the book. But just as she'd started on the first box, Elle had hurried down the stairs in a bright yellow sundress.

"You're helping me clean for the bed and breakfast," she said, grinning, and before Mae could answer, Elle shook her head. "You're helping me," she repeated, challenging her with the brown eyes they shared. There was a price for Elle's silence about Cage, and working for her all morning was it. Mae had just slipped out to the porch to leave some food for the strays when something drew her attention.

It was the rocking chair, moving slightly in the breeze. And draped over its seat was her canvas bag.

Mae walked toward it slowly, dread pooling in her stomach. The bag was too flat and too light and her hands shook as she opened the flap, saw her pocketknife in one of the sleeves. Then she looked inside. The ribbon was at the bottom, curled up like a sleeping snake. The book was missing.

"Mae!" Elle's voice carried from inside the house. "Mae?"

Mae went through the bag again, nursing a tendril of hope, and then glanced at the lawn, just in case it had fallen out. But there was only the sandy driveway full of puddles from the rain. No book. Feeling desperate, she searched the empty canvas once more.

A small piece of paper was sticking out of the corner pocket. It was a little scroll of cigarette paper, its edges yellowed. Mae snatched it up and unrolled it—instead of tobacco inside there were words. The writing was messy, written in a hurry:

> Mae, you dropped this. I kept her book,
> might help me remember something.
> Meet me at her hideaway. Nightfall.

Nightfall. It was midmorning now, a lazy warmth in the air. She didn't like being apart from the green book, but at least she knew who had it. She let out a breath and leaned against the door, the heat warming her as she closed her eyes. Cage had seemed innocent at the cemetery last night. It was in his gaze: oculesics, she'd read about it. His blue eyes hadn't wavered from hers when she'd asked him about Ro. His pupils hadn't moved side to side either, which usually meant a lie. Cage Shaw was either very good at hiding things, or he hadn't hurt Ro. Or perhaps he just *believed* he hadn't?

"Mae!" Elle shouted again from inside the house. "Where are you?"

If she wanted the book back, she had to meet Cage later. Mae opened her eyes to the sun and then stepped inside the house, locking the door behind her. "Hope you didn't throw out anything while I was gone," she called into the dusty foyer. When she turned, she stopped in her tracks.

Lance was in the dining room, sitting at the old table near the archway. He waved to her, and Mae forced her legs to move. She felt nervous, on edge, but she was always this way around other people; she never knew what to say, especially to guys who were suddenly friendly after years of acting reserved. Being around this new Lance was like trying to paint blindfolded—she didn't know what colors to choose; she didn't even know what sort of palette she was working with.

"Look who snuck in through the kitchen door while you were outside." Elle nodded at Lance, who rocked back in his chair looking pleased with himself.

"Hi," Mae offered, because both Elle and Lance seemed to be expecting something from her. Her grand-dad was sitting with his eyes half closed in the window seat, the Bible on his lap and a sprig of lantana poking up from his suit pocket. A real smile slipped out before she remembered the green book.

"You promised to help me clean all day," Elle said, giving her an extra-meaningful look, "and yet I sense some heel dragging." She had changed into a pair of dark jeans and a black tank top. A red bandanna that matched her nail polish was tied around her neck. "Time to pay what's due."

Mae turned out her pockets. "Hate to disappoint, but these are pretty empty," she said, surprised to hear a burst of laughter from Lance.

"Far from it." He leaned back in his chair again, sending it on its hind legs. "What did Ro used to say?" The wood groaned under his weight, which was mostly muscle and tan skin. "'Time is more valuable than money.' Remember the rest, Mayday?"

Lance's chair tilted farther, and then the front legs thudded to the ground. His eyes were on hers under that curly brown hair. "'You can always get more money . . . ,'" he said, trailing off like he was waiting for them to finish.

"I don't remember," Elle said, "how does it end?"

"'But you can't get more time,'" Mae said. "'Usually.'"

"Ro always added the *usually*, didn't she?" He smiled and Mae found herself smiling back. Besides Cage, it was the first time in a long time that someone had said her sister's name in the house, and she was grateful.

"Well, now it's time to clean, boys and girls." Elle pointed at the remaining pile of boxes by the table. "I'll take those. You take the ones by the chair, Mae."

Mae tugged a box over and felt Lance's hazel eyes on her, like he wanted to ask her something but was holding back. He used to look at Ro that way, only softer, less sure of himself. She'd caught him once or twice staring up at her sister's window from the yard or peering through the garden hedge while Ro dug near the gift cherub, burying her silver box under the earth. Lance's constant watching had started at thirteen, and at fourteen he'd gotten bolder, leaving Ro notes with messages like *Every day I want to be near you* and *I've never met anyone like you*. Mae hadn't known anyone like her sister either, but she'd never left her notes about it. Ro had said Lance was sweet and harmless, and she'd treated him like a kid brother, even though he was only a couple of years younger than her.

"Can I help with anything, Elle?" Lance asked. Elle raised her eyebrows, looking as surprised as Mae was. They'd never seen this side of him—he'd always been shy, except around Ro.

"Sure," Elle said, and then grinned. "Why don't you start on the box next to mine?"

Mae cut in; she couldn't help herself. "Just don't throw out any old photos." She nodded toward her granddad, who'd fallen asleep. "He wouldn't like it," she said, though that was only partly the truth. If she couldn't read the green book today, then she could at least find out about Hanna and Grady—where it had all started. "And I'm collecting the old albums," she added quickly. "I don't care about anything else."

"Got it," Lance said. "Keep the Kodaks, trash the

rest." He turned as Elle lunged past with an armful of what looked to be old Sears catalogs and a random corset. "Hey, what's the bandanna for?" he asked.

"My lungs," Elle said, her voice muffled through the fabric. "They're pristine, minus that one time I tried my dad's cigarette." She pulled the bandanna down to talk some more. "I don't want to be inhaling century-old filth. You know what dust is? It's human flesh. It gets everywhere, in your mouth, your hair . . ."

Mae almost laughed. Elle loved being dramatic. The dust was probably more like sand, mold spores, animal dander. She imagined a painting—dust floating in a shaft of sunlight, Ro standing in it, the light catching her hair and spinning it gold—and then Lance was rocking in his chair again, making it creak with his weight, and Elle whirled suddenly, flinging a rag Mae's way. It sailed past her and landed next to the bookshelf in a heap.

"Are you just daydreaming in your sweatshirt over there," Elle asked, "or helping clean for the B and B?"

"There is," Sonny shouted from the foyer, "no bed and breakfast!"

"There's your answer," Mae said, kicking the rag back toward her sister.

"Oh, your dad's home." Lance popped up out of his seat, vaulted over the next one, and jogged out of the room, the keys in his pocket jingling. At the archway, he saluted their granddad, who'd woken from his nap, and then winked at the girls as he left.

"Hey, Sonny," Lance said. "My dad wanted to ask you

about one of our horses. It . . ." He trailed off, and Mae tried to ignore a twinge of disappointment as she opened the box in front of her. Inside was a pile of antique picture frames. She made herself focus on them. Why should she care if Lance was still in the room or not?

"Okay," Elle said, "put everything into yes, no, and maybe piles." She turned toward the foyer. "We need all of this cleared out for the *bed and breakfast*!" She yelled the last part and Mae winced, waiting for Sonny to tell her off.

Except this time Elle only got silence. Her dad was on good behavior with a guest around. And then it occurred to Mae why she hadn't wanted Lance to leave: he brought a lightness inside the house, the way he smiled at everyone, kept the conversation upbeat. Blue Gate hadn't felt happy—it hadn't even felt normal—for the past year. It was like Ro had sucked out all the light when she'd gone and left them with nothing in their dark hearts but a couple of matches between them. Lance was like having another light around.

Mae glanced up and saw Elle's progress and then hastily unloaded more frames. The pictures were miniaturized versions of the oil paintings hanging in the foyer. She dug through them quickly, trying to appear like she was categorizing them; she was actually looking for Hanna, but none of them were labeled.

"Two to zero," Elle said, stomping down on an empty box with fervor. "I'm winning."

Underneath all the picture frames was a tangle of

crocheted wire hangers, and Mae put them in the "maybe" pile for Elle to sort through. When she went to crush the box, she noticed something wedged under the cardboard at the bottom.

A photo album. It was old and falling apart, its spine bent, its pages a light saffron. Her fingers started tingling as she picked it up. She expected it to smell like dust or mold, but instead there was a tinge of sweetness: the scent of icing, powdered sugar. It was overpowering, so strong she had to ask, "Elle, are you baking?"

Her sister turned, wielding a box cutter. Her auburn hair was in sweaty tendrils against her neck. "Am I baking? While it'd be nice to have some homemade muffins in the oven ready for paying guests, we don't yet have a bed and breakfast." She cut open another lid. "Am I baking," she muttered. "I have to do everything around here."

Elle zeroed in on the window seat, a fired-up look in her eyes. "Granddad," she shouted, "you can help too instead of just sitting there!"

Their granddad nodded but didn't move from his seat. He was staring at the album Mae was holding. When she looked down at it again, something hot and sweet seemed to brush against her face. *Open it, Mae. Open it.*

She raised the cover and held her breath as dust billowed out. When it finally cleared, she saw a picture of Blue Gate, long ago, probably back when it was first built. The photo was in black-and-white, that faded-looking monochrome that made the house look distant and unreal, like it hadn't really existed at all. A range of dark trees was in the background, shutters flanked the windows, and a small, pale path led to the grayish porch. Mae imagined the way it would have looked: blue would go into the sky, red ocher for the door. The colonnades a blinding white, the closest thing to snow this far south. The wood on the porch layered in golds and browns, the shade of the whiskey that her dad drank.

She turned the page to another black-and-white image of Blue Gate, now with people clustered on the porch. In the center was a tall man in a vest with eyes that glared. A watch chain dangled from his pocket and an oil lantern was on a table beside him. He was standing next to a woman in a rocking chair. The woman held a black parasol over her head, and her shoulders were stiff, her too-thin waist cinched tight by her dress. Everything about her seemed pained, though her long dark hair was in a girlish braid, a ribbon tied at the end.

Next to them, standing a few paces away, was someone Mae recognized. Young Grady Cole wore his shirt rolled up at the sleeves and a bent hat. His light hair was shaggy, his eyes angled from the lens. He looked about seventeen. Beside him was a much younger boy—probably his brother, though Mae hadn't seen many pictures of him around the house. She frowned, remembering what she'd heard once. Long ago, one of the Cole children had run away. Could it have been him? The boy's chin was jutting out and he had a big smile on his face, like he couldn't contain it. His suit pants were muddy at the knees too, as if he'd been playing right up until being called in front of the camera.

Half of the picture had come unglued from the page, and she lifted it. A date was inked onto the other side. *1859*. Someone's cursive. *Grady Deacon, Grady II, Jacob, Rose Louisa*.

Mae glanced back at Rose Cole. She looked thin, even frail, but the hint of a smile was at her lips. Mae's grand-dad had mentioned that she was from the North. She'd refused to own slaves, which was a point in her favor, even though Mae didn't know much else about her. Apparently she'd never hired servants either, despite being sick for most of her life. Her husband was a doctor, so maybe she had all the help she needed. Or her boys might have looked after her. Blue Gate would have seemed even more isolated back then, surrounded by miles and miles of trees. Had the Coles ever left the house, or was their only company each other?

Mae studied the younger boy again—Jacob. He and Grady were night and day. Jacob was grinning at the cam-era, while Grady hadn't even bothered to turn his head in the right direction. He was gazing off to the side, like something had caught his eye. The high grass in the yard was empty, but at the edge of the yard—what was that?

Mae brought the picture closer. There, just beyond a large oak, was a strange blur. She squinted down at the photo. The thing next to the tree was out of focus, almost hazy-looking. Probably whatever it was had been moving at the time the photograph was shot, since everything else in the frame was crisp.

She peered closer, tilting the album. The blurry shape was a person, she was sure of it. The more she looked at it, the more she was certain: The Coles hadn't been alone in the photograph. Someone had been watching the house, and Grady had noticed. And the expression on his face . . . he looked apprehensive.

A shadow fell across the page and Mae jerked her head up. Elle was standing over her with a plastic garbage bag in her hand and the bandanna around her face. Mae waited for her to shout out the cleaning score, but Elle only leaned in.

"See?" she said. "That's why this place would be perfect for a B and B." She tugged at her bandanna. "Blue Gate is charming and historic and what have you. All sorts of things happened here in the old days. Remember? Keep turning."

She collapsed down beside Mae, the chair groaning under her weight. Mae flipped the page and saw Grady's father again. His watch chain was dangling from his pocket as he stood next to his wife. Rose Cole was propped in the center of a massive four-poster bed, her long dark hair spread out behind her like a fan. She looked even paler than before.

"She's the one who got real sick, right?" Elle asked, sliding off her ballet flats and then fluffing up the cushion behind her back.

"They called it brain fever," Mae said. "It was probably meningitis."

She flipped the page and Elle gasped. There was another photograph of Rose in the bed, except this time her eyes were closed and something was off about her. It was hard to say what exactly. She was just lacking . . . something vital. An essence.

"Is she dead?" Elle whispered.

Mae nodded. "I think so." Taking pictures of the recently deceased seemed morbid—but then again, wasn't it a little like her sketching Ro now that she was gone? So that she'd never forget her, even if her face disappeared from memory. If that happened, you had to rely on photographs. The first portrait Mae had ever drawn was of her mother. Her short, light brown hair and thick bangs, sharp cheekbones and oval-shaped green eyes. She'd traced everything from an old picture, because she didn't have any memories of her, not one.

Elle turned the next page and then shoved it away. "My God," she whispered.

Mae pulled the album toward them with her fingertips and stared at it. Distantly she registered that her granddad had hobbled over from the window seat and was standing at her shoulder, leaning on her chair for support. She felt like she needed something to lean on too.

The picture in front of them was nothing like Rose's. Grady's mother had been lovingly portrayed in death— her hair cleaned and curled, her eyes gently closed. But this second picture was cruel. It was Grady's father—

unmistakably—someone had taken the time to print his name on the image.

That ink in the corner was the easiest thing to look at because nothing else was. His clothing was torn and dirty, as if he'd fallen or been dragged. His shirt was ripped open, his chest exposed, a wide gash near his heart seeping blood, a dark stain pooling on his pants. His eyes were the worst part. They were open, so pale the irises almost looked white, and they were staring at nothing at all. He was slumped against the side of the house—no ceremony about it—an oil lantern inexplicably set by his hands. Whoever had taken the photo hated this man, hated him even after his death. The remnants of a story Ro told her long ago came to mind.

"He was murdered." Mae's voice felt hoarse and she cleared her throat, aware all of a sudden that no one had spoken in a long time. The three of them had been staring at the picture, half entranced, probably all thinking the same thing: *Why?*

She looked over her shoulder to find her granddad nodding, his eyes still on the album, a sadness in them that hurt her to see. What did he know about the Cole history? So much was trapped inside him, his speech dammed in his throat, his hands curled in on themselves. She wanted to learn about Hanna, and to know more about the ancestors who'd written in the green book before Ro had. But the dangerous part about asking questions in life was not being ready for answers. She hadn't been ready for this.

Her sister started flipping through the pictures, faster

now. "Everyone was afraid of the Coles," Elle said, her voice hushed. "But no one ever did anything about it because the Coles were rich. At least, they were, till little Grady Junior or whatever went crazy after his father died. Maybe he's the one who killed him."

"What are you talking about?" Lance was standing in the archway, his hands shoved into his pockets, that easy grin on his face.

"Someone way, way back in our family," Elle told him.

His name was on Mae's lips, but she held it in. Young Grady II, who'd started the green book, his signature penned at the top of the inside cover. Ro said once that he'd been sent to an asylum, but she'd always loved embellishing for thrills, just like the only time she showed her the green book. Back then, Mae shut her eyes instead of looking because she'd been terrified. Because the book had reminded her of something. Of following her sister into the woods one day, trailing her lacy white dress, a basket in Ro's hand . . . A hint of the memory came to her and then was gone.

Mae's heart fluttered. She realized Elle was still talking about Grady. Lance was standing on her other side now, smelling of cologne as he leaned over her, his chest grazing her shoulder while he looked at the album. Elle tugged a picture loose and fanned herself with it, her eyes going to Lance like she was waiting for him to ask for more.

"So what happened to the guy?" he finally said.

Elle gave him a grin. "He spent years building additions to the house, and blew all the family money wandering the world, that sort of thing. But no one really

137

knows what he was searching for. That's what Ro said." She finished her story and turned to their granddad. "I was a good listener, believe it or not," she said. "Bet you didn't think so, did you?"

He grappled for his writing pad, and then licked the tip of his pen and wrote a single word:

IMPULSIVE

His gnarled hands turned back to the picture of the house that they'd looked at before, with young Grady Cole on the porch. Mae peered down at him.

"Did you know him?" Elle asked. Mae was shocked when her granddad nodded and then wrote on his writing pad.

LONG LIFE

His hands opened and closed like he wanted to write more. Then he was pressing the pen down again and Mae felt Lance lean in closer to look.

NO GOOD

"Was he guilty?" Mae asked, and her granddad shook his head as if she was missing the point. He tapped the writing pad with his finger and added another word.

NO GOOD DEEDS

She'd heard that phrase before, maybe from Ro? But then the trilling cursive rose up in her memory and she remembered seeing it in the book. "What do you mean?"

Her granddad's blue eyes went faraway, lost in thought, and his fist holding the pen started to tremble. Mae reached out to grab his hand. She squeezed his fingers and then his eyes were on her, coming into focus. He smiled a little, just on one side, and crushed her hand back.

"Anyway, are we getting sentimental over old pictures or are we cleaning?" Elle wiped at her forehead and left a streak of dirt behind. "Granddad," she said, way too loud again, "if you're going to keep all those frames, we'll have to put them in your room." She glanced at Mae. "Will you take them to the attic? I'll keep cleaning."

"Enough for the both of us?" Mae asked.

"Very funny," Elle answered, rolling her eyes. "But hurry up."

"And promise you'll come back," Lance said, reaching out to tuck a strand of hair behind her ear.

Mae sidestepped him, letting her hair fall across her eyes so he wouldn't see the surprise in them. "I promise nothing. And remember, please don't—"

"We know," Elle said, letting out a gusting sigh. "You're so demanding."

Mae laughed at the irony as she put the stack of frames into the empty box and then topped it off with the album. She heaved up the box and carried it out of the room, halting when she got to the foyer.

Scattered across the wooden floorboards were guns

and bullet belts and knives, spread out beside piles of coveralls and giant flashlights. Sonny was crouched in the center of it all, rifling through a duffel bag, a pair of binoculars around his neck.

"What are you doing?"

"Brought this up from the basement." He didn't turn around. "To get ready," he said, like that explained everything.

Mae's stomach tightened. "Ready for what?"

He looked over his shoulder and glared at her. "You're standing in my light, Mae." He was so quick to use the possessive—all shoulders and strength, Atlas carrying the world on his back. She stepped out of the stream of sunlight and he grunted something unintelligible and went back to his duffel bag. The box was digging into her fingers, so she started up the curving steps and then heard footsteps behind her.

"Thought you could use a hand."

She didn't have to look over her shoulder to know it was Lance. A smile was at her lips that she couldn't hold back. This might be her chance. "You could get the door," she told him, "but I've got the box."

Something grazed her elbow and then he was at her side, his T-shirt so white it hurt her eyes. "It's half your size," he pressed. "Let me take it."

The frames were heavy but she tried not to show it as she reached the first landing. "This box is the least of my problems," she said, the words off her tongue before she could stop them.

"Maybe, maybe not," Lance teased, sounding cryptic.

She could feel him watching her, matching her pace. Her heart quickened as he stayed even with her, all the way to the back steps. The walls narrowed in on them as they finally reached the top, and he jogged ahead to open the door, the attic shadowy without a light on.

"After you," Lance said, smiling again.

CHAPTER 12

MAE SET THE BOX ON the table as Lance followed her into the attic. Her stomach tensed with a flutter of nerves. They were alone now. Should she just come right out with it?

"Why does your grandpa stay up here, anyway?" Lance asked, standing too close beside her.

"It's one of life's great mysteries," Mae said, and that was true because she'd asked him plenty of times and had never gotten a straight answer. "He likes the view, mostly."

"Long way up, though. You'd think after the stroke . . ." Lance shoved his hands in his pockets as he scanned her granddad's bookshelf. "I still feel bad about it."

Mae bit the insides of her cheeks, the pain keeping her from the memory of that day. How her granddad had collapsed when he saw Lance carrying Ro's body. How she'd almost lost both of them, all at once.

"Ro was real close to your grandpa, wasn't she?" Lance looked her way, worry crossing his face. "Sorry. You probably don't want to talk about her."

She shook her head—there was so much to talk about, but she still wasn't sure where to start. Ro would dive right in.

"Actually, I do." Her eyes teared up and she turned, letting out a cough like she had dust in her throat, and then turned back. "Why'd you leave?" She hadn't known what she was going to ask until it burst out. "After it happened."

Lance shrugged, rocked on his heels. His gaze settled on the window, the one overlooking the woods and the bay beyond.

"I needed a change," he said. "Wanted to clear my head. It just about killed me."

He stopped then, realizing what he'd said. An uncomfortable silence stretched between them, and she couldn't help herself. "Because you felt guilty?"

The pain on his face disappeared, replaced by confusion. For a moment she caught a glimpse of the old Lance—the guy who was always lurking in the shadows, trying to catch her sister's attention—but the confidence returned and he nodded.

"Yeah, you're right," he said, watching her. "I wished I could have saved her. Wished I could've got there in time." He sighed. "Think about it, Mae. Each day ends up being a series of moments, some big, some small, and I know that's the one I'll regret the most. That day. That moment I missed." He stared out the window again and she knew he was looking at the bay in the distance. "To tell you the truth, my dad wanted me gone last year so I'd quit asking so many questions. Quit talking about Ro every night." He shook his head, let out another frustrated sigh. "Do you know what that's like? To spend every day thinking about how if you'd just been a little earlier, found her a little sooner . . ."

Mae's heart clinched and he glanced up at the ceiling and then back at her again.

"You probably do," he said, his eyes full of understanding. He ran a hand through his hair, crossed his arms like he didn't know where to put them. "I loved her, Mae."

She searched his eyes, trying to catch him in the lie, but it wasn't there. He'd loved her. He'd loved Ro, and Cage had too. They all had, but that hadn't been enough to save her.

"Any more questions?" He sounded hoarse, like he was trying not to break down in front of her.

"Lots." Maybe it was hurting them both, but she needed to keep him talking. "Can you tell me what happened again?"

Lance stepped toward her. "Everything's in the police report," he said, his voice softer now. "You know I made an official statement, Mae."

She'd read it. A hundred times over. "Yes. To your dad." She gave him a loaded look, let the words hang in the air.

He shook his head and then smiled as if half amused, half disappointed in her. "Kind of how it works when he's a cop."

"What about the differences in what you said to my dad and what you wrote in your statement?"

Lance nodded slowly, stared at the ground for a breath like he was thinking about what to say. "Like what?" he finally asked. His hazel eyes held a challenge but she wasn't going to back down.

"You told my dad you thought Cage killed her." She was watching his face. Lance's jaw was firm but not clenched, his gaze steady. "But in the statement you only mentioned that you saw him standing over her."

He nodded again. "That's true." He took another step and seemed suddenly taller, his skin darker, tanner, everything about him magnified. She fought the urge to back away, put distance between them.

"Why'd you say that to Sonny, then?" Mae asked. "Tell him something like that when you weren't sure?" All of the not-knowing of the past year rose up in her throat and she wanted to cry. "Do you really think Cage did it?"

Lance rubbed at his forehead, leaned against her grand-dad's bookcase. "At first I did, but I—" His voice cracked. "I remember that day, clear as clear. I just don't know what he was doing. He was either holding her, or . . ."

Mae felt herself flinch, and Lance saw it too. "I should quit talking."

"No. Go on." She shoved her hands into the pockets of her jeans to keep them from shaking. "Please."

"I wanted it to be his fault," he said, and now he wasn't

looking at her anymore, like he was embarrassed. "I never liked him, Mae. He kept to himself. Never noticed anyone but her. Never spoke to anyone but her."

Her eyes narrowed. Didn't he realize he was describing himself too?

"That's not a reason to think he killed her." The black door in her mind flung open and she threw all her sadness into it, all her anger. She had to stay focused.

"I know." Lance rubbed at his forehead again, his shoulders tensing. "That's why I left it out of my statement. Would've just sounded jealous anyway."

"So instead you told my dad you thought Cage did it."

"I don't know what I saw, Mae." A hint of frustration in his voice now. "Maybe I shouldn't have said that, but I'm allowed an opinion. I found her." He walked over to the box on the table, his elbow grazing her arm as he passed. "I saw Cage standing over her body. I saw the blood. He ran off when I shouted at him. And that's the truth."

Her heart felt tight as it all sank in. Surely she hadn't gotten Cage wrong? But he ran. And she'd known it all along. He ran.

Lance's hair fell over his eyes as he pulled the lid off the box. Inside were the old photographs, all those faces gaping up at her, the younger Grady's near the top. The black-and-white daguerreotype couldn't hide his lankiness or that impression of being restless to the bone. It reminded her of herself—how she felt right now, how she'd felt all year—and she stared at him and knew she had to try harder.

"Tell me what else you didn't say in the report."

Lance smiled, but he looked sad. "Kind of seems like you're interrogating me," he said, forcing a playfulness into his words. Maybe he couldn't stand the pressure in the room either. Maybe that heavy sadness that was pressing down on her was pressing down on him too. "Planning on keeping me a prisoner up here?"

Mae folded her arms across her chest. "Do I have a reason to?"

"No, but I wouldn't really mind, long as you were here." He stepped toward her and she could smell his cologne again, and something like sand and salt—that scent from being outdoors in the sun. "Listen, I know there's things I could have done better," he said. "I know that." His words struck her as odd, but his eyes were serious when he looked her over; she could see the depth of his gaze. "Mae, I want the same thing you want. I—"

"Lance?" Elle's voice filtered through the open door. "Mae?"

They both turned at the sound of her shout, and then Lance shrugged.

"Best not get in trouble with both of you." Suddenly his hand was on the side of her face and he was leaning toward her, warmth radiating from his skin, his hazel eyes pinning her right where she stood. "Believe me," Lance said, his voice breaking, all his words coming in a rush, "I would have done anything for her. I still would."

And then he was gone, his footsteps pounding down the stairs.

Mae was left alone in the attic. Frustrated, she shut the cardboard lid over Grady's picture. She hadn't learned anything from talking to Lance, not really. And she'd gotten nothing from Cage last night.

She sat down on the edge of the table. Maybe Lance would open up to her if he trusted her more. He'd seemed honest enough, willing to talk, but her gut told her he was holding back. She needed to go downstairs and small-talk him, start slow. Use every minute before nightfall to lure out whatever he wasn't telling her about Ro.

As she stood, gearing herself up for the task, she heard a scratching noise. She took a step toward the stairs and heard it again. It sounded too loud to be mice. Her next thought was Lance; but she'd seen him leave. Maybe it was another bird, or some small animal had gotten trapped inside the attic?

Beyond her granddad's tidy room was the storage space, full of stacks of old furniture and books, over a century of clutter, all put away behind the newer plywood wall. The sound had come from back there. Curious now, Mae started into the warm shadows. This was the unfinished part of the attic, lit by the window on the far wall.

A wail came from somewhere—slow and drawn out. The room was still, and she couldn't see anything hiding among the boxes. She kept going, treading as lightly as she could, all the way to the back of the attic. When she got close to the window, she felt fresh air against her skin—the glass pane was crooked, halfway open. The scratching came again, and her breath went shallow as she realized it was coming from beneath her.

Mae hesitated and then heaved a nearby box aside to clear some space. A small rug was rumpled under it and she pulled it away, revealing warped floorboards with wide cracks between them. Had an animal gotten trapped down there? She shoved the box with her shoulder to move it against the wall, but it was stuck. She shoved it again, glancing down to see what it was caught on, and then sank to her knees.

A brass hinge. She was staring at a pair of hinges in the floor. In another moment it registered: she'd found a trapdoor.

A chill shot down her back. Running her hands along the wood in the opposite direction of the hinges, she found a dime-sized furrow in one of the boards. She hooked her finger into the little groove and lifted.

A wave of heat hit her face as she stared at a narrow ladder, dropping away into darkness. Her heart quickened. Why had she never seen this before? And the bigger question: What was down there?

The scraping was louder now and Mae tensed. Part of her knew she should find a flashlight or go get Elle. But the other part of her couldn't turn away. It felt like she was on the edge of a discovery and if she blinked it might disappear. *Don't blink.* She gripped the floorboards and then started down the ladder, one foot at a time, going slow to let her eyes adjust to the dimness. When she got to the last rung, she was in a tunnel—some sort of crawlspace underneath the attic floor, running along the wall of the house. It was dark and narrow and hot, and hard to breathe.

Ahead light splintered through a small hole. The ceiling slanted even lower and she ducked down, her fingernails digging into her palms as she veered deeper into the tunnel.

And then the end came into sight. It looked as if it had been boarded up recently, planks of blond plywood stretched over what appeared to be a brick step. Mae turned, searching the corners of the tunnel, but nothing was on the ground. No animal lying there hurt, nothing to make that scratching noise she'd heard.

She stepped closer to the barrier. In the trickle of light, she saw that the boards nailed to the upper half of the boundary were dusty. She ran her hands over the wood and her fingertips hit air. An opening.

A brick at the base had been pushed through: there was a hole to the other side. The scratching started up again and she bent down, her pulse thudding in her ears.

Something was definitely in there *now*—it needed help—just beyond the barrier. She yanked the wood at the edge of the crack, trying to make it bigger. A plank swung loose and then gave way in her arms, and she staggered back, setting the board down and grabbing the next one. She tugged harder this time, dust showering her face as the wood pulled free. Now the gap was big enough to squeeze through.

"Hello?"

Mae heard the sound of breathing. Her heart was skidding in her chest as she forced herself to step through the hole she'd made. And then she was on the other side.

It was dark, the air blanket-thick.

She took a small shuffle forward, her foot knocking against something sharp. It thudded to the floor and she leaned down, her hand finding a box no bigger than her palm. She picked it up, its contents rattling—a box of matches? Her fingers worked fast to open it, strike a match.

There was a whiff of phosphorus and she gasped, blinking, as the light flared over glass. At her feet was an oil lantern, just like the one in the old photographs. She stared at it in disbelief and then the wail came again, behind her. Mae whirled and saw glowing eyes.

In the corner of the cramped space was the little black stray. It huddled against the far wall, trembling.

How had it gotten all the way in here? But she didn't even know where *here* was. She'd expected the tunnel to winnow out, leading to another doorway or trapdoor, some other location in the house, but the small flame revealed yet another barrier, closing in the cavelike space. The cat had somehow found its way in and gotten trapped.

She lit the oil lantern and knelt down, holding out her hand. "Here, it's okay."

The cat flinched away before circling toward her, its nose nudging her wrist. She ran her hand over it, felt its ribs sticking out. It was half starved, its fur clumped with dirt and cobwebs, dried blood between its claws—it'd been trying to scratch its way out. She took another look along the floor for the calico, just in case it had gotten trapped too, but didn't see it.

"Come on, let's get you out of here," Mae said, picking it up. "I'm glad I found you," she whispered. It was small and warm in her arms, and she thought of the breathing she'd heard—too loud to be from the stray. Her imagination had gotten away from her in the darkness of the tunnel.

When she turned to leave, the light fell over the wall and she froze. In front of her was a charcoal drawing that spanned the entire length of brick. She held up the lantern to get a better look and felt her jaw drop.

At the top, near the ceiling, was an arc of stars and the moon. A foreign word was written beside it in capital letters. *CHANA*. She whispered it aloud and then remembered seeing it before. In the green book, maybe, jotted in a margin. It was so hot it was hard to think and she didn't know what it meant. The lantern was flickering across the wall, casting shadows, and she wanted to leave, to breathe fresh air again, but her eyes were seduced by the charcoal.

Underneath the moon and stars was a rectangular shape, jutting up from what was meant to be the ground. It was a sketch of a grave. The cat trembled in her arms and she tucked it closer as she squinted at the drawing. Leading up to the large headstone were little lumps spaced out in a row.

A trail of animals. A bird, a cat, a snake, and a deer, or a horse, maybe. All sleeping, their eyes in the shape of little X marks.

Not sleeping, then. The animals were supposed to be dead.

Next to them was a woman in a dress, rising up toward the charcoal moon. She was suspended—there was air underneath her feet, almost like a ghost. Standing on the ground beside her was another figure, this one darker, filled in like flesh.

Mae searched for a signature and found a small scribble in the bottom corner. Setting the heavy lantern on the floor, she crouched down to read it, but the artist had left only a single word, followed by numbers. *Psalms 3:5*. A Bible passage.

Sharp pinpricks ground into her arm. The cat was digging in its claws as it trembled. Mae felt the same way inside. Anyone in her family could have drawn this sketch, even Ro, and someone had tried to keep it hidden by walling up the room.

The cat wriggled again, letting out a cry this time, and Mae shifted it in her arms. "You're right," she whispered, "let's go."

She picked up the lantern with her free hand, carrying the cat in her other. One last glance at the charcoal and then she wedged through the small opening and raced into the tunnel and up the ladder, shutting the trapdoor behind her. She quickly pushed the rug and the box over it, trying to make it look exactly how it was before. Maybe this was why her granddad never wanted to leave the attic, insisted on sleeping up here too. Maybe he'd been trying to protect its secrets.

The cat squirmed, its claws hooking into her thin shirt. "Come on. We'll get some food in you." The stray twisted itself, diving off her shoulder. It hit the floor, darted onto the box she'd just moved, and then jumped up to the windowsill.

"No," Mae said, making her voice soft. "Come down."

Before she could coax it further she heard a piercing whistle, and the cat lunged through the opening, disappearing out of sight. Shocked, Mae ran to the window, expecting to see the stray clinging to the roof or sprawled on the ground.

But there was only the sandy driveway, the beech trees by the old fountain, the woods swelling out under dark clouds.

She held on to the windowsill, a tingle creeping down her spine. Her chest felt tight from all the dust, and she took in deep gulps of fresh air. The tunnel, the cat, the drawing, the book, everything whirled in her head, and she didn't know what door to put it behind and she didn't want to hide it away anyway, because she needed answers. She blinked, leaned farther out the window as she gazed at the lawn below. What was that?

She rubbed at her eyes. Someone was standing by the fountain, staring at the house.

CHAPTER 13

AROUND HIM THE WOODS HAD gone quiet. He was at the Coles' beach—a tiny spread of sand that hooked inward, sheltered by trees that bordered the dunes. Ahead of him the narrow dock reached across the water. The pilings underneath it were thin and shadowy, clumps of seagrass rising up around them. He hoped that being out here on the beach where it happened would help him remember.

It was dark for late afternoon. The morning sun had been replaced by low-hanging clouds and the smell of rain. Cage struck another match and held it above the book he'd taken from Mae's bag. He tried to find the line he'd been on, something about *viselike headaches*. It had caught his attention, since his own head felt like someone had shoved a tire iron into it and was prying open his skull.

He huddled over the log he was sitting on and focused on the page toward the end, near the missing back cover. Ro had told him about that too. She'd seen the book intact when she was a kid and thought her grand-dad had hidden part of it from her. He didn't know if she'd found the other half, but wherever it was, it wasn't here. The page in front of him had a list, with *Signs of the Raised* at the top. He wanted to search through the writing as much as he could, in case it'd jog some memory. He was tracing his steps like his mother always said to do, as if his memory could be found like a lost set of keys. *Forget where you put them? Trace your steps.* Here he was, holding the very book Ro had shown him, but it wasn't much help. Instead he'd gotten stuck on this list.

He'd laugh if his head didn't hurt so much. The page was like the horoscopes Ro used to trawl through. *Viselike headaches, great thirst.* General enough to rope in just about everyone. His headaches were from the gash on his head, not from being *raised*, whatever that meant, and he was extra-thirsty from being dehydrated. Simple.

Cage dropped the spent match at his feet and struck another. When the light flared, he read the end of the list again.

Throat like scorched earth, great thirst with dreams of water. Hunger dwindles, food soon forgotten. Sleep broken by visits from those now gone. Painful steps, painful breaths, passing between two worlds. Visions of the dead and whispers. Breath that comes and goes, the body overrun with magic.

It was absurd, and none of it had anything to do with him. But he couldn't remember the last time he'd eaten, and his thirst was constant. *Throat like scorched earth.* He'd drunk half the rainwater tank at the barn already and could drink the other half right now. And what about the hallucination he'd had of Ro at the cemetery last night? *Visions of the dead and whispers.*

If he thought it was more than a dream, he was bullshitting himself. But he could remember every detail. Ro with her hair wet, standing in front of him. Water glistening on her skin. Blood on her teeth as she'd smiled. She'd seemed as real as anything—real as the barn and the boat and the trees around him. Here he was, back at Blue Gate, all of last year a wide-open blank, and now he was either hallucinating or . . . or he was seeing Ro.

Cage looked down at the page again and hated himself for thinking it possible. *Sleep broken by visits from those now gone.* If this part of the book spoke of things he'd experienced, then what if the rest of it was real? That raising ritual, the one Ro had talked about. *I know I can bring my mother back. I've come close before.* She'd been so serious, and he'd laughed at her.

He wasn't laughing anymore. *Painful steps, painful breaths, passing between two worlds.* Maybe the motorcycle accident had been worse than he'd thought. Maybe he *hadn't* walked away from it. What if Mae had done the ritual? What if she'd found the book and tried it, and instead of Ro coming back, it'd been him? Or it'd been him *first*?

His stomach turned to lead; he wasn't thinking straight. His mother would be doubled over cackling—she'd be telling him the accident had given him brain damage. She'd say he was being a fool. She'd spit out that word. *That's what love does*, she'd say, *makes you a fool*.

Except last night in the woods he'd seen Ro. It hadn't just been a dream or a hallucination. He'd seen Ro and then passed out. Asleep for what, ten hours, twelve? Lucky no one had found him. He'd woken up on the dirt and grass, right outside the cemetery gate. His hand on the book.

He wasn't going to leave Blue Gate now, not yet. Not if he might see Ro in the woods again. If she was only a dream, then so be it. If he got caught by Sonny or that cop Childers or by Elle and her rifle, then so be it. But at least he'd see Ro. And then he might know more about what had happened. About what he'd done to her.

Cage felt hot, unbearably hot, and his headache was in full force. He lit another match and flicked to the last page, the one with the smudge in the corner. *A Ritual for a Raising* was at the top, and then that clumsy scrawl. The whole thing reminded him of a folk song or a hymn, at least until the blood part. He read it again.

Please follow carefully:
Harbor love in your heart,
while in your hand
hold the loved one's belongings.
Then begin the offerings.

For death feeds life
as blood feeds the ritual,
and little creatures show the way.
A cat for nine

And that was it. Did he really think those few words would bring someone to life? He shifted on the log and felt it dig into his jeans, and then flipped backward from the last page, rifling past another heading, *Putting to Rest the Raised.*

Another wave of heat hit him, and he couldn't think. The pages fluttered and settled as he peeled off his shirt. The bruising on his chest was spreading. He breathed through his teeth and then stared down at Ro's book. Before, he'd never wanted anything to do with it. It reminded him too much of his mother, the way she used to tease him about the father he'd never met. *You got magic in your blood, that's what your daddy always said. What a joke. A lot of good it did you.* And now here he was, reading a book of spells. He'd done all he could to avoid it before, but now he was desperate to understand it, to remember everything Ro had told him about it. If it all came back to him, all of his memories, then maybe he'd remember the one thing he needed to.

The day she died.

His lungs felt like someone had taken a fillet knife to them, and he clenched his jaw, tried to breathe. After counting to ten he lit another match, held it over the ink, and then stopped. The match shook in his hand.

Ro's handwriting was all over the page he was staring at. That slanted alphabet, he'd know it anywhere. The lines blurred, and he wiped his face with his sweaty shirt so he could see.

> *Part of being gifted this book is that we're supposed to write in it. It's meant to be a living thing, meaning everyone who gets it keeps adding to it. Now it's my turn.*

His heart was going wild in his chest. The match ran out, singeing his fingers, and he dropped it onto the sand. A hiss as he struck another one, holding the flame out. The next line was simple, and unexpected:

A Ritual for Love

It was followed by another list that he couldn't get his head around. It reminded him of a poem, and he hated poetry, the way it got stuck in his head like a bad song and hardly made any sense. But this was her handwriting—it was something from Ro, and he could imagine her saying the words aloud as he read them. It felt like she was sitting right beside him. Like they'd just come in from a swim and here she was, perched on the log with him, her skin cold from the water and her hair smelling of salt.

A Ritual for Love Is This

Open mind, soft heart.
Listen, then speak.
Keep no secrets
unless they hurt.

Always talk
with words or deeds
& remember to say
thank you.

Cage balled up a fist, focused on his raw knuckles to keep from shouting out. It was painful to know she'd written this, to wonder if she'd really loved him. What if she'd kept secrets from him, thinking they'd hurt? He let out a breath, checked the woods around him, and then turned back to the book. The next line was still in her handwriting. *A Ritual for a Ritual* was in darker ink, like she'd run her pen over it several times. It seemed like more poetry, but he read on anyway, couldn't stop if he tried.

Old mouth warned,
spoke of danger.
Young hands buried it

under the thorns.
Little statue watched on,
along with other eyes.

It looked like a few more lines had been added in a hurry. The match glowed over her writing, burning down to his fingers again.

As per the instructions
this is the direction.
What was torn out
is now underground.
If it's raising you seek,
then dig.

The rest was blotted out, blackened by ink. He turned to the next page, but it was a blank, a big nothing. He flipped back and read it once more, hesitating on the lines about the little statue and the thorns. Ro was talking about the gift cherub in Blue Gate's garden—she hadn't tried hard to disguise it. She'd found the other half of the book and buried it, that much was obvious, but the rest didn't make any sense. He skimmed the pages that followed, trying to spot more of her writing. There were too many sketches and different sets of handwriting packed together, and he'd always been a slow reader.

Cage swore aloud. He'd taken the book from Mae hoping it would help him remember, but it was only making him more confused. The book felt hot to the touch and then his whole body felt hot, almost feverish. His hands—they were dirty, full of soot or maybe it was grease, and he was slick with sweat. Water, he was craving water.

He looked up at the stretch of sand, the hulking dock where they'd found her body almost a year ago, if he believed her sister. To him, it felt like he'd been here a few days ago taking out the sailboat with Ro. That was the last thing he remembered doing with her. The dock and the fight, and then the crash . . .

"Ro," he said aloud, because he couldn't help it.

A rustling came from behind him and Cage jerked, stared into the woods. Nothing was there. Another wave of heat hit him. He was sweating, dripping on the book. It looked like it might storm soon—no one would be at this beach for a while. He could cool down in the bay and then read some more. He set the book on the log and took off his stolen boots, his jeans. The air felt good against his bare skin, and the pebbly sand was rough under his feet as he walked to the dock, all the way down to the water.

Home is the sailor, home from sea. Remembering what Ro used to say sent a chill through him. He knew she'd be grinning at him if she could read his mind right now, and maybe she was. Who knew what came after death, where you went. Preachers said heaven, old folk said haints, and some said nothing came after. He thought of his friend back in Ohio who'd touched an electric fence over summer break and died. Their neighbor in New Orleans, dead for a week before anyone found him. His uncle's wife, killed slow by cancer. Maybe they were all still here somehow. If there was a choice to stick around, Ro would take it. She wasn't the type to give up easy.

A little wave rushed at his feet, the foam hissing and bubbling and cold on his skin. Cage strode out into the bay, shivering as the cool wet edged up his thighs. It should've been warmer this time of year. He was freezing, but he kept going, his jaw tight, his hands tucked under his armpits.

When the water reached his stomach, he dunked himself under like an evangelist being saved. The coldness rushed over him, his ears, his mouth, his eyes, everything. He lifted his head up, taking in a monster breath before going under again. It was ice to his head, and his pulse thrummed in his ears. *Boom. Boom. Boom. Boom.* He could hear his heart beating, the blood running through his veins.

Keeping himself down, he let the coolness prickle over him. Then he surfaced with a gasp, splashed under his arms, rubbed at his buzz cut gone feral, gargled a mouthful of gritty salt water. He waded toward the dock before he lost all feeling in his legs. The water was so cold it was fiery. It streamed down him as he made his way back to shore, his limbs stiff. And then, just as he was striding onto the beach, he saw it—a smear of blood in the sand. It flashed at him and was gone, and he yelled out, lunging from the water.

Ro was found right here by the dock, that was what Mae had told him. If he kept tracing his steps, maybe he'd remember. It had to come back to him, all of it, not just flashes.

Cage braced himself against one of the pilings and thought of that day, what had happened in this very place. Ro'd been shouting at him, but what else? He slammed the back of his head against the wood and got nothing but pain. He was shivering now; he needed clothes.

Home is the sailor, home from sea. His heart was pounding so hard he couldn't breathe. *And the hunter home from the hill.*

Overhead a flock of gulls shrieked and then settled on the sand nearby, huddling around a dead fish. When they all turned their beaks at once, he followed their gaze.

Someone was coming out of the woods.

Cage ducked around the piling, flattening himself against it. He took a breath and peered out. It was a man with a fishing rod, and he was standing near the dirt access road. The fisherman stepped onto the sand, looked down the beach. Cage stayed flush against the piling and tried to quiet his breathing. No shout came, but everything inside him was tense. Being naked made it worse. Like those nightmares where he was stuck at school without a scrap of clothes and everyone was laughing. He needed to get to the trees, get back to his clothes, grab the book and run.

He heard the squeaking sound of footprints on sand, followed by a thud on the dock. The boards creaked overhead as the steps grew louder and then stopped directly above him.

Next came the metallic whir of a lighter being flicked, the stench of cigarette smoke. After a minute, the fisherman started to whistle. It was an old tune, one that Ro used to hum. Cage peered up through the slats, his heart pounding.

Sonny Cole was right above him.

He was crouched on one knee, jabbing cut bait through a hook. The long brown ponytail under his cap was impossible to miss. Cage pressed himself against the piling, hoped Ro's dad wouldn't look down. He knew Sonny kept a pistol in his tackle box.

Don't move, don't. His breath was so loud, he was sure it'd give him away.

And then Sonny shouted.

Cage stiffened, his heart in his throat. But Sonny wasn't looking down at him, aiming true. He was facing the woods.

More footsteps now, someone's heavy tread through the sand. Cage thought at first it might be the old man—Ro's grandfather and Sonny used to fish together—but instead a younger voice called out a greeting, swung down some lawn chairs on the dock. "Thought you'd come out here."

"Where's your dad?" Sonny sounded gruff, just how Cage remembered him.

"Saw him on the way over from your place. He spilled coffee on himself in the truck. Went back home for jeans and another drink."

Cage's fists tightened. Lance Childers was above him. He was trapped here under the dock until the two of them went farther out or left altogether. Being late afternoon, they'd probably be onto the trout, given the flooding tide. Once they got stuck into it, he'd have to move—fast.

"He better not bring that dog with him," Sonny said. A hook jingled on a fishing line, and the boards groaned overhead. Ro's dad was walking down the dock now. If Lance followed him, Cage could leave without them seeing. He stared through the slats, waiting.

"Good that you're fishing again." Lance shifted in his lawn chair and pulled off the hat he was wearing. "You casting or what?"

Sonny grunted. A long minute of quiet stretched out. Cage held still, hearing nothing, and then squinted up through the planks at Sonny. After another minute, he glided the line back overhead and then suddenly whipped it down, the rod snapping in his hands with a loud crack. He dropped the pieces onto the dock before kicking them into the water.

"You okay?" Lance stood up so fast he knocked his chair to the ground. Cage got ready to bolt—here was his chance—but Lance stayed where he was. Then came more footsteps, moving toward him. Cage crouched low as Sonny sank into one of the lawn chairs.

"Can't do it. Can't fish anymore." His voice was raw. "Reminds me of her."

Another long silence. Should he make a run for it now? Hope to Christ they didn't see him?

Sonny spat and then cleared his throat. "Tell me about that day."

Cage went cold at those words, like he was back in

that freezing water. *That day.* He knew exactly what day he meant.

"I already told you," Lance said. "I don't think it'd—"

"Why don't you tell me again." Sonny sounded strung tight, impatient. "From the beginning." It was a challenge, or maybe the strain in his voice was from missing his daughter.

Lance let out a sigh. "I found her on the shore," he said after a minute. "He was bent over her, holding her."

Cage sucked in a breath—it was him they were talking about. His feet were heavy, welded down, his heart firing in his chest. He couldn't run now if he wanted to. He was stuck against the piling. He had to hear, had to know.

"Go on."

"Something didn't look right," Lance said. "The way she was just lying there."

"Why'd you show up?"

"I'd come to fish; sometimes Ro and me fished together, you know that." Lance let out another jagged sigh. "And then I saw him; she was . . ." He trailed off. "She was lying on the sand. He was trying to hold her, or shake her. I wasn't sure which, but I shouted out."

Cage's body went to stone. *One, two, three.*

"And he looked up at me, at least I think he did, and then he was running. He just dropped her down on the sand and took off."

"I'll kill him," Sonny swore. "I'll kill him if he did it."

He meant it, it was in his voice. Cage kept as silent as he could.

"Don't blame you," Lance said, "not for a second."

"Why didn't you follow him?"

"Because of her," Lance said. He coughed. "She was still on the sand. She didn't move. I went down to the water, and when I got close I saw . . ." He stopped. "Sir, pardon me, but—"

"Go on."

"When I got close, I saw the blood. Her head was bleeding. There was blood on her mouth. Her eyes were . . ." He stopped, seemed to pull it together. "They were all black. That's when I checked for a pulse. Didn't feel anything. My phone never works out here—"

"Did you notice anything else?" Sonny shifted in his chair, the metal legs screeching across the wood. "Anything at all?"

"Well," Lance said, "y'all's boat was tied up."

"Show me where."

Cage heard their footsteps moving farther down the dock and knew he couldn't wait another second. Go, go, go. *Now.*

He sprinted across the sand toward the trees, expecting to hear a shout. Every muscle was straining, and he could almost hear it—their yells, their hollering, a clap in the air, the meaty thud of a bullet in his back—but nothing came. He made it to his clothes and then ducked down behind the fallen log. They hadn't seen him. A shred of luck. He pulled on his shirt and jeans as quick as he could and then dared a glance at the dock. Sonny and Lance were looking at the bay, their backs to the woods.

Cage ran off toward the barn, glad to grow the distance between them. Halfway there he realized what he'd done—

Ro's book, he'd left it on the log. *Christ.* He turned and raced back. When the ground got sandier under his feet and he heard the tide, he knew he was close. At a break in the trees he saw the dock. Only one man was still out there, but he couldn't tell if it was Lance or Sonny.

He slowed down, wary now, going for stealth over speed as he headed toward the fallen log. When he got close to it, he stopped.

Near the branches on the other side was a blond girl. She was standing by the log with her back to him.

Ro?

But she was too small, too young. The girl was holding something in her arms and straightaway he knew what it was. He couldn't call out to her, but he couldn't let her take the book either. Grabbing her was a bad idea too. She'd scream and it'd all be over.

The girl turned away from the beach and set off into the trees. He didn't have any choice but to follow.

She moved slowly, her head bent over the book. She was trying to read as she walked. He kept his distance, stepping from tree to tree as he stalked her.

The girl's hair was a knotted mess down her back, and she was barefoot. Maybe it was the neighbor kid who lived on the other side of the woods. The one Ro used to baby-sit. She was related to the cop somehow, had one of those hippie names, he remembered that now. Daisy? Apple? *Fern.* He'd only met her once, so she probably wouldn't recognize him—and he needed that book; it wasn't his to lose. He had to call out to her, ask her for it. That cash he'd taken at the hospital was rolled up in his boot. He'd offer to pay her for it if she didn't give it to him outright.

"Is that you?" The girl had stopped walking. She was peering into the woods ahead. "You can't scare me, I know you're there," she said, turning suddenly.

Cage crouched behind the trunk of an oak and waited, trying to figure out who she was talking to.

"I'm serious," she said. "I saw you just then. Don't try to scare me."

Maybe she'd spotted him. He chanced a quick look. The girl was still standing there in the woods, staring off to the side at nothing he could see.

"Just come out already."

He thought about stepping out, asking her for the book, but then—

"Wouldn't waste my breath scaring you." It was Lance, walking into view now. "What's that you got, little cousin?"

Cage pulled back behind the trunk and sank low to the ground.

"Nice, give it here," Lance said, and then the girl cried out like he'd yanked it from her. "Holy shit, Fern. You found it." He sounded surprised. "I've been looking for this. Know who it belongs to?"

Cage's chest flared tight and hot. Maybe Ro had shown

the book to Lance too. He shook off his jealousy, tried to focus.

"Yeah, it's mine," Fern piped up. "Finders, keepers."

Lance laughed. "I don't think so." There was a scuffling sound—the girl was trying to grab it back. "I might let you look at it," he said. "If you're lucky."

Christ, he was going to keep it. Mae would be furious with him.

"You got any of those pills?" Lance asked.

It was a weird thing to ask a kid, and suddenly they were beside him, walking right past the oak, close enough for him to touch. Lance was studying the book's front cover and didn't look his way. He could hit him and take it, but the girl would yell.

"Mom skipped her shift," Fern said. "Didn't bring any home."

Cage held still, unsure of what to do. And then something strange happened. Fern looked over her shoulder. Her eyes landed on him—she was staring straight at him, he could've sworn it.

A tightness gripped him as he waited for the girl to call out, get Lance's attention. Instead she frowned a little and then turned back, kept walking.

As though she hadn't really seen him at all. As though she'd seen *through* him.

CHAPTER 14

MAE RAN DOWN THE STAIRS and threw open the front door. No one was in the yard—no man standing in a hat, glaring at Blue Gate. No one was at the tree line either, those dark oaks hemming in the house from all sides. A coldness was at her neck as if she was being watched, and when she went inside, locking the door behind her, the foyer felt airless. She couldn't hear her dad or Lance and Elle either. The house had emptied out while she'd been in the tunnel, and it seemed like she'd returned to some other place, where her family didn't exist anymore. But when she passed the dining room, she found her grand-dad asleep in the window seat, his chin resting on his chest and his Bible on his lap.

He nodded awake and waved her over. She hesitated for a moment, thinking again of the attic. What was he hiding about their past? Everything she'd found in the house so far was odd, but the way he'd acted around the book . . . That was fear. And even when they'd gone through the album earlier he was spooked, on edge. Now his blue eyes looked clear, calmer. He pulled one of the garden's pink lantanas out of his pocket, presented it to her, and then fumbled for his notepad and scratched out a line.

NOTHING LIKE BEAUTY SLEEP

She put a smile on her face because it would make him happy. "Keep sleeping, then," she said, and he grinned. It was their joke. With all that had happened last year, he was the only one who tried to keep a sense of humor, who took the time to remind them that he cared, even though they were all missing Ro.

"May I borrow that Bible?" she asked.

His eyebrows rose, and then he pointed at the bookshelf by the table instead of handing her the one beside him. Another edition was on the bottom shelf, next to the old encyclopedias he used to read aloud when they were younger.

"Just want to check something." It wasn't a lie, but her face flushed as she turned the thin pages to the right section. Psalms 3:5.

I laid me down, the verse started, and Mae's eyes locked on those four words. *I laid me down*. She didn't have to read the rest to know what it said. She'd seen it before, on Hanna's grave in the woods.

> *I laid me down and slept; I awaked,*
> *for the Lord sustained me.*

Whoever had chosen the epitaph had also been the artist in the hidden tunnel. Mae shifted, tried to hide her unease. She slid the Bible back onto the shelf, knowing what she had to do. Her granddad shook his head when she asked if he needed anything—he was always worried about being a burden—but she brought him some sweet tea anyway to drink on the porch. She spent the rest of the afternoon searching the house for more hidden tunnels. Elle and Sonny weren't around to ask questions, and the search kept her mind off meeting Cage at nightfall. But even after checking every closet, and knocking against walls in every bedroom to see if they were hollow, she didn't find any more secret passages. Blue Gate was hiding them. Or someone was.

It was almost dark. Clouds were smothering the sky by the time her dad had left the house to go drink with Childers, Elle leaving right after him for a party. Mae steeled herself as she finally made her way toward the woods. Her pocketknife was in her hand, and she'd decided to shove a hammer into her bag, just in case. She turned the knife over, the metal cool on her skin. She wasn't sure if Cage was innocent, but she knew what she wanted from him— she could feel it all throughout her body, like diving into shocking-cold water. What she wanted from him, what she craved, was the same thing she wanted from Lance. She had to know the truth about what happened with Ro.

The sky seemed even darker when she reached the tree

line, and she clenched her bag strap as she started on the trail toward the barn. The woods were thick here, full of tupelo and black gum and cypress. If you didn't know your way, it was easy to get lost, especially in the fading light, the whole sky moving toward a purplish dusk. It was the color of blood coming to the surface—a bruised color that matched her heart.

As the ground grew softer, wetter, the old cabins came into view. Overhead the leaves blocked the last dregs of light, turning the clay foundations into shadows. There were a few decaying walls, a gap that used to be a window. Mae weaved through the ruins, passing a crumbling chimney and then the old well. Spanish moss hung down from the surrounding branches, grazing the round stone rim. Just as she walked past it, there was movement ahead. She tensed, peering into the woods. But she could only make out the lean trunks of trees, the clotted undergrowth.

Then she heard footsteps behind her, near the cabins. She spun, saw nothing. A moment later the footsteps were on the other side of the well. A tingle shot through her. There was the sound of something dragging across the mud—it was everywhere, moving through the trees. Someone was circling her.

Cage? His name was on her lips, but she stayed still, barely breathing, her eyes straining in the dusk. The woods were a deep gray, full of shadows. If she could hardly see, maybe this other person, or thing, couldn't either.

Everything went silent, and then all of a sudden the dragging was back—farther away now.

Mae's feet were riveted to the ground. She clutched her knife, took another long breath. The footsteps waned, but she held still for a few minutes longer, her eyes searching the woods. The trees around her were so thick it was hard to see. As she stepped out from behind a massive oak, her stomach went cold.

What was that, in the distance?

She gripped the knife tighter and stepped forward. There, some yards ahead, was a rope strung from a branch like a noose. The rope was thick, the dark shape at the end of it dangling a few feet above the ground.

It cut in and out of sight as she moved toward it, branches scraping her arms, her face. When the rope came into view again, she gasped at what was hanging from it.

A cat, slowly spinning in the air.

Her heart ratcheted in her chest. She ran up to it and grabbed the rope, started cutting. After a couple of swipes the animal swung loose. It was limp in her arms, and she set it on the ground where it lay still. She couldn't see anyone nearby as she crouched down and touched the cat's fur, her hand shaking. It was the little black stray.

Just that morning it had crawled out of her arms and escaped through the attic window. Surely someone hadn't just killed it, hung it up like this. And then it all clicked into place and she froze.

A cat for nine.

Mae's chest clamped up. She didn't want to believe it. She tried to fill her lungs, to breathe, but her ribs felt trapped. She dropped the knife onto the ground and stripped to her tank top, then wrapped the cat in her sweatshirt. If Cage had done this, then he was sick. He was sick in the head and she needed to—

"Mae."

She stood, grappling for the knife. She thrust it out in front of her, but no one was there.

"Mae, it's me."

And then he was stepping out from behind a tree, his hands up.

"It's just me," Cage said, his voice soft, almost coaxing. His face was barely visible in the growing dark, but he looked confused by the knife—his head tilted to the side just a fraction. Was that his trick? He pretended he didn't know anything, like he was innocent, so she'd feel sorry for him?

"Everything okay?" He stepped toward her. "Thought you'd know to meet at the barn."

"Don't come any closer," she said, thrusting the knife higher. Her eyes had adjusted enough in the dimness to see him. His gaze dropped to the knife and then went back to her.

"Come on, Mae," he said. "This again?" He took another step—like he thought she didn't mean it. One more and he could almost reach her. He was getting too close.

"Don't move." She pointed the blade at him, her other hand grasping for her bag. "Don't." But her voice sounded faint now, weak to her own ears. She felt like she'd been tricked, sucker punched. Her dad didn't trust him, Elle didn't, neither did Lance. The list was getting longer, and she'd refused to see it.

"Mae, I—"

He took another step forward, and she swung her bag as hard as she could. The canvas collided with his face and the force of the hammer hitting bone traveled up her elbow. Something came from Cage's lips—a soft wheezing sound—as he sank to his knees and fell over. He lay on his side, one of his arms at an awkward angle, his eyes shut. She felt a surge of panic. There was blood on his temple, on his dark hair.

"Hey!" The shout startled her and she bit back a gasp. It was her dad. "Hey!"

"Over here!" The yell was closer now; this time it was Childers. Bright orbs flashed, winking out when they were blocked by the trees. They'd followed her. "Answer us!"

Mae looked down at Cage, saw how he was slumped. She should call out to them. She should tell them everything she knew, even though it wasn't enough yet.

Just as she was about to yell, she heard a small sigh, a rustle. *Cage?* But he was still on the ground.

"Hey, Fern!" Childers shouted. "Fern, get yourself over here!"

Mae crouched down, her breath trapped in her lungs. Why were they looking for Fern? Was she hurt? Did Cage—

And then came the girl's answering shout, too close. "What!" The men were trudging over a nearby hill, their flashlights pooling on the ground, throwing streams of light across pine needles and mud. Mae heard the pitter-patter of Fern's footsteps nearby. The girl came into view and stopped a few feet from the shredded rope, and Mae shrank back into the shadows. Fern wasn't looking at her, but she *was* close enough to see her. Something wasn't right.

"Your mom's worried," Childers called out. "Now come on home."

Mae pressed herself against a tree, hoping Cage was shielded by the bush he'd fallen next to. If they saw him . . .

"Fern, scoot yourself over here," Sonny said. "I'm tired of walking."

Her dad was getting closer, near enough to spot the rope. One of the flashlight beams almost grazed its edge and Mae sucked in a breath, the bark digging into her shoulders. She could see it unfold: her dad pulling a gun, shooting Cage as he lay passed out on the ground.

The light fell on the tree beside the one she was hiding against and she flinched. Another tingle flashed down her neck, holding her voice captive. Surely they'd see the rope. Any minute, any minute—

A shadow shot past. It was Fern, running into the beam of light.

"All right, let's go home, Uncle Chill-chill!" she yelled, trampling her way over the brush, her curls bouncing in the flashlight beam as she sprinted toward the house. Fern was running away from the rope—almost like she hadn't wanted Childers and Sonny to see it.

The tingle was back at Mae's neck, her body's way of saying *This is the feeling of having wool pulled over your eyes.* Fern knew something, she was deliberately drawing her dad and Childers away from the dead cat on the ground. Away from Cage.

"Your mama's gonna tan your hide!" Childers called out. He stopped walking toward Mae and turned to watch Fern, his flashlight pointed at her as she ran in the opposite direction.

"Come on now," Sonny said. "Girl probably just wants attention."

Mae shivered. It seemed too much of a coincidence that Fern had been in this part of the woods, the same place where she'd found the cat. But Fern wouldn't have killed the animal. Even if there was some cruel streak in her, the tree limb seemed too high for her to throw the rope around, and yet . . . Was she wrong to have hit Cage?

Mae couldn't make sense of it, so she stayed down, keeping small. She waited in the dark until her dad and Childers were gone. By that time her shoes had sunk into the mud and Cage still hadn't moved from the ground. She stepped closer and then felt a bolt of fear.

He wasn't breathing.

CHAPTER 15

"CAGE!" MAE HISSED, SHAKING HIM. He was sprawled in the brush, still lying on his side.

Her heart was fast in her chest, and she tried to remember what to do—she'd read about it after her granddad's stroke. Clear the airway, start compressions, rescue breaths. He couldn't be dead; she couldn't have killed him.

She rolled him onto his back and put the heel of her hand on his chest, ready to push, and then all of a sudden she felt his ribs lift. She gasped, her heart thudding hard.

"Can you hear me, Cage?"

His lids were fluttering open. She could see the whites of his eyes, his face in a grimace. "Ro?" he asked. Now he was looking over her shoulder, staring so intently that she felt a chill.

Mae whirled, saw a cluster of trees in the moonlight. When she glanced back, his gaze was on her. "Did you— did you punch me?" He sounded dazed. A welt was swelling above his temple.

"Not exactly."

He rubbed his head and sat up, slowly, like he might pass out again.

"What happened?" he asked.

She decided to go with the truth, even though she felt embarrassed now, as if she owed him an apology. But it wasn't all her fault—and she still didn't know what he'd done. She kept her knife close, staying alert.

"I warned you to keep back, but you didn't listen."

"My mother says I have that problem." He tried to stand and swayed instead. Mae scrambled to her feet, wanting to keep her advantage.

"Well, now you've got a lot more." Her voice came out sharp and she watched for a reaction.

But Cage didn't seem defensive or on edge, or the least bit concerned about the frayed rope hanging beside them. He leaned against a tree for support and sighed out a breath through his teeth. "Mae, I need to tell you something."

"Tell me about that." She pulled the flashlight from her bag and pointed it at the rope.

"What about it?" He glanced at it, and then back at her. A trickle of blood was running down his face. "What's it for?"

He seemed genuinely confused. She beamed the light at his body and stared at him without saying anything, letting the quiet of the woods grow between them. Still looking dazed, he picked up the edge of his T-shirt and wiped the blood at his temple, the muscles in his arm flickering in the light. Nothing in his stance made him seem guilty. He looked baffled more than anything, and wary of her, and another seed of doubt worked its way into her heart.

She flicked off the flashlight and stuck it into her back pocket, letting her eyes adjust again. Maybe he hadn't hanged the cat. Maybe she'd guessed wrong. There were so many questions to ask—but it'd be smart to get inside first.

"Barn," she said. "Now."

He nodded, and she gestured for him to lead, her hand on the knife in her pocket. A minute later they were walking up the hill, the moon lighting their path. The back of his shirt was dirty, and so were his jeans. She watched a leaf flutter past his arm as he pushed the barn's side door open and disappeared inside.

She ducked after him. The light inside was dim; she found a couple of large flashlights on the counter near the boat and flicked them on, keeping Cage in sight. He had bruising near his cheek, a cut near his temple. She cringed, tried not to show it. "Are you okay?"

"Been hit worse," he said. "You must have a killer hook."

Guilt was creeping in. But she'd made a decision in the moment, thinking it was the best one she had. "It was a hammer," she admitted, feeling even worse.

His eyebrows shot up. "A what?" He put a hand to his head as if reconsidering his level of pain.

"In my bag. I had a hammer in my bag. Still do." She wanted to apologize but her throat felt tight. Her mind flashed to the stray—it was still outside, wrapped in her sweatshirt, and now she needed answers.

"The note you left me," she said, holding her bag close. "Did you remember anything about Ro?"

He stiffened. Then he shook his head, quick, like he had something to say but wasn't sure it'd come out right. "I was hoping to. Thought maybe the book would be a trigger, but it wasn't." His hands went to fists. "Mae, did you ever try the ritual?"

She crossed her arms, her body tense. "You saw it in the book. . . ." She felt spurred, ready for a fight. So it was him—it had to be. He was testing her, seeing what she knew.

He stared at the ground, blinking, as if trying to work something out. "Ro mentioned it before, but I—" His voice cracked. "I told her I wasn't interested."

She let the question loose. "And are you now?" He glanced at her, his blue eyes giving her nothing. "Tell me," she pressed. "Did you try it?" *Did you slaughter the cat?* Because if he did that, then what else was he capable of?

He looked away, running a hand through his dark hair. The skin along his knuckles was raised, bunched up in a row of scars. "I asked you first."

"Of course I haven't." She was the one who should be asking questions, not him. And the magic wasn't real; it couldn't be. She only cared about the book because it belonged to her family—because it had belonged to Ro. And whatever she'd written in it might bring Mae one step closer to knowing what secrets she'd been hiding before she died.

185

But now Cage had doubt on his face, like she was the one who was lying. "I've got an idea," he said. "Hear me out," he added, as if sensing she was about to protest. The flashlight was directly behind him, glowing over his skin, his dark hair. "Please."

Confusion swirled in her stomach. Every time he was around, she felt like this. There was something she was missing. She walked past him to the small kitchen, needing space to think. The faucet was hooked up to a rainwater tank, and she filled a glass. It tasted metallic, gritty, but she drank it all and filled the glass again before turning back.

Cage was watching her with his hands shoved into the pockets of his dirty jeans, his forearms rigid with tension. "Things have happened that I can't explain," he said.

His gaze narrowed on her as he walked forward and took the glass without asking, downed it all in one gulp. He wiped his mouth with the back of his hand, his eyes still on her. "I was gone nearly a year, Mae. A whole year I can't remember."

The water felt like it was roiling in her stomach. "I don't know what you're getting at," she said, trying to draw in a breath that wouldn't come. She knew exactly what he was saying, only there wasn't enough air in the barn, she wasn't getting enough oxygen to think. She hadn't tried the raising ritual. All she'd done was find the book in Ro's room. "Whatever it is," she said, "you're wrong."

He leaned toward her, the glass tight in his fist. "How

do you know for sure?" he asked. "You want me to just give up on her, is that what you're saying?" He was six feet of fury, Vesuvius in the flesh. "That the best you got? Just forget about her?" His jaw was working, biting something back.

Don't flinch, don't look away, don't blink—she could hear her sister even now. Ro would stare right back at him, hold her ground, so Mae kept her eyes on his, didn't move.

"How can you do it?" Cage's voice had fallen to a whisper. "Keep it all inside? Stand there so calm?"

She didn't feel calm. Her heart was thudding hard, and she wanted to yell and kick something. She wanted Ro alive just as much as he did.

"You told me she's been dead for almost a year, Mae," he said. His neck was tense, his shoulders flexing with anger under his thin T-shirt. "That right, or have you forgot already?"

"A year in a week," she shot back, her anger fueled by his. How could she ever forget? It was always on her mind, burning a hole in her. It was in everything she did every minute of her life.

"Then why," Cage asked, his voice tight, "why can't I *remember*!" He whirled and heaved back his arm, throwing the glass against the wall.

Mae flinched as it shattered, shards skidding across the cement floor. That was the problem—Cage couldn't remember. She had no reason to trust him. No one did.

She could feel her heart striking her chest—she could hear it. She took a step away from him. And another, and another, until her hip caught something sharp—the kitchen counter. Glass was cutting the thin soles of her shoes; one of the bigger shards had landed by her muddy Converse. It sparkled, winking off the beam from the flashlights on the counter. She looked up and saw that Cage's jaw was clenched. His blue eyes were intense, glistening with anger or grief, she wasn't sure which.

"I'm sorry," he said. "But there's something I have to do."

She shook her head—this was the confession she'd been waiting for. "No." She kept her voice steady. "It's not real, Cage. It's . . . a fantasy."

His eyes dropped from hers at last, and finally she could breathe again. He swayed on his feet, rubbed his head like it was aching. "What if there's a chance, Mae?"

Could he be right . . . ? She thrust the thought away. There was desperation in him now, that was all it was. She should get what she came for and leave.

"I need the book, Cage." Her sister could have written something more in it—it was her best lead. And it didn't belong to him, it was Ro's, and Mae wanted it back. She made fists with her hands to keep them from trembling. "Now please give it to me."

Cage leaned against the sailboat. He sighed, his hair dark against the tarp, his face pinched with pain. "I don't have it."

It felt like the breath had been knocked from her. "What?"

"I'm sorry," he said again. "The kid, that girl, she took it." He kicked a piece of glass.

"Fern has it?" Mae's skin was tingling. If Fern had the book, then . . . She thought back to how the girl had been standing next to the hanging rope. Surely she hadn't killed the cat, not on her own. She couldn't have, she—

"No, Lance does," Cage said. "He grabbed it off her in the woods. I saw him."

Mae's skin went prickly again, like she was standing underneath a humming wire. Was he lying?

Cage stepped forward, his boots crunching over glass. "We have to get it back," he said. "I have to try every . . ." He trailed off, shook his head. "Christ," he muttered. "She believed in it."

Mae's heart was thudding faster. A thread of a memory tugged at her—Ro dressed up in the woods, a basket in her arms—and then it was gone, the black door in her mind shuddering on its hinges. "If you lost it, then what does it matter?" She felt hopelessness rising in her chest. What could she do for Ro if she didn't have the book? Lance and Cage were the last two people to see her; they had to know more than they claimed. They must. And if Cage was telling the truth—if he wasn't trying to smoke-and-mirror her—then for some reason Lance wanted the book too.

Cage turned back toward her, but his gaze was a long way off, staring at something she couldn't see.

"What if it doesn't?" he said softly, like he was talking to himself. "What if there's another way?"

189

CHAPTER 16

BLUE GATE, 1859

GRADY'S COVERED IN BILE. HIS mother heaves again and this time nothing comes up. She gasps and he lays her head back on the pillow. *Please hurry*, he thinks. *Please*.

Jacob runs into the bedroom, his face streaked with tears. "They're here!" he shouts, and a moment later Pearl and Hanna are in the doorway. Pearl takes one look at his mother and swoops to her side. Grady lets himself glance at Hanna and he's pulled into her dark eyes, that tint of amber in them. Her skin looks even paler inside the house, paler than the sheets his mother lies on. Her red scarf is tied around her hair, and she's wearing a loose cloak over her dress to hide what they've done.

"Can you help her?" Grady asks, his voice raw.

There's a whispering sound and Hanna moves to the other side of the bed. It's his mother, trying to talk. Hanna leans over to listen and then straightens.

"Can't save someone who doesn't want saving," she says softly.

"What do you mean?" Grady asks, but he knows, deep down, and it feels like a blow. His mother's headaches have gotten so much worse. She can hardly speak and never leaves the house, complains that her chest hurts too. Would he wish her a life like this? Shut away at Blue Gate forever?

His mother's eyes flutter open. "My boys," she says. There are rivers of sweat on her forehead and her skin is shiny like the lantern beside her. "I hope you understand," she whispers, "why I wanted them here."

"To help you!" Jacob shouts, and presses his head against her shoulder.

"Here," Hanna says softly, offering a cloth to Grady. She's not wearing the ring he gave her—not in this house, not yet—and her fingertips are stained with ink. As her hand touches his, he feels a lightning bolt of warmth. He holds the cloth to his mother's face, wipes her mouth as gently as he can.

"Last time it was morning for her and now it's the night." Pearl runs her palms over the air above the bed, tracing his mother's body without touching her. "The mornings always pass."

His mother's eyes open again. Her eyes are blue, like his, but a darker blue, the color of the bay. "I'm ready," she says. "I'm going to Amelia."

Jacob cries out and Grady doesn't know it, but he is shaking his head no. Amelia died the day she was born, the day his mother was dying too, until he fetched Pearl from the woods. Now his mother needs to live—she needs to get well again. He reaches up with his free hand and pulls off his hat because his scalp is hurting; everything hurts when he looks at her, especially his heart.

Beside him, Hanna's eyes are watering. Little dark pools that the light catches. She strikes a match and then the smell of sage is thick in the air.

Help her, he begs silently. *Help her, I know you can*, and Hanna looks away. For a moment her hand is on the roundness of her stomach. But he can't think about the baby now. It's all gone wrong. He was going to tell his father and mother, he was going to ask for their blessing, but not now. Not like this.

"I love you both," his mother says.

Grady tries to repeat it back like Jacob does, but it feels like there's a stone lodged in his throat. A door slams somewhere in the house, followed by loud footsteps up the stairs. Grady's heart lurches as his father bursts through the doorway. When he sees Pearl, his bag drops to his feet, his stethoscope clattering to the floorboards.

"What's this?" he shouts, turning to Grady. Then he whirls on Jacob, who looks like he's about to cry. "Out!"

"Yes, Papa," Jacob says.

Grady knows his brother won't argue, no matter how much he wants to stay. As he rushes from the room, Grady tries to explain. "I thought . . . ," he starts. "It's just—"

"I told you never again!" His father is shaking he's so angry. "How dare you invite them inside this house?" His blue eyes narrow on Grady as he steps forward.

"I—" Grady tries again, and now he can tell Hanna is staring at him, waiting for him to defend himself, and Pearl is staring too, her arms folded across her chest, her dark gaze assessing him.

"It's fine." His mother lifts her hand. "It's me who asked them to come."

Grady's father picks up his bag from the floor. "I'll help you, Rose," he says. "Not these . . ." He waves a hand at Pearl and Hanna. "They're *unnatural*," he hisses.

Grady wants to protest, but a floorboard creaks and suddenly Hanna's brother is in the doorway. The ax is in his hands and his eyes are like two bits of coal. Grady doesn't know who to be more scared of—his father or this witch boy in front of him.

"There's no problem, is there, Doctor?" Pearl asks.

Grady's father looks like he's about to yell when there's a sputtering noise and his mother sits straight up in bed. "Please," she begs, and they all turn toward her.

"Rose?" his father says, and now he sounds worried.

"Please listen." His mother drops back down on the pillows. Her eyes are open, but they don't seem to focus on anyone. No, she is staring at the ceiling, the same way an animal sometimes stares at nothing at all. Grady follows her gaze. He sees only whiteness, unlike the ceiling in his room, which is painted the color of the sky. That was his mother's idea, so that no walls would ever bind his thoughts.

"I'm ready to go," she says. "I'm ready, Pearl."

Grady wants to protest. Pearl is supposed to heal his mother, like she did before. He looks at Hanna, who nods so slightly he might have imagined it. This is her way of asking if he's ready too, because last time he was not. Because last time, when his mother was dying in labor, he ran into the woods and found the witch's cabin, even though he wasn't supposed to. He begged Pearl to help his mother live after his father said there was nothing more he could do—that she was dead and so was the baby. And Pearl had come to the house and she'd shut the bedroom door and then, hours and hours later, it opened again and his mother was standing, her blue eyes blinking. His father had been horrified.

Hanna is still looking at him but Grady doesn't give her an answer. He can't, because every answer will be the wrong one. So he holds the cloth over his mother's forehead and dabs at her skin. He wants to bear what she's feeling; he wants to take her pain and carry it so she doesn't have to. Look how thin she is, all bone. How could she carry anything at all?

"I'm ready," his mother says again.

Pearl stares Grady's father down as if daring him to speak. Then she strides to the bed with Hanna, each with a rosary dangling from one hand, a muslin sack in the other, their lips moving but no sound coming out.

"Rose," his father says, desperate now. "Can't you hear me?"

Her eyes finally settle on him. "It's you," she says. She grits her teeth in what must be a smile. "Take care of our boys," she tells him, and Grady's heart tightens. "Be kind to each other." Her head falls to the side but her lace dress is rising near her ribs—she's only asleep.

And then she opens her eyes, and her gaze is on Hanna's stomach, and then Grady. "Listen," she whispers.

"Rose," his father tells her, "I'm right here, Rose."

Grady touches her hand, but she's staring at the ceiling again. He can't see what she's fixated on, he doesn't see us here like she does; he doesn't know that we're all around her, trying to make her passing easier, just like Hanna, who's whispering for her to let go, let go. And just as Rose reaches out to us, right as she slips into our arms, she tries to warn Grady; she tries to say "Be careful," but it's already too late.

CHAPTER 17

CAGE SLOWLY TRACED HIS FINGERTIPS along the strands of Mae's hair, not touching her, but close. Asleep like this, with her back to him, she almost looked like Ro, and he wanted to lie down beside her. But her hair was longer than Ro's, and she was smaller. She was darker than Ro too. It wasn't just her eyes, it was her gaze itself—like she was constantly measuring the world and had found it lacking. Ro saw the world as her own ocean, ready to be mapped, but Mae saw riptides and currents and whirlpools and knew to be cautious. She wasn't a girl who touched or let you touch her. Like an animal that way, like water that slipped through your fingers.

He reached out again to wake her. His hand grazed her cheek this time, close enough to feel the heat from her skin. She stirred, but her eyes stayed closed, her canvas bag under her head like a pillow, a flashlight tucked into her pocket. After he'd apologized for throwing the glass, Mae had talked to him for what felt like hours, trying to help him remember what happened on that last day with Ro. He'd been telling her about the hospital when he realized she'd fallen asleep next to him.

He got to his feet, deciding to let her rest. Then he strode up to the sailboat and hoisted himself onto the deck. If what Lance said was true, this might have been the last place Ro'd been alive. Had he lost his temper, hurt her? Why was that day a blank? Think. *Think!* He ran his hand over the wheel, the cubby's small hatch. The shadowy deck was like being underwater, swimming through a sunken ship.

He hopped down from the railing and onto the cement. Mae was still sleeping in the shadows, except something felt wrong about it. Ro should be lying here with him, not Mae. She might be the only person in the world on his side, but Ro came first and always would. It was simple: her before anyone else. The pit of his stomach churned when he thought of what he needed to do. Grabbing a small spade, he opened the barn door, shut it quietly behind him. Somewhere far off a dog howled, but Cage pressed on through the trees, careening his way over shrubs and bushes until he finally saw Blue Gate. The house was towering in the moonlight, its windows and edges dark. It was near midnight and the lights were off—they should all be sleeping.

He crouched down in the cover of the trees. Clouds were gathering overhead, throwing shadows over the crumbling old brick. He looked at the porch, checked for movement behind the pillars but saw only the empty rocking chairs, the porch swing creaking on its chains. His lungs felt like they were smothering in the humidity, and he took in a deep breath, needing courage. He searched his back pocket and pulled out what Mae had given him tonight. It was the picture that used to be taped up on the wall of the barn—she'd pocketed it for safekeeping.

Now he angled the photo at the moonlight. *R.C. & C.S.* It was the shot of him and Ro on the dock. His hair was buzzed short and his eyes were more bloodshot than usual. Ro was just golden, like the locket around her neck. She'd come from a swim and smelled like salt water when she'd leaned on his shoulder. Her reckless smile made his throat ache.

He swallowed hard and then glanced up at the dark hedge, imagining what he'd need to do if her dad caught him. Mae had warned him against coming here tonight, but he didn't have a choice. If Ro had buried the other half of the book, he'd find it. There might be more about the raising ritual in it, and then he'd try it and know for sure. He had to try, no matter how unhinged Mae said he was. His mother would call him hopeless—*Good thing your daddy didn't hang around to see you now.* She'd reel over in a fit of coughing, trying to catch her breath. *Sooner you realize your lot in life, the happier you're gonna be, lucky boy. Quit thinking so big.* Cage could see her point—he'd always had an imagination. The day he'd glimpsed Ro, he imagined being with her, as impossible as it seemed. Now he was going after the impossible again, and it was waiting for him in Blue Gate's garden.

The tall hedge enclosing the garden was so thick there was no way to pass through. He found the metal gate, but it was locked and didn't give when he shook it. Then he saw it—at the corner of the house was a cast-iron downspout that ran parallel to the hedge. A way across.

He gripped the flashlight between his teeth and hoisted himself up, dug his boots into the brickwork as he climbed. The spout was slick but he kept his hold. When he made it past the top of the hedge, he counted down from three and then jumped, falling to his knees as he hit the damp earth with a thud. He held his breath and looked up.

The house was still silent like some guard dog he was trying not to wake. Lightning burst overhead and lit up the windows and the garden, the thorny rosebushes next to the stone cherub. As he stared at its single eye, a whispering noise swept across the surrounding woods and then water was pouring over him. Pellets of rain beat down upon the mangled garden, the statue, but he wasn't leaving until he got what he'd come for.

When he stepped behind the hunch of the cherub's wings, the rosebushes guarding it clawed at his legs. Crouching down, he pulled the spade from his pocket. There was a patch of mud in front of the statue's feet like the ground had already been disturbed, but he plunged his spade in anyway and started to dig. The hole soon filled with muddy water.

If it's not here . . . The thought wormed its way into his head and he gritted his teeth. He dug in the rain and the dark, thinking only of her. Lightning struck, closer this time.

Home is the sailor, home from sea. And now he was here again, back at Blue Gate, hacking at the earth. The rain rushed over him, water was everywhere. A few feet down and still nothing—only mud and rocks and a swarm of tree roots long dead.

The rain slaughtered him, filling the hole, and he wondered if someone else had gotten to her hiding spot first. That sent him into a frenzied dig.

"Cage."

He froze. Mae's voice was soft, like the rustle of leaves. He turned toward the house but saw nothing in the dark.

"You here?" he asked, his throat raw. He knew he sounded like a kid—he felt like a kid, curled up in a ball in his mother's apartment alone. The rain was making him hear things and he couldn't tell what was real anymore and what wasn't. He wanted to yell, strike his fists against a wall, but instead he slammed down the spade.

It clanked when it hit the earth.

Cage leaned forward, searching the wet ground with his fingers. Lo and behold, something solid—sharp. He worked the spade around the metallic edge and then grabbed the thing that was buried and yanked it from the mud.

Lightning flashed again and illuminated the ground. *Home is the sailor, home from sea. And the hunter home from the hill.* A metal box lay in his hands. As quickly as he could, he shoveled the pile of dirt back into the watery hole, patted it down.

Behind him, a footfall.

He turned and saw shadows in the garden, a dim light by the gate. A whining came from the hinges, and his head was pounding, harder than the rain, and he couldn't see, everything was going white in the downpour. And then she walked through the rain and was standing in front of him, her hair loose around her shoulders and soaking wet.

"I told you not to come back," she said.

Her voice sounded strange and he blinked, the face in front of him blurring. Mae was staring at him like he should know better than to be outside in this storm. She was drenched; she needed to get out of the rain too.

"I've got it," he told her. "Now I'll know what to do." He let out his breath and turned to Ro's box, lifting its tarnished lid. The moldy stench hit him with a force as he huddled over it to look inside.

It was empty.

No, *no!* This was his plan, and he was risking everything for it—*one, two, three, four . . .*

"Is it there?" Mae whispered.

The box was empty. A single shred of paper was curled at the bottom, and that was all. He felt like the rain was coming from inside him; he was drowning in his own sadness. He was sure she'd buried the hidden half of the book here. *What was torn out is now underground. If it's raising you seek, then dig.*

He pulled out the shred of paper, held it up. Its ink was running, and even in the dimness he could see it was nothing, just a note in pink pen, half destroyed by water and age. The rain poured down over it, and then Mae grabbed it from him, shoving it into her pocket. All he wanted was to raise Ro, but there was nothing here—it was just another one of her games, or someone had taken it. He'd failed. He couldn't remember what he'd done to Ro that day, and he couldn't change it, he couldn't bring her back. Not without her book.

"It's gone," he said, "she's gone." As he said it there was a clap of thunder, and through the rain Mae looked like Ro. "I think I need help," he told her. "What's wrong with me?" He was talking to Mae, to Ro. "I . . . I see you, I hear you."

She stepped forward, she was so close now. "I see her sometimes too," she said. The rain was flooding her face, her hair, everything. "And I hear her."

Christ, she even smelled like Ro, that scent of cloves and mint and something sweet. Her shirt was soaked through, and she was staring up at him, so serious.

"It's not real," she said, her voice faltering. "It can't be." His head was aching. The rain stung his skin, thrashing at him as he tried to listen to her. "Do you . . . ?" she said, and then stopped. She blinked at him through the rain. "Do you really think the ritual could work?"

A flash of memory: his motorcycle hitting the guardrail, the slide into the kudzu. All that green, he was tangled up in it. Lots of blood, streaming in his eyes. He hadn't been able to get to his feet; he hadn't been able to move. He shook his head, felt like crying. "I don't know, Mae."

"I want to believe." She looked down at her hands.

Her eyelashes were wet from the rain and she was standing beside the hole and the empty box and the water was everywhere around them and he felt like it was washing him away, into the earth, into the hole he'd dug. "I want to believe she could come back," she whispered.

Cage saw her shoulders rise and fall. He realized she was crying, and then he could move, and he did. He pulled her against him, holding her because it was all he could do.

"Mae," he said. His arms tightened around her. Mae pressing against him felt good, and he couldn't help himself, he breathed in the smell of her hair like he used to with Ro.

She tilted her chin to look at him. Instead of moving away she held still, staring up at him through the rain. The water on her face, on that hair of hers, her neck.

He tried to back away, but his legs wouldn't work. She was standing between him and the house, trying to protect him even now, and then his thumb was on her lips and he didn't know how it had gotten there and he was going to kiss her, it was all he wanted, and the next thing he knew she was pulling out of his arms, stepping back.

It was over.

The rain pelted down between them, and she was staring at him, her head tilted to the side, her wet hair darker than Ro's. She wasn't Ro, she was Mae, and he'd almost gone and lost the only friend he had left. His head ached, but it was nothing compared to what he felt inside.

"I'm sorry," he said, except now he was so ashamed

he couldn't stand to look at her. She was too much like Ro, only she wasn't, she would never be, and this was all wrong. It was his head—it was going funny on him again, the pain sharp and steady.

Another streak of lightning split the sky, and he turned and stumbled for the gate and shoved it open, needing to get away, to leave. He ran to the edge of the trees, and only then did he stop to glance back at the house.

It was dark. Something panged inside his chest, and Christ, he couldn't think of Mae alone in the garden. He had to think of Ro.

He should walk toward the highway, hitch a ride to his uncle's place. But he couldn't go there, not now. Not like this, drenched and desperate. He needed to clear his head first. Dry off in the barn, sleep, think.

Cage stumbled deeper into the undergrowth. The rain had eased, but everything around him leaked, like the entire world was a boat with a hole in it and it was sinking and always had been. The branches were dripping; the leaves were dripping. He raised his head to the sky and held open his mouth, caught a few drops. He was so thirsty, and dizzy too—he hadn't eaten all day. Just a little farther, just a little farther. He started running, trying to find the barn. It was close, not much longer now. He kept going, charging forward, falling and picking himself up again. It felt like someone was following him, and he didn't recognize the trail; nothing in the woods looked familiar. A huge tree that he didn't remember blocked his path. He wandered around it, and instead of seeing the barn he fell onto sand.

He was on the beach. It didn't make sense—he'd been walking toward the barn, but here he was. A white-hot pain pulsed in his head and he shut his eyes and then opened them.

The sand was wet. The clouds parted and the moon fell down on the black water, a round pool of light, all the way out in the center of the bay. The water was calm and flat, like it had never rained at all.

And there in front of him was the dock where it had happened, where they'd found her body. *Think, Cage, think.* His insides were burning, but he rose to his feet, stumbled over the sand dunes, through the seagrass. And then, at the far edge of the dock, he saw it. There was something resting on the planks. It looked like—

"Ro?" His legs were taking him over the sand. It sloped down toward the water and he fell and got up all in one motion, pushed forward until his boots were clapping over the dock, pounding like his heart. At the end of the dock was a figure hunched over.

Ro—it was her. It was her. She was in a black dress, and it was pooling out behind her on the planks. There were feathers on the dress. Feathers, and Ro, her face turned to the side. He could see her chin, her nose, and underneath were the feathers. They were everywhere. A pile of feathers and claws and . . .

He sank to his knees. *This isn't real, this isn't real.*

He blinked and rubbed his eyes, but the blackbirds were still there, the pile of dead birds, and now he could smell them. Sharp and sweet, the stench of decay.

Cage leaned over and emptied his guts into the water. Heaved again and again until there was nothing left to come up. As he wiped his mouth, he saw it in the water.

Her pale face, floating down, down, down.

And then he remembered what he'd done.

CHAPTER 18

MAE WAS SOAKING WET, HER hands covered in silt. She'd cleaned up the muddy hole in the garden, hurrying so her dad wouldn't wake up and find her outside. The house was quiet and dark when she finally let herself in and pulled off her soaked Cons.

She made her way to the kitchen without turning on any lights—the hallway was a hazy silver path. Water pooled under her feet where she stood on the kitchen tiles; she'd left a trail of wet footprints across the floor. She felt cold to the bone, and her fingers were numb. It was hard to believe that Cage had just run off like that, though part of her hoped he'd leave Blue Gate—it might be better for everyone. She shivered, and the coldness felt like it was coming from inside her heart. Her dad would say that she needed warm milk, but what she really wanted was coffee, something to sharpen her mind, help her think things through.

She set her bag on the counter and went into the

pantry for the jar of grounds. As she reached for it, she heard hinges squeak—the door was swinging shut. She bolted toward it and slipped, the pantry going dark as the latch clicked. She felt panic rising as she rattled the knob. It was stuck.

The flashlight was still in her pocket and she pulled it out and turned it on, found the string that was dangling above her and tugged. The bulb flickered and then settled, orangey and dull, casting shadows over the cereal boxes and tin cans on the shelves around her.

Mae tried the door again, but it didn't budge, no matter how hard she shoved her hip against it. Her heart seized as she realized the problem: the lock was on the other side. She was trapped.

She flicked the flashlight off, wanting to save its battery. The pantry was so deep she couldn't see how far back it went, and staring into the shadows made her uneasy. She still felt shaken up from finding Cage in the garden, digging in the storm. And now she was locked in here, and soaking wet, her bare feet streaked with mud.

The pantry's orange bulb dimmed, and Mae shook the doorknob again. If she called out for her dad, he'd want an explanation. But Elle should be sneaking home any minute—she usually slipped into the house just after midnight, when Mae was supposed to meet her at the front door in case their dad was awake, so he'd think they'd gone out together. So far her sister hadn't told anyone about Cage, and Mae couldn't risk making her mad by calling out for Sonny and getting her in trouble.

So she'd have to wait for Elle. Mae tucked her wet hair behind her ears, took a deep breath. She hated sitting still. She crossed her arms, trying to stop shivering, and then saw a large cardboard box shoved underneath a shelf. She must have missed it this morning when she dragged the others into the dining room, intent on finding out more about Hanna.

Mae tried the door again. The sound of the rattling knob was the only thing she could hear. She rubbed her face, tried to push from her mind all the ways she'd messed up lately. To distract herself, she went over to the box and pulled off the masking tape on top. Inside were more photo albums, but of recent years. She grabbed one and sat down on the box, her wet jeans leaking onto the cardboard lid.

When she opened the book, she realized what it was. Not a photo album like she'd thought. A scrapbook. Ro's name was written in bright red ink on the inside cover. Mae knew that she and Elle didn't have a memory book like this, but their mother had packed this one full.

The first page held a copy of Ro's birth certificate. She'd been born at the same hospital where their mom died three years later. They'd never been able to talk to Sonny about it, but Ro had explained it in no uncertain terms. They came into existence and their mother died.

Mae turned the page and saw a picture of her mother holding a serene-faced baby Ro in a hospital bed, a slender plastic name tag looped around her wrist and a huge white pillow propped up behind her. She looked as if a light was glowing beneath her skin, like there was a flame held to her green eyes. Even her brown hair shone. She seemed so alive, so radiant—and then she wasn't, just like that.

Mae knew her dad would always blame her and Elle, even if he didn't realize it. Her eyes stung and she flicked past more baby pictures, stopping at Ro's first birthday. Sonny had a party hat on and was laughing so hard he'd thrown his head back, while a gleeful Ro was in a high chair, the red velvet cake missing a huge chunk, her chubby baby fist holding it up in triumph. That man with short hair, the one who was howling to the moon with laughter, looked nothing like the dad she knew. At the table next to Ro was their granddad, a napkin draped across his stomach, a silly grin on his face as he held up a spoonful of icing, toasting the camera. Her mom must have taken the photo—even then she was invisible, forever out of reach.

Mae skipped a few more pages, one of them stapled with Ro's first drawing of what seemed to be a horse, probably inspired by the Childers' stables. Next came a report from Ro's preschool teacher. Ro was described as *creative and charming, a pure joy*, but the teaching assistant had also made a note: *She's inventive with the truth and likes to get her own way.*

Mae shifted on the cardboard lid, felt it bend under her weight as she turned to the end of the scrapbook. Then she stopped, her heart missing a beat.

On one of the last pages was Ro, wearing a white

Easter dress, a black ribbon in her hair and a basket in her hands. She was standing near the garden hedge, the green leaves rising behind her. She was about eight or nine years old—which meant someone besides their mother had added the picture to the scrapbook.

Mae stared at Ro, an odd sensation creeping down her spine. She actually *remembered* her in that dress. She remembered the white lace and black ribbon, and Ro running out to the woods, and something heavy in that Easter basket. She remembered following her through spiky grass, and more snippets of memory that didn't make sense, stitched together crookedly like the sequence of a dream.

Looking at the photograph brought her back to that day. How she'd hidden while Ro stooped over the basket. How her sister had taken so very long with whatever she'd been doing, her back to her, that white dress sweeping over twigs and leaves. Mae had been watching and hiding, wanting to play a trick like Ro always did. Waiting patiently to spring out and scare her. But when Ro had finally turned, oh, when she'd turned, her dress had been a different color.

The dress was a different color. Mae sucked in a breath and slammed the scrapbook shut, feeling her heart race. The black door in her mind shook on its hinges. She knew there was something important to remember, but it was gone now.

She stood and rattled the knob again, but she couldn't hear Elle or anything outside, and suddenly it seemed too dark, too dusty. The air felt ominous, weighed down—if she didn't get out, she knew something terrible would happen. She could pound a can against the wall until someone heard her. But then, who was she hoping would help? If she woke up her dad, he'd see how muddy she was and ask what she'd been doing, and there was no way her granddad would hear her. When she'd checked on him earlier, he'd been slumped at his desk in the attic, a piece of paper spread over his Bible and his head resting on his forearms, already asleep.

Mae glanced around the shelving, growing even more claustrophobic. Maybe there was another door; maybe the back of the pantry linked up with a tunnel or a crawl-space? She'd searched every bedroom in the house today, looking for hidden tunnels, but hadn't thought to check the kitchen. Maybe there was a way out.

Stepping farther into the gloom, she ducked past cob-webs. The walls narrowed and then turned at a sharp angle. Back here most of the shelves were bare—no one had used this part of the pantry in a long time—but on some of the shelves were jars of preserves. They were packed together, clustered in dusty rows. Food jammed and pickled years ago and stored here, under the staircase, because it was cool and dark and more protected than the basement.

The ceiling slanted downward, and Mae lowered her head and kept walking, surprised that the pantry extended even farther. When she finally reached the end of it, she found an old wooden cabinet in a corner. She ran her hand along the far wall, hoping to feel a latch or a doorknob, but there was nothing.

Just as she turned away, ready to yell for Elle or Sonny, she stopped. The faint stream of orangey light was spilling over the brick to her side, and she noticed something strange: a long, narrow crack behind the row of shelves. Mae stepped close and then gasped.

It wasn't a crack—it was a line of charcoal. Someone had written on the stonework.

Come back. Come back. Come back. Come back. Come back. Come back. Come back.

It was everywhere. The same words over and over again, a hundred times over. She put her finger to one of the marks, felt the dark chalky smudge. How long had it been here? *Come back. Come back. Come back. Come back.*

She shivered, tamping down a sudden feeling of alarm. She traced her finger underneath the cursive as she moved past the bulky shelves, shifting jars to keep the charcoal in sight. Someone had wanted to cover it up, placing the shelves in front of it, lining up the preserves to block it. The lettering snaked all the way to the wooden cabinet in the corner and disappeared behind it.

Mae shoved the edge of the cabinet. It didn't budge, it was too heavy. An urgency overtook her and she opened its drawers and started emptying them out—there was china, a tablecloth, a pipe. When she was finished, she shoved the edge of the cabinet again, and this time it shifted. It took her another few minutes to push it far enough. Then she grabbed the flashlight from her pocket and beamed it behind the cabinet, on the tiny charcoal scribble.

And there was its origin. A dark looping figure eight. *Hanna.* When she touched the lettering where it sloped upward, a sliver of the brick fell, dusting her feet. A dent in the wall?

She touched it again, and this time the brick groaned backward, opening. It was a small door, no higher than her hip. She blinked, her pulse quickening as her flashlight cut through the dark haze. Beyond the pantry wall was a cavelike enclosure. Coldness streamed from it, and a smell of mold.

The flashlight trembled in her hand. She let out a breath and crouched down, ducking into the darkness. As she straightened, the bright beam flooded another wall a few feet away. The space was cramped, the ceiling low. The stale smell hit her and she pulled her shirt over her mouth. The flashlight splayed across the floor and her heart nearly stopped in her chest. *CHANA 4 CHANA* was written in the center of the room, next to a circle drawn in chalk. Inside it were four glass jars of various sizes placed in a row. They had dusty lids and their glass was foggy and full of debris, hazy shadows. Mae gripped the flashlight as she stepped across the cold floorboards, holding the beam steady on the jars.

A greasy residue had collected on the surface of the first one, and chunks of a hairlike substance were at the bottom. Floating inside the jar was a pale cat skull.

Bile rose to Mae's throat, and her legs felt weak as she pointed the flashlight to the next jar. Behind the debris was a coiled snake, some of its scales still intact. The third jar was as foggy as the first and she stepped closer, already guessing what she'd find. A bird claw was scraping against the glass at the bottom.

That left the last jar, the biggest one. She had to see inside; she couldn't stop herself.

She squinted at it, the light hitting the glass. She reached out and tilted it and the debris trapped inside spun in circles, shifting and floating. Bits of tissue swirled in the murky water, and long dark hair was layered at the bottom. Her stomach knotted up as she shifted the jar another inch. Then came a tapping sound.

The smear of a hoof smacked the glass through the globs of floating tissue. She gasped, her flashlight jerking back. A hank of what looked like the horse's dark mane fluttered at the bottom, next to bone.

God, who would do this? She tried to swallow, but her mouth was dry and she felt like she might be sick. She wanted to run back to the pantry, get out of the cold and the dark and the smell that was everywhere. Instead she shut her eyes and thought of Ro, and then she opened her eyes and looked straight at the thing that scared her, just like her sister would have done.

Next to the jars was something bright and red. She edged forward, bending down to touch the redness—it was a cloth. Soft, folded into a square, with stains on it and dark embroidery.

Mae stared at the designs around the hem—vines and flowers and herbs. Without thinking, she grabbed the cloth. She backed away, nearly tripping on her own feet, the flashlight lurching across the brick walls as she turned and crawled through the small doorway, closing the thick door behind her.

The pantry bathed her in orange light; she stood in its glow and caught her breath, the spidery handwriting on the walls blurring in front of her. *Come back. Come back. Come back.*

A wave of dizziness overtook her and she shut her eyes. It felt like the floor was canting, ever so slowly, about to capsize underneath her, as if she was back on the sailboat with Ro. And then she heard . . . *what?* Someone breathing next to her.

Her eyes shot open.

There was no one in the pantry, no one hiding beside the cabinet—she was just imagining things. And tonight Cage had said that everything was mixing up in his head. The storm had drenched them both in the garden, and she hadn't listened to him, hadn't wanted to listen. She could see him now: crouching over Ro's tarnished silver box, the raindrops glistening on his face and his dark hair, the gift cherub behind him pale and huddled. Cage had straightened, so tall, water streaming off him the way it streamed off the sides of a house in a storm. His body was tight with anger, but how he held her had been soft. His hands warm, threading through her hair, holding her close.

Mae shoved the cabinet against the wall with a burst of adrenaline and then launched herself forward, wanting out of the pantry. She stumbled past the jars of preserves, feeling disoriented. Instead of fruit or jam inside them, now she saw hair and fur and bone. She blinked—her eyes were playing tricks on her. The shelves were cavernous, dark, closing in on her. Cage had told her not to follow him and she'd let him go, only she shouldn't have. He'd been half out of his mind, and there was no telling what he'd do. He'd asked for help. He'd asked her for help, and she'd let him go. Her breath rushed from her lungs as she threw all her weight against the pantry door, but it still held strong. She slammed into it again, her shoulder stinging. The door didn't move.

Just as she was about to yell out, pound against the ceiling, she heard her name. A whisper, just outside the door. The handle started to turn. She was so shocked that she stepped back, knocking her elbow against a shelf.

The orangey haze fanned out across the tiles as the door slowly opened. She glimpsed a face in the darkness ahead, and then the light was flicking on. Elle was standing in the kitchen with the pocketknife raised.

"Jesus," her sister said, setting down the knife near the bag. "What are you even doing in there? And why are you all muddy?"

Mae blinked back tears, not wanting Elle to see. "You wouldn't believe me if I told you," she said, grabbing her hand. "I thought you'd be home earlier," she choked out.

"Sorry. I stayed to talk with Lance at the party." Elle blushed and shook her off. "He's coming over tomorrow for dinner."

Mae could tell she was excited, and she wanted to say the right thing, but every time she blinked she saw spidery black handwriting crawling under her eyes. She reached for her sister's hand again, needing to feel something solid, something real.

"You're filthy," Elle said, pulling away for the second time. She sighed, crossed her arms over her tight black dress. "So that's me, but you haven't told me what you were doing in there. And why do you have a flashlight?"

She wouldn't even know where to start, so she stepped past Elle and lied. "I was out painting in the garden," she said at the sink, flipping on the tap to wash her hands. They were shaking under the stream of water. "I came inside and then got locked in the pantry. Accidentally."

When she turned back, Elle's gaze was narrowed on her. "You never do anything by accident."

Mae dried her hands on a towel. "I'm just glad you let me out." The sigh came from deep inside her before she could hold it back. "Thank you."

Elle gave her a look and then shrugged. "Whatever. I'm going to bed."

Mae could tell Elle knew she was lying. Her sister's disappointment on top of everything she'd seen was too much. She thought of telling Elle the truth—it was about to spill from her. How Lance might have Ro's book, and the secret rooms in the house, and about Cage, how she'd messed up tonight by letting him run off. But instead she bit down on her lip until it stung. She had to stay quiet. It was safer that way.

"You really do need a shower." Without saying anything more, Elle turned and walked off.

"Night," Mae whispered, still feeling shaky as she picked up her bag, tucking away the cloth she'd found. She leaned against the counter, watching her sister tiptoe down the hallway. After she heard Elle's bedroom door click shut upstairs, she went to the foyer and pulled on her damp Cons. She stepped outside onto the porch and sucked in deep gulps of fresh air, trying to get the mold out of her lungs. Trying to forget what she'd seen.

The rain clouds had cleared and the moon lit her path. She started running—she wanted to put space between her and the pantry, and that hidden, cavelike room. *Come back. Come back. Come back. Come back.* Grady's words echoed with every step, and she thought of Cage. *Come back. Come back. Come back.*

The woods were moving around her, the trees swaying, the scent of rain still in the air. Before she knew it there was the small hill and the rise of the barn ahead. The side door had been left open a crack and Mae glanced over her shoulder and then squeezed through.

Inside it smelled musty, and the white tarp was pulled over the boat. The skylight let in just enough light to see.

"Cage?"

Her stomach tensed with worry as she looked around. His boots were gone. The fridge was shut, the cord unplugged. All the cups were back under the sink, and the other flashlights were put away. There wasn't any garbage on the floor, no fruit peels, no roll of toilet paper. The little raft he'd slept on wasn't in sight.

All was quiet, undisturbed. As if he'd never been here at all. A cloud passed over the skylight, and dark shapes moved at the edge of her vision. A dog howled somewhere far away.

"Cage?"

She switched on her flashlight, its beam rippling out. She thought he was sitting in the far corner, but it was just a stack of chairs, a rag on top.

What she'd do to see him—the bob of his dark hair, his smile that had to be earned. She wanted him to step out from the dark the way moonlight can break through clouds over the bay. Onyx water, the moon ghost-white. She could see it as a painting, and she could imagine him appearing in front of the boat. But he didn't.

Because he'd left Blue Gate.

She lowered the flashlight and leaned against the wall, her heart heavy. It felt like she already missed him—how he'd listened to her, how they'd been able to talk about Ro. How around him she felt like maybe, just maybe, anything was possible.

A wave of exhaustion hit her. She thought of everything she'd seen that day, then checked her bag for the cloth. She pulled it out, letting it unfold in her hands. It was an apron, long enough to graze the floor. The embroidery along its edges was intricate, its flowery vines twisting around a large square pocket. Mae traced the thread with her finger and noticed that the inside of the pocket was stained black. She turned it inside out, then nearly dropped the apron.

Grady Cole was staring at her, and so was a girl she'd never seen before.

On the cloth was a sketch in black ink, so perfectly rendered that it almost looked like a photograph. Written at the bottom, a single line: *Grady and Hanna, always.* Mae's heart spiked. Hanna! She thought back to the grave in the woods, the confession in the green book. *I love Hanna, I love Hanna, I love Hanna.* Here she was, finally. And she was with Grady.

Hanna was looking over her shoulder, her mouth unsmiling. She was striking: high cheekbones, guarded eyes. Her forearms looked slim but strong, as strong as her jawline. Her body was facing Grady's. His chest was blocked by the curve of her shoulder and her long dark hair, and his hat was hiding part of his face. Mae stared at the writing beneath the sketch again. It was a tight cursive—Grady's handwriting—and she drew in a breath.

It was Grady, all of it was Grady. He'd written in the green book and on the walls of the house over a century and a half ago; he'd sacrificed the animals, trying to raise Hanna. Had he done it? Had she returned?

Mae shoved the cloth into her bag. It was too much, all

of it. She fought the urge to sink to the floor, to stay in the barn until she saw Cage again. She wanted him in front of her, that dark hair, that cut near his temple. But he'd left tonight, and she'd let him go.

She forced herself to walk to the door, tug it open, step outside. There was something slender and shadowy beside the nearest tree. She flicked on her flashlight, beamed it at the cowering thing. Then her heart leaped into her throat and she held back a scream.

CHAPTER 19

RO SHRIEKS WHEN HE TIPS a water bottle over her. "Your turn to get wet," he says.

She pushes him toward the edge. "You jump first."

He can't resist her, and she knows it. "Come after me."

She gives him another push. "Always." Then she's laughing behind him as he dives into the cold jolt of the water. He shoots down and opens his eyes in the brackishness, turning toward the faint hull of the boat. Instead of Ro diving after him, a lure drops into the water. She's playing one of her games.

He kicks hard and breaks the surface. There she is on the deck, grinning in an old straw hat that somehow suits her, her sun-bleached hair over both shoulders, her locket dangling.

He treads water, keeping warm. "You gonna jump in?"

"Nope, decided to fish," Ro says. "Have I got you hooked yet?"

"Who haven't you hooked?" he asks, and it's meant to

be a joke, but he thinks of Lance and jealousy hits him. He doesn't know what Ro sees in him.

"Your face is going all funny," she says, casting again.

He grabs the ladder and hauls himself up. If he tells her he's jealous of her friend, he'll set her off. If he points out how Lance is always hanging around her when he's at work, she'll just laugh, say he's harmless. But now she's waiting for an answer, and he has to tell her the truth. That's the promise they made.

"I was thinking about you and Lance."

"How many times do you need to hear it? There is no me and Lance."

He knows this, deep down. He hates sounding possessive—it reminds him of his mother—but he keeps talking anyway. "I don't trust him."

Her eyes narrow. "Funny. That's what he said about you."

Cage's jaw clamps down, and for a minute he forgets to breathe. "Ro . . ."

"What?" Her voice has an edge; they're so near to fighting he can taste it. "I said, what?"

He shakes his head, tries to spit the bitterness out. "Nothing." But she doesn't like one-word answers, so he finds something else to say. "Thought we were heading in soon." They were adrift in the bay, nearly back at Blue Gate, close enough to hear the birds on the shore.

"We are." Her nylon line glints in the sun and then disappears into the water. He's probably ruined the whole day by bringing up Lance. Everything he's planned, just because he had to open his mouth.

"Cage?"

"Yeah."

"I love you."

She looks at him with those green eyes, and he can't say it back—he's still pissed off a little. But she smiles anyway and he loves her even more.

A moment later her line starts bouncing. She's looking sly in her red bikini and that crooked straw hat.

"You get all the luck," he says.

She grins. "I got you."

And then his stomach goes to shreds, and he knows he has to do it. Not many things scare him, except for this; he lies awake at night thinking about it. Here's his chance, while it's just the two of them. He opens the small hatch and finds what he hid.

When he turns back, there's a halo of light around her—the sun's behind her and the effect is something magic. Then he drops to his knee, because his mother has always told him that's the best way. The deck is digging into his skin, and his throat is dry, even though they're surrounded by water that seems bigger than the sky itself. But Ro is bigger than all of it—she is everything to him, and he says her name aloud.

Her line's still bobbing when she turns to him. Her eyes widen at the box in his hands, and the rod splashes into the water. Then he knows he's got her attention.

He needs to go through with it before he loses his courage.

"I don't have a speech or anything," he says, "but I have this." He holds up the box and opens it. "Will you marry me?"

She grins like she's about to say yes, and then he's grinning too. But when her gaze settles on the ring, all of a sudden she stops smiling. Her hand goes to her mouth and she's shaking her head. He falters for a second, almost lets go. Looks down at the box to make sure the ring hasn't fallen out. But it's sitting right there, gold and red in the sun, and he can't figure out why she's not smiling anymore.

She's staring at it, so he does too. Maybe it isn't good enough? It's the heirloom ring with the rubies on top, what his mother gave him after he drove home this summer. He went back to tell her he met a girl, someone he loved more than anything. More than a new motorcycle, or having friends who weren't scared of him, or getting a job out of high school so he wouldn't have to worry. When he turned to leave, ready to head back to his uncle's, his mother grabbed his elbow, shoved the box into his hand. *Go after her*, she told him. *Don't let her go*, and for once she wasn't so bitter. *Good luck*, she said. *That's the ring your dad gave me. It's yours now.*

He's thinking all this as he holds it out, the very best thing he can offer, and Ro looks at him and finally speaks. "Where's it from?"

His heart is firing in his chest because it's not supposed

to be like this—it's *supposed* to be a one-word answer. He gets to his feet. "What?"

"You heard me." There's fire in her voice, and he can't believe this is happening.

"I didn't steal it," he says. "It's a family ring." He thought she'd like the oldness of it, the meaning behind it, and here she is looking at him like he's done something wrong. "I wanted it to be a surprise."

She doesn't answer him, and he can feel the worry snake move in his stomach. He wants to start over again; he wants another chance.

"If this is about money," he says, "I'll keep working for my uncle."

"Your uncle who lives here. In Gulf Shores." She sounds different; she's not acting like herself.

"I could get a job for more somewhere—"

"Cage," she interrupts. She's shaking her head again; she's upset. "This is bigger than both of us." Now she won't even look at him. She's staring at the ring. "God. The engraving . . ."

He touches her elbow but she shakes him off, her eyes still on the ring. The dock is in sight now and the worry snake coils around his neck and he wonders what he did wrong. "Ro, talk to me."

"How were we to know?" Her face is drained of happiness, and it scares him. "This is bigger than both of us, Cage," she whispers again, and he wants her to stop.

"Just tell me what you mean!" His yell is out before he realizes it, and her green eyes narrow on him.

"It *is* what I mean," she says, and he grabs her hand. "Just back off!" she shouts, and the wind sweeps away her words, carries them out to sea, and she's staring at him now, breathing hard. He's vaguely aware that the boat is drifting closer to the dock. They'll hit it soon.

"My book, Cage. Don't you get it?" The sharpness is gone from her voice, but she's still talking nonsense, and she hasn't said what counts—she hasn't said yes.

He steps away from her. An excuse, that's all it is. They've got to dock any minute and the snake is gnawing on him, biting down. She's looking out over the water now, all the fight has left her. But his temper's burning through him, and he tries to hold it back. He's been so wrong.

"How are you so calm, Ro?"

She turns. Her eyes search his face like it's something she's only just now seeing. "Start from one because it's better than nothing." It's her thing to say when she knows he's angry. "I guess we can laugh or we can cry, Cage. Or count to ten and take a deep breath."

So that's it—she's made it pretty simple. Play by her rules. Don't ask questions. Somehow he manages to move his feet, to steer with one hand while she pulls on a T-shirt and leaps to the dock, ties figure eights around the cleats.

She finishes, but he's stuck on the boat, still holding the box with the ring. When she sees him standing there, she hops back on for him, almost like the old Ro—the one he thought would've said yes. But instead she says, "Let's go home."

"Just take this," he says, and folds the box into her hand because it's the only thing he can do.

"But—"

"It's for you."

She touches his shoulder and then draws back like it hurts her. "We can talk about this later," she says. "Okay?"

He still hasn't moved, and she's almost at the edge of the boat when he slams his fist into the wheel. "Ro!" he calls out.

She turns, and her look is telling him it's going to be okay and he swears he hears faraway bells chiming, a song to match the magic that's always around her, even now. "What?"

There's no going back, so he'll lay it all out. "I love you, no matter what. Until the day I die, and then some."

She smiles, but it's a sad smile, and the box is gone now, shoved into her shirt pocket. He won't ask her if she's wearing the ring, he won't make this any worse.

"I know," she says, her eyes still on him, as she steps backward, except she trips on something, or twists her ankle, because she's falling. Before he can reach out, before he can yell, she disappears over the side and there's a loud thump, an earsplitting crack—*no, no, no*—and he rushes to the edge.

There's blood on the dock, there's blood and he can't find her anywhere and then he panics, he yells out her name again and again. His heart is wild in his chest as he searches the water, but he can't see her, she hasn't come up, and then he thinks he sees her, a curling tendril of blond hair. He dives after her, his whole body screaming inside as he hits the water, arms outstretched, reaching, grasping. Where is she? *Where?* His hands close on something and he pulls it, but it's only seaweed. He shoots up for more air and dives down again, opening his eyes in the murky water. He can't find her; he can't see anything except the hull of the boat. The water is warm in places and cold in others but she isn't here; it's light and dark and full of tiny creatures but not her, not her. He kicks deeper and feels his heart skidding and when he turns to get air there's a shadow hovering above, floating through the green.

It's her—her body, her face. *Ro!* He kicks up and grabs her. He pulls her toward shore, everything inside him straining as he drags her in, tugging her onto the sand.

"Ro!" he shouts, and he turns her sideways, tries to get the water out of her, but she's bleeding, her whole head is sticky, and her hair, her red suit, no, that's blood, that's blood. He hits against her ribs and breathes into her mouth thinking, *Cough*, thinking, *Breathe*, and her eyes are wide open, *Breathe!* He hears her whisper his name, but when he puts his hand against her neck there's no pulse. Her eyes are wide open but not looking, and then there's a shout, someone's running at him—it's Lance, maybe he can help, please help Ro, but Lance starts yelling, and there's a gun in his hands, and now he's screaming at him, something that sounds a lot like *What have you done?*

CHAPTER 20

CAGE SAT UPRIGHT, GASPING FOR air. He shuddered, felt chilled. Everywhere was cold. He had a bad feeling inside and his bones were aching, deep down to the marrow. It was dark around him and the air felt hard like a wall.

There was warmth on his chin and someone was turning his face as light flared. He squinted, threw his arm up to shield his eyes, but the movement seemed to take forever.

And then a girl appeared in front of him. A pretty pixie face, dark golden hair. She looked like . . . The name came to him slowly, like he was still half asleep.

"Mae?"

"Don't worry, I found you. I'm right here."

The bad feeling came back and his head was about to split open. He felt chilled inside and everything was shivering. Something was wrong.

"You're soaking wet. We need to get you out of those clothes."

He was cold, but the voice was soft. He wanted to hug it, but he couldn't see it.

"You must have passed out. I thought you were dead."

No, he wasn't. Everything hurt too much for him to be dead.

"Cage?"

And then Mae was in front of him again, and she was tugging on his shirt.

"Lift your arms."

What was she doing? "No, wrong," he said.

The pressure on his arms was insistent. "You're soaked through." It went dark and then light again and there was no more wetness on his chest.

"Pants next," Mae said.

Warm hands were on his waist and she was unbuttoning his jeans. But Ro! "Mae, we can't."

Her face was a blur in front of him and then time sped up and she said really fast, "Cage, that's not what I'm doing!"

His jeans peeled off with a yank, but it was far away, like through a tunnel. Now he felt less cold. He looked down and saw he was naked. Wet sand was all over him and he was sitting on a raft, but underneath the plastic wasn't water, it was cement. The barn, he was in the barn. The light was still shivering around him and there was a clattering in his ears. Something soft passed over his head, his chest.

"There," he heard, and that golden hair was back in front of him. She was so pretty. He could see her goodness and she didn't even know it. Dark blond hair, pixie-face Mae. She was floating past him, he tried to catch her.

"I need to take you to the hospital."

"No!" Not now, no hospital. He couldn't go there.

"What?"

No hospital, not again. Bad idea. A hand was on his forehead.

"You're burning up, Cage."

Burning, yes, he was burning where she touched him. He could feel the heat from his insides, but his skin felt damp as the cold surged over him and the blackness came down.

"Cage? *Caaaaaaaa...*"

The girl is driving so fast Cage thinks they might die. He tries to relax into the passenger seat as her red car veers down the one-lane highway, going deeper and deeper into the Alabama woods.

He looks over at her and thinks he's dreaming. She's gorgeous. Red bikini strings tied around her neck, sea-green nail polish, and a grin that makes him feel lucky. Her blond hair's still wet from the ocean, from nearly drowning in Gulf Shores, where she coaxed him off his uncle's boat and into her car.

"I want to thank you with dinner," Roxanne says, her eyes on him instead of the road. "Since you rescued me and all." This is what she promises: a real Southern home-cooked meal in an antebellum home. She tells him

he should be careful, though, because the Coles have secrets, and then she laughs. He wonders again how he got
to be in the car.

She grabs the rearview mirror and adjusts it. He can
see the reflection of the two younger girls in the back.
They're fifteen or so: one tall and curvy, one petite and
lean. He's embarrassed when he catches the smaller girl
looking his way.

Her name is Mae, he remembers, shifting in his seat.
He met her on his morning break—he was eating a ham
and cheese sandwich on the pier. All of a sudden there she
was, a girl in jean cutoffs and one of those Hanes V-necks,
way too big for her. She asked about his uncle's boat, what
he was fishing for. She asked if she could sketch him too.
She was real nice, easy to talk to, and he hadn't wanted to
go back on the water. He looked for her again that afternoon, but she wasn't on the beach. And that was when
he saw Roxanne. That was when he saved her in the water
and his life changed. After he pulled her out, Mae and
the other girl came running up, and when Roxanne in-
troduced them as her younger sisters he tried to hide his
shock. He knew then he should probably say something
to Mae—an apology, or a hello to show he remembered
her—but Roxanne did all the talking, and the moment
was gone.

"Where'd you go there, sailor?" Roxanne asks, grinning at him. The force of her smile gets him right in the
gut and he grins back. She makes a sudden turn off the
road and the car shoots down a gravel driveway lined with

oaks. The radio blasts and she starts singing the Rolling Stones as loud as she can and he can't take his eyes off her.

Then she's pulling up beside an old fountain, and as she does a shadow falls across them. Next to the car is a huge run-down house swarmed by ivy. Its high walls are bluish and ugly, and darkness gathers in its corners, hemmed in by trees and overgrown bushes. The air is thick with the stench of undergrowth, as though the weeds are waiting to reclaim the house and everyone inside it. Instinctively he doesn't like the feel of the place—not the house, not the wide yard, not the woods around it.

But then he looks at Roxanne, and he can't help but smile. She's humming the song from the car, only slowly, off-tempo. *I see a red door and I want it painted black. . . .* He knows he's been sucked into the riptide that she is, but he doesn't care and follows her jean skirt and tank onto the rickety porch. The wood has fallen away in chunks, and the porch swing hanging down from thick chains is swaying even though it's empty, and the row of rocking chairs is doing the same. The decaying pillars tell him the house was once grand but has been cast into some sort of purgatory. Everything is ragged except for the door, which is red and newly painted.

The younger girls trail behind them, probably unsure what to think about him being there. Roxanne grabs his hand and he feels the way he did when he first rode a motorcycle, that excitement bordering on queasiness, a charged-up anticipation that the world is going to get better. She gives a loud rap on the iron knocker, and a minute later the door creaks open to a dank foyer. Standing a few feet away in the stairwell is an old man, practically ancient. His white hair is smoothed to the side and he's wearing a suit even in the summer heat, a flower in his jacket pocket like he's on his way to a prom.

"I didn't even have to open it," he says, and then turns to Cage. "Hello there, young man!"

"Hello there yourself, young man," Ro says, teasing him. "We've brought a guest for dinner, Granddad."

His face brightens, and he nods. "How do you do, son?" he says from his place on the stairs. He's clutching the railing as if afraid to let go.

"Good, sir. Thank you." Cage glances at Roxanne to see if he's said the right thing and she squeezes his hand. He feels like there's a generator inside him kicking in, his whole body buzzing with her touch.

"Well, come on in," the old man tells him, and Roxanne pulls him inside, the girls right behind them.

Cage glances up at the oil paintings on the walls and at the dusty chandelier suspended from above—it looks as if the old crystal might come crashing down any moment. The foyer is strangely cold, the afternoon shadows turning everything dark and watery. The doldrums, he thinks. The house reminds him of stagnant water, yet this girl lives in its depths like some sort of siren, the kind his uncle talks about.

Roxanne takes his hand and pulls him deeper into the house. It creaks underfoot as if to protest each one of his steps, wanting to spit him back out. Deeper into the house they go, and deeper still. Now he's being led down a narrow set of stairs by his golden girl, who tugs his hand and sends shivers up his arm. And then they're in an unfinished basement filled with outdoor gear.

It's a raised basement; the windows meet the soil outside so that the room is half underground. There's a stench of something Cage can't name, and it's hard to breathe. He isn't used to so much humidity in such a cramped space, not after spending the start of the summer on a boat with the wind and water around him.

"Home is the sailor, home from sea," Roxanne tells him, and grins like he knows what it means.

And then, looking out the window at the crested ground that meets the glass panes like a wave, Cage realizes why the house seems so strange. It feels like a sinking ship.

"This way," she says. He is taut in her presence, and she is like a flame. She leads him past a table piled high with fishing supplies, long fillet knives and tackle boxes and trophies and bright lures in different colors, and someone emerges from the shadows. A man with a long ponytail, a rag in his hand, a knife.

"Cage, this is Sonny, my dad," Roxanne says. Sonny looks him over, doesn't smile. Goes back to cleaning his knife.

"Nice to meet you, sir." Cage forces himself to remember her dad's name, to make a good impression—but it's hard to think about anyone but Roxanne. This blond ray of light next to him is warming his skin, warming him everywhere. There's something off about the house, about her dad, but she is *home*. He feels like he's known her all his life. Or maybe his life only started when he pulled her from the water. And he can do better for her, no matter what his mother might say. This time he can do better.

"Come on, stranger." Roxanne takes his hand. "Don't want you getting lost."

Then she's leading him back up the stairs, her two sisters orbiting like moons, and Cage wonders, all of a sudden, how he came to be surrounded by girls and rotting wood. He's already in love, and it could be the end of him. A bad feeling takes hold, but he shrugs it off and gives her hand a squeeze, never wanting to let go—

"Cage!"

He jolted upright, his breath ragged. The shirt he was wearing clung to him; he was drenched. He blinked and looked around the barn. A water jug was beside him, and a bowl with a washcloth. Blankets were at his feet, and he was sitting on something spongy.

And someone was in the barn with him, watching from the shadows.

After staring at the girl for what seemed like two minutes, three, an avalanche of sweat began to run down his face. The sensation heightened in the silence; he felt the sweat pouring from him.

Still this girl said nothing. She stayed in the shadows, studying him. He could see the whites of her eyes and the shadow of her hair and she seemed familiar but he didn't know her. He wanted to move away, only his muscles felt like sludge as she took a step toward him.

"Who are you?" he asked.

And then she darted forward, too fast to track, and a hot white flash stung his cheek.

Cage blinked, opened his eyes. "What?"

He was flat on his back, looking up at the ceiling of the barn, and Mae was kneeling over him. She was angry, her brown eyes sharp. No, not angry—*worried.*

"You wouldn't wake up. I didn't want to hit you, but you wouldn't wake up."

He brought his hand to his cheek. It stung and his skin felt like sandpaper; his insides were thin and brittle, about to break. It was hard to move.

"Don't mind waking up to you," he finally managed, trying to hide how sick he felt.

She laughed—it was like a sigh and a laugh together. "You're coherent," she said. "At last." She brought her hand to his forehead. "Your fever must have broken."

"I had a fever?" It explained why he was weak, sweaty.

She held a glass to his lips and he drank, but it hurt to swallow. The water was cold in his throat, in his gut. He wanted more and drank it all down and then leaned over and threw up, right on her shoes.

"Sorry," he said, wiping his mouth. "I'll clean that." But when he tried to stand, his legs gave out. He shivered; it was awful being this sick in front of her.

"It's fine," Mae said, glancing down at the mess, her nose all wrinkled up. "You need to rest. You've been in and out all night."

He'd never known what being this sick felt like; he'd always thought it was something you could shake off if you tried. But this tiredness, this—

Mae touched his forehead again. "You're still hot." She bent down and squeezed the washcloth into the bowl of water and then put the damp cloth on his face. "You didn't recognize me just then." The cloth was cooling him down, and she was so close that her breath brushed across his neck. "Your eyes were open, but you weren't looking at anything."

"I don't remember."

"I think you were dreaming." She dipped the washcloth into the water again and wiped at his temple. "You kept talking about Ro in your sleep. The things you said—"

"Mae." Her hand was slick when he took it. No, *his* hands were slick. There were shiny beads across his skin—he was leaking, sweating everywhere. He felt cold and hot all at once, and he dropped her hand. "I remember what happened. I didn't kill her."

"I know." Her voice sounded funny. "I heard you in your sleep. I heard everything."

"It was an accident. She . . . she tripped."

Then Mae was leaning into him, her arms wrapping him in a hug, and he didn't want her to let go. "I believe you," she said.

Smart Mae, sweet Mae. She didn't know how good she was. "You might," he told her as she pulled away, "but no one else will."

"I have a plan." Her lips pursed and she sighed. "Cage, there were things you said that only Ro would . . ."

She was still talking, but his head was rushing—it was heavy, waterlogged. It felt like a whirlpool was spinning in his skull, and he couldn't think. He tried to stand and collapsed back onto the raft.

"Are you okay?"

Mae's voice was fading. He stared up at the skylight and it started fading too. The air was doing strange things. It was curling in on him.

"Can you hear me?" Mae was farther away now; the air was forming a wall between them. He couldn't see her anymore. "Cage, your eyes are black!"

And then everything dropped away, and the kudzu, it was crawling up his legs, up his arms, over his face, his nose. Green, so much green, he was buried in it. He opened his mouth to breathe and the vines filled his throat and then a bright light was shining through the vines, shining every-where and—

The sun's beating down on the deck, blinding him. It glints off the bay, off the metal fasteners on the boat. An empty Coke can is on the counter and a map sticks out from under a coffee mug. Something seems off. He feels like he's been here before, like he's in a dream.

The map ruffles in the wind and the can tips over and there's a loud burst of laughter. "Cage! Over here!"

"Ro?"

He turns and finds her sitting on a deck cushion behind him, her blond hair lifting in the breeze like smoke. "What kept you so long?"

He feels dizzy—he must be dreaming. "You're not alive anymore," he says.

She laughs and pats a cushion. Chipped green nail polish is on her fingers. "Takes more than a little water to get me. Anyway, I come bearing a message."

"What message?" And the next thing he knows he's sitting beside her on the cushion, but he doesn't remember moving. He lifts his hand to touch her hair. "Your head . . . You were bleeding before."

She smiles and kisses his cheek. "Doesn't matter here."

He feels confused. "Am I dreaming? Where are we?"

"We're on the sailboat, Cage. Don't you recognize it?"

In front of him is the small hideaway hatch, the mast, the railing. Everything is just how he remembers it.

"And there's the dock at Blue Gate," she says.

He looks to where she's pointing. The dock is small at first, but he blinks and then it's larger—they're tied up next to it now. Something shadowy is in the center of the planks.

Dead blackbirds, piled on top of each other. He turns to Ro, feels like he might be sick. "Who did that?"

She puts a finger to her lips and shakes her head. "He'll hear you," she warns. "He's always watching."

"Who?"

But then she only winks. "And up there," she says, "is the island." A few billowy clouds are in the sky. "See all that green?"

Something drops down from the cloud. It's a vine, a ladder of kudzu. His eyes follow it up to a hovering island of green. His head hurts and he remembers his tire hitting the guardrail, the motorcycle flipping.

"Please come back with me." He wipes his hand across his face, tries to figure out what to say. "You always told me you'd take care of your sisters. And your dad, he needs you. And I need you."

"You only think you do." She kisses his cheek again, but all he feels is coldness. "I miss you, though. I miss the small things, stuff you wouldn't think."

"Like what?"

Ro tilts her head, runs a finger down his arm. "The way my dad squints when he can't make up his mind. And watching Mae paint, how she loses herself in it. Driving at night, Elle falling asleep on my shoulder." She looks at him—her eyes are so green, glittering like cut jade.

"I remember being young too," she says. "Dressing up in the old clothes in our attic." She pulls her hair back and he sees how pale her skin is, almost transparent. "I made the twins wear these big bell-shaped dresses, while I got the straw hat and a vest made out of animal skins."

He can't help it, he laughs. She laughs too and touches his hand. Her fingers trail softly over his forearms.

"I can only do small things now," she says. "Blowing a door open, or making the jewelry box sing."

The sky seems to ripple like they're underwater. He rubs his eyes—he doesn't know what she's talking about, but she needs to listen. "Come back with me, Ro."

Something moves behind her. It's the wind, fluttering through the bird feathers on the dock. He doesn't like the stench, and as soon as the thought comes he smells sweetness, like cake in the oven, sweet cream and vanilla, and Ro is reaching for him.

"Just hold my hand for now. I like how it feels, the firmness of it." She threads her fingers through his, chilling him all the way up his arm. "That's what life is, it's feeling things." There's metal against his knuckle and he looks down.

"You're wearing the ring."

"*Our* ring." Her voice is slow, drawling. "Remember that. That's my message."

Why is she talking so strange? Her lips are moving, but the words don't match up. Something twists inside him. "Stay with me."

She leans in, kisses him slowly, kisses him like she's drinking him in, and then she stops. He can feel something shifting in the air. She puts her finger to her lips. "Shh."

The boat pitches, strains against its ties, and Ro slides away. He tries to run to her, but he can't move; his legs feel paralyzed. Water is lapping against the hull, but it sounds off, like it's only an echo of water, not real at all.

"Cage?" She's standing on the other end of the deck, just a few yards from him, but it's far enough that he can't touch her. "There's only so much time." She's at the edge of the boat now, still facing him. "I'm right here," she says. "I'll always be here."

Except she's not moving toward him, no, she's lifting her foot, and it's going in the wrong direction, it's going backward.

"Don't!" he shouts, but she's stepping back, and it's happening all over again, her foot missing its mark, coming down on air. She's smiling at him like she's forgotten that she's going to fall, that he doesn't save her, that her head hits the dock and splits open, that he doesn't find her in the water in time—she's forgotten that this is how she dies, this single step away from him. He yells her name as she disappears over the edge and all of a sudden everything goes black, dark and fluttering and sharp, and claws and wings are scratching at his face. The blackbirds have risen up and swarmed the sky.

CHAPTER 21

BLOOD POUNDED IN MAE'S EARS as she stared at him, fear gripping her chest. He'd fallen at her feet, passed out on the floor of the barn, nearly bringing her down with him. "Cage," she said, grabbing his shoulder. "Cage, wake up."

His ribs moved, he was taking jagged breaths. He felt hot, so hot. Maybe he was just sick or maybe it was a concussion from when she'd hit him with the hammer. Should she call an ambulance? Drive him to the hospital herself?

She tensed, uncertain. He'd told her no—made her swear not to—but she couldn't bear to see him like this, sprawled on the cement. She ran over to the little raft he'd been sleeping on, put it beside him, and then tried to drag him onto it again. If only she knew what to do, or knew a doctor she could call. Fern's mom was a nurse, but she worked the night shift and she'd tell Childers everything.

If he got any worse . . .

"Cage," she said, "wake up." She could hear the alarm in her own voice and her eyes flicked to the door. He needed help. Could she even leave him like this?

When she looked back at Cage, his blue eyes were wide open. She gasped, startled, and then reached for his hand.

"Stay awake," she said, hoping he'd tell her he was okay, but he didn't speak.

A single flashlight beam was still streaming from the countertop near the sink, over the stretch of cement floor. He was looking in the opposite direction, at something in the shadows.

"I'd never hurt you," he said, but he wasn't talking to her. She knew he was talking to Ro again, just like he had the whole time he'd been sick. She'd heard everything that had happened; it had spilled from him in his sleep.

She touched his head as gently as she could. There was sweat on his brow, sweat shining in his hair. He didn't move from where he was lying on the raft.

"Cage," she said again. She grabbed the washcloth from the bucket beside him and pressed it to his neck, trying to cool him off. "If you can hear me," she said, hiding the fear in her voice, "just blink or nod, okay?"

He stared into the distance just beyond her shoulder. "Ro."

Mae clenched the rag tight. "Cage, look at me."

His blue eyes were unwavering. He seemed possessed—straddling some other world that she wasn't part of. Seeing him like this made her believe anything was possible, even ghosts, even magic.

"If we're already dead," Cage said, "can we die again?" He nodded like he was getting an answer. "Almost a year," he murmured.

"Stop," Mae said. "Stop it!" She clamped down on his wrist as tight as she could. "Look at me, Cage."

He wrenched his arm away and yelled for her sister. Mae threw her hands to her ears. The sound was awful; she felt it all the way in her bones—it was like he was dying, his heart breaking. She didn't know what to do, so she lay down next to him on the raft and wrapped her arms around him.

"Ro's here," she said, and he stopped midshout, his head angled away from her. "I'm right here," she whispered, "I'm here next to you."

Just like that his body relaxed and his breath started evening out. His skin felt hot against hers. She glanced past him at the flashlight's waning beam and then stared at the taut line of his neck, the bulk of his shoulder, the sharp muscles of his arms, his back, and then up again to the dark crop of his hair. After what seemed like a long time, she tilted her head enough to look at his eyes. They were shut: he was sleeping. His jaw was relaxed now, everything was relaxed. He hadn't killed Ro—it'd been an accident. He loved her sister. He would always love her. He'd made himself sick over her death, digging out in the storm for the rest of the book and finding nothing.

Mae froze, remembering. She slowly reached into her pocket, not wanting to wake him. Her fingertips hit a scrap of folded paper. With everything that had happened that night, she'd forgotten about it. She slid it out now and raised it in front of her.

It was a piece of wide-ruled notebook paper. Ink had leaked over it in the rain, but now it was dry, the paper crinkled, a smudge of dirt from the garden on one edge. She unfolded it and stopped breathing.

Ro's handwriting was slanted across the page in pink-colored pen. The first part was completely destroyed—the rain had splattered the ink, and she couldn't make out more than a letter here or there. But halfway down the page it was readable and her eyes widened on a line.

A bird for vision.

Her mind flashed to the trail of ants, to what she'd found underneath Ro's bed and what she'd seen hidden away in the pantry. She knew what would come next—Blue Gate had already shown her.

A horse for the passage.
A snake for new skin.

Mae's heart was thudding as she read the rest of the slanted pink writing. A streak of water had run down a crease, taking a few letters with it, but she could still make out the words.

Laid out in a row of four,
only this will open the door.
Then save the most brutal for last:
Chana for a life,
Since all should be equal.
Do these tasks and see the return,
except if the earth has traveled the sun.

The notebook paper was trembling in her hand. Ro had made a copy of the raising ritual and buried it under the gift cherub. The first part—the beginning of the ritual—had been destroyed by the rain, but everything else was legible. And she knew where she could find the rest. It was in the green book, on the thumbprint page. She could get it back from Lance, and then . . .

And then what? It was late, she wasn't thinking clearly. A feeling of hope was sneaking up on her, and that was a dangerous thing. Look where it'd gotten Cage.

He was still deep in sleep, his body warm, nuzzled next to hers. Just for a moment she let herself lean against him, her breathing starting to match his. Everything inside her felt heavy, tired, and what she believed and didn't believe was blurring together, the boundary as thin as the space between her and Cage, and she felt warm, so warm.

Mae opened her eyes, shocked she'd fallen asleep. The redness of the setting sun beat through the skylight, throwing orange rectangles along the cement floor. God, how long had she slept?

She got to her elbows and sat up, and then touched the back of her hand to Cage's forehead. Warm but not burning up. She stood, trying not to disturb him. His breath was steady, his big hands loose at his sides, the wet jeans and shirt she'd pulled off of him drying on a chair beside them. He wasn't sweating much anymore. He looked like he was going to be okay. They'd been sleeping for what— all day?

Mae let out a shuddering breath. His fever seemed better; maybe he'd just sleep it off now. She stared down at him, rubbed her forehead. Ro's sheet of notebook paper was lying on the floor, and she folded it up and put it in her pocket.

Lance had the book, that was what Cage had told her. She bit her lip, the sharpness focusing her mind. Elle was supposed to meet Lance today at the house for dinner, that was what she'd said last night. If he was there, Mae could try to get the book back. Maybe that would be enough to help Cage, give him a reason to pull through his fever, snap out of whatever dream he was lost in. And maybe it'd be enough for Ro too. . . .

"I've got a plan," she whispered, and then she turned and left, grabbing her bag on her way out, suddenly afraid to say goodbye.

Outside in the woods she felt better. The air was muggy—she guessed it was already seven, eight in the evening. When had Elle said Lance was coming over? She rushed down the path toward Blue Gate, trying to convince herself she really did have a plan. She barely watched where she was going; her feet led her home, her mind still on Cage as she stumbled into the wide yard. The grass was soggy from the rain, but now the sky was clear, a red tint across it.

Past the gargoyle fountain was Childers's truck, and her heart ramped up. Her dad's truck wasn't in the driveway—he must be out. The house soared above her, pink and bluish in the fading light like something strangled. Her granddad was standing at the attic window, waving. She waved back, knowing he wanted her to come and say hello. That could wait—she needed to find Lance first.

She ran up the porch steps and shoved her key into the lock, stepping inside. The sunset was pouring through the foyer windows, basking the portraits in red. Grady Cole winked at her in the stippled light, and she turned away from him, heading toward the back of the house. The pipes were groaning in the walls—someone had the water on—and the smell of baking bread, buttery and starchy, was in the air. It was her turn to cook tonight, but Elle must have started without her.

Mae rounded the corner. The kitchen was empty, the pantry door shut, lidded pots simmering on the stove, three place settings stacked on the countertop. Maybe her granddad wasn't feeling well enough to eat? He'd seemed fine yesterday, even leaving one of his notes for her and Elle. *Love you, dear little twins*. It'd made her smile, but Elle had rolled her eyes. She never took the time to sit with him anymore. Lately, Mae hadn't either. She should check in on him now, look for Lance in Elle's room on the way up.

She started toward the back stairs, but then heard footsteps on the other side of the house. Too fast for her granddad, too loud for even Elle. Lance, then? The front door was clicking shut by the time she reached the foyer, half out of breath. Through the window she caught the bright white of his shirt as he strode across the drive toward his dad's truck.

She threw open the door. "Lance!"

He stopped and turned, a smile spreading across his face. The old fountain was right behind him, his hazel eyes and tan skin a stark contrast to the stone. His shirt was another fitted one and his hair was ruffled and wet like he'd just showered. Even from here she could smell the foresty scent of his cologne. Seeing him made her smile too, and she was surprised at the lightness in her step as she walked toward him.

"Hey there, Mayday," he called, waving her over to the truck. Was it just her imagination, or was there a raw enthusiasm in his voice, like he was genuinely happy to see her? "I was hoping I'd run into you."

"Me too," Mae said. She glanced at the truck beside him, but he stepped in front of her, leaning against the passenger door, his hands tucked into his pockets, completely and totally relaxed. Nothing like the old Lance. The pale guy in the black band shirt who used to follow Ro at a distance until he could close in. Mae had liked his T-shirts before, the way he'd always wore a different band's, but his shyness had eclipsed everything—it had been a wall between him and the world, and only Ro had been invited in.

"What's up?"

Mae felt a jolt of nerves and tried to mask it. She liked this friendly side of him, this new Lance she was just now getting to know. Coming on too strong about the green book might put him on the defensive. She stalled. "Seeing you at the house again is almost like old times."

Lance shrugged. "What can I say? I like Blue Gate. Like the Coles even more." He smiled, his dimples flashing. Out here, standing close to him in the sunlight, she felt like she was seeing him for the first time. His eyes were green around his pupils, rimmed by a golden brown that exploded outward, like a dying star.

"It kind of feels good to own that, actually," he said. "I was way too shy before to admit it."

Curiosity got at her. "What changed?"

He looked toward the house. "When someone you love dies, it makes you think about life in a different way, I guess. You would know."

Everything inside her went still. It was the way he said it—like he really cared how she felt, what she'd been going through. How had she lived next to him all these years and not known this side of him?

"Whenever I'm around you, I want to talk about Ro," he said. "Your turn to talk first."

"Is that how it works?" She gripped the bag strap at her shoulder. The air was thick with humidity, and her hair felt hot against her neck. She noticed Lance watching her, a smile on his face, and held her bag tighter. "Actually, I wanted to ask you something."

"Good," he said, and laughed. "Otherwise I'll end up running my mouth and you'll never get a word in edgewise."

"I don't mind." Except she did. The question was on the tip of her tongue. Cage had sworn that the green book was with Lance, but now she felt like she was accusing him of stealing. She blew out a deep breath, her heart going staccato in her chest.

"You should see your face," Lance said. "You're always thinking about something, aren't you?"

"Usually."

"And your brain just goes *tick tick tick tick* in the night and you can't ever sleep. Have I got that right?"

She liked nights for thinking, when no one else was awake. And she hadn't gotten enough sleep lately, not with worrying about Cage. "I could use some more, that's for sure."

"You and me both," Lance said. "Come here just a minute." He stepped forward and slung his arm around her shoulder, the gesture so quick she was pulled against the truck with him. "That's better. You looked too uptight."

"I like it that way," Mae said. "Keeps me alert."

Lance laughed again as if she'd made a joke. The truck felt warm on her back, and Lance's arm was warm too. Out here in the brightness, the idea that he had the book seemed hard to believe. Maybe it was just a misunderstanding. He probably had no idea what it was. The charcoal drawing in the tunnel, the dead animals in the pantry, the hanged cat in the woods—those sorts of things didn't belong in daylight. They were sepia-toned, from a different era; they didn't mix with the scent of Lance's cologne or the gleam of custom paint.

He tilted his head to meet her gaze. "Hey, you okay?"

She needed to hurry before she lost her courage. "I wanted to ask"—she could barely get the words out, barely even take a breath—"if you have a book of Ro's."

Lance raised his eyebrows and then smiled again, disarming her. "I have a lot of books from her," he said. "What are you after?"

Her stomach tensed and she swallowed down her nerves. "It has a green cover. A green leather cover," she added.

"Which one?"

What did he mean, *which one*? She glanced at the house, but no one had come outside yet. "It was a book from our family." She stopped then, unsure of how much to say. She felt awkward. If he'd opened the book, he already would have known to return it, and if he hadn't, then . . . She pulled away from him, facing the truck now, putting distance between them. Lance was still leaning back, looking like he had all the time in the world.

"It has a list of names inside it," she said. "You couldn't miss it."

His eyebrows crinkled up, and he rubbed at his curly

hair. "You know what? Fern came across something the other day in the woods. Could be what you're talking about." He went around to the driver's side of the truck and she followed him. "I left it in here. Been planning on dropping it off at your house, since we found it on your property and all."

He opened the door and leaned over to reach into the truck, giving her a view of the twin pockets of his blue jeans. When he turned, the book was in his hands. "Is this what you want?" he asked.

There it was, right in front of her. Her heart was going so fast in her chest she thought she might faint. "Thanks." She grabbed it, tucked it into her bag, and then glanced at the house—no one was at the windows, her granddad hadn't seen them.

"I better get going." She took a step back from Lance, clutching her bag. Why had he taken so long to give her the book? He seemed happy to help, but he wasn't telling her everything.

Lance shut the truck door and then tilted his head at her. "You know what I like most about you, Mae?" His voice was so low she could barely hear him. "I like how you've always judged me, in your quiet way." He held up a hand like he expected her to protest. "Even now, you're deciding whether to judge me." He looked down at the gravel, seemed to be thinking. The sunlight caught the gold in his hair. "You see what you want to see, and that keeps me on my toes. I even think you used to hate me."

She fought the urge to take another step back. "I didn't," she said, "I don't," but her chest felt tight, and she crossed her arms. She didn't hate him; she just didn't trust him.

He stepped toward her, closing the distance between them. "Hate and love are strong emotions. They make us do things . . . we don't expect to do. They clutter up the mind."

What was he talking about? She suddenly felt exhausted—the past few days had worn her down, and she didn't understand what he was getting at.

Lance shrugged, and there was a little crease in his brow, like he was concerned about what would come out of his mouth next. "But if I've got that wrong, then maybe you think better of me now?"

She peered up at him, at the setting sun behind his back, the large house to his side surrounded by trees. Blue Gate looked quiet, peaceful. He'd given her the book, just like she wanted, and that showed a measure of trust.

"I do," she told him, which was true. She *did* think better of him than she used to, even though he was keeping things from her. But she'd been keeping secrets too. Too many to count.

"Good." He was smiling again. "Because I think the world of you."

Her heart skipped with surprise. Before she could say anything, his hazel eyes shot toward the house. Mae saw his eyebrows rise ever so slightly, and she turned and let out a gasp.

Ro was standing on the porch near a rocking chair, her long blond hair streaming over her shoulders.

CHAPTER 22

IT WASN'T RO, IT WAS Elle—she'd bleached her hair, and she must have put on self-tanner. She'd wiped off her usual red lipstick and gone natural, like Ro's just-got-done-swimming look. Somehow she looked leaner, all athletic limbs and her hair wavy from air drying. Mae couldn't look away. How had she never seen the resemblance before? It was like a Picasso suddenly rearranging itself into a realist painting. Seeing her like this flipped the world upside down—some sort of magic had taken place.

Mae watched, half fascinated, half wary, as her sister stepped off the porch and cut through the grass toward them.

"Your hair . . . ," Mae started.

"I just did it," Elle said, unable to keep the grin off her face. She even sounded more like Ro, as if she was deliberately lowering her voice. "Do you like it?"

Mae fumbled for an answer, and Elle's face fell. "It's—"

"You look stunning," Lance said. "Sorry for cutting you off, Mae, but I couldn't hold back."

"I was just going to say"—her eyes darted to Elle's and saw hope there, and a strange, giddy anticipation—"the very same thing."

"Thanks." Elle's smile was back in full force as she turned to Lance. "I thought you were just grabbing something from your dad's truck. Nice he lets you drive it instead of that old one," she said. "Come on, Sonny's at the bar, so we've got free rein."

"Free rein of what?" Mae asked.

"Sweet," Lance said, throwing his arm around Elle. "The place is all ours. You joining us for Elle's specialty, Mayday?"

"Probably not," Elle said before Mae could ask what he meant. "Mae's been disappearing lately. I'm guessing she'd rather go off and paint instead of hang out."

"Funny," Lance said. "I took her for more of a reader."

He winked and Mae held her breath, wondering if her sister would catch on, but Elle was already heading back to the house and was tugging Lance along. Mae stared after them for a moment. Elle's blond hair was so much like Ro's, and her legs were tan and strong. It was like their sister was here again, like she'd come home. Mae tore her eyes away and looked down at her bag. She felt the weight of the book inside, and then opened the flap just to be sure.

There it was. The two coffins on the front. She should show Cage. Go check on him in the barn and let him know she had it. Maybe then he'd feel better, pull out of whatever was making him sick.

When she glanced up again, Elle's hand was still on Lance's wrist—she was leading him into the side yard.

"It's back here," Elle called out, and then laughed at something Lance said. Mae felt a pang in her heart. She couldn't let this imitation Ro out of her sight, not yet. It wasn't just the bleached hair; it was the mannerisms too. Elle would have never grabbed Lance's wrist like that—that was always Ro's territory, and now here she was, barely distinguishable from their older sister at a distance. Mae watched as she rounded the back of the house, Lance still in tow. There was the sound of a key scraping against a lock, the creak of a gate. Without another thought she trailed after them, ducking down by some bushes beside the edge of the house. When she peeked out, Lance's white shirt was disappearing into the garden.

She eased her way forward, her steps quiet through the grass in the yard. Giving the rusted gate wide berth, she made her way to the hedge. Her heart felt like it was being called by Ro, like she was beckoning to her. She wanted to see her again, just a little longer. When she peered through the hedge's sharp leaves, she gasped.

Her sister was staring straight at her.

Mae ducked back, waited for a yell. It didn't come. A few seconds passed and it still didn't come. She leaned in again and parted the leaves, wincing as their sharpness dug into her hands.

The garden had been transformed. It was aglow with

candles, and iron lanterns hung from a wire. The house loomed over everything, stately in the way that only old houses could be. In the wavering light, Blue Gate seemed as though it had been heaved a hundred years into the past, generations ago.

Mae stared at her sister, unable to take her eyes from her. She was sitting beside Lance at the wrought-iron table set with steaming plates of food. He tipped his chair back, his hands threaded behind his head, and then said something Mae couldn't hear. A minute later they began to eat, and she realized she was starving, that she hadn't eaten in a long time, and that watching this mirror of Ro was making her aware of the emptiness inside her, the hole that her older sister had left.

She closed her eyes, imagining the black door where she kept all the Ro memories, all the sadness. It needed to stay shut, but it was hard to keep it that way with Elle like this, somehow eating exactly how Ro used to. Ro had been the type to delicately rip off each section of a tangerine with her teeth, savoring the juice on her tongue with every bite, while Elle would just peel it and eat the thing whole. Now she was savoring each forkful of whatever she'd made—Mae saw bacon and grits and what must have been a quiche, and warm fluffy biscuits covered with jam and cream. It must have been a practice run for the B and B, breakfast for dinner, but they were eating like kings.

Lance leaned back in his chair again, listening to Elle talk about her plans for Blue Gate, how it'd be good for

Sonny to run a guesthouse. Before, the occasional prize money from his sport fishing had been enough to pay the bills, but he hadn't gone out on the water all year.

"Besides, I think it could really work," Elle was saying, slathering more jam on her biscuit. "I mean, isn't it nice out here?"

"It's beautiful," Lance said, but he wasn't looking at the garden; he was looking at Elle.

Mae stiffened, suddenly feeling protective. She leaned in closer, the leaves of the hedge spiky against her face, the thorns scratching at her forearms, her hands. The pain was welcome; it helped her think. Ro had always said not to let a guy close unless you knew exactly what you wanted, but Elle had never taken her advice, and right now Mae was worried for her sister.

"You know, Ro made breakfast for me once." Lance reached out to tuck a strand of blond hair behind Elle's ear. "And then we went to the dock. It was real early, before class. I caught a ten-pound grouper and she came up empty-handed."

Mae wished she was close enough to read his eyes, see if he was lying—carried away by the moment and bragging when he shouldn't. Ro had always outfished anyone.

"She was furious with me, smoked half a pack of cloves afterward. Probably one of my favorite memories of her." He laughed softly. "She was different from most people. Had different ideas about the world, you know? With her, it was like the terms of the universe didn't apply." He looked up at the sky, seemed to study it. "And she could do just about anything too. You ever hunt with her? She never missed. I was always jealous because my dad and Sonny worshipped her."

"Maybe . . . ," Elle started.

Don't say it, don't say it, Mae thought, squeezing her eyes shut. Her sister would be devastated if he turned her down. Because Elle wasn't like Ro, not on the inside. She was always getting upset over some guy not calling. She'd walk around the house like a zombie for days. Right now Elle's face was lit up, and Mae wanted it to stay that way.

"Maybe we could go together sometime?"

Lance took a drink from his glass, seemed to consider. "Are we talking fishing or hunting?"

"Both," Elle said, her fork clinking against her plate as she set it down.

Lance shrugged, and Mae stopped breathing for a moment. Then he smiled. "Why not?" he said. "We'll start with fishing. No better time to be out on the water."

"You've got a deal." Elle wiped her mouth with her wrist and made it look elegant, exactly how Ro used to. It was like she'd been practicing. Mae stared at her sister, trying to figure her out. The look on Elle's face made Mae realize she hadn't seen Elle happy—really happy—in a long time.

"I tried a little fishing when we were kids, but when we got older it was mostly just Ro and my dad who went out. I want to get good at it."

Mae felt her insides twist. Lance's hand was on Elle's,

and they were gazing at each other like they might never stop. She knew she shouldn't be watching, but she couldn't turn away from the sister who was so much like Ro.

She gripped the waxy leaves of the hedge, their tips biting into her palms while she stared into the garden. For some reason she thought of Cage: how he'd stood there in the storm last night, how the rain had seemed to wash him down to his very essence. And now here was Lance, somehow made warmer by the candlelight, leaning in to kiss her sister, getting closer, closer, the light flickering across their faces, and then—

"What are you doing, Mae?"

She stumbled back at the same time that the chairs scraped across the cobblestones. When she turned, she saw Fern leaning against the hedge, seemingly oblivious to the thorns. Her little blond curls were hooked in the leaves, floating up above her head as she smirked.

"Lance says to never get caught when you're spying," Fern sang out.

"Isn't it past your bedtime?" Mae whispered. Her neck blazed with heat.

"I spy better than you," Fern said. "I spy on you all the time and you don't even know it."

"Never admit to such a thing," Mae said quickly as her sister rounded the hedge looking furious.

"What are you doing?" Elle asked, her voice sharp.

The truth would sound too strange—*I couldn't help but stare at you because you look exactly like Ro*—so she didn't say anything.

Fern started giggling, and Elle folded her arms across her chest and glared. "I don't know what you're up to," she said, "but I'd appreciate it if you'd give us some space."

Lance strolled around the corner with his hands tucked into his pockets, his white shirt luminescent in the fading light. "Or join us. It's much nicer on the other side, I promise."

He grinned at Mae, looking like the same person who'd opened up to her in the attic—the guy who seemed like a friend. Almost.

"I've been searching all over for you," Fern said to her cousin. She stepped away from the hedge, yanked her hair loose from the leaves. "Mae here was just having a little look-see. Be careful around her."

"Was she?" Lance said, and grinned.

"What the hell, Mae," Elle said. She was holding one of her elbows like Ro used to, the other arm dangling against her hip. "There's plenty of food. I already saved you a plate."

Mae's eyes watered. That was what Ro would say.

"We're pretty much finished anyway," Lance added. "Best breakfast for dinner I've ever had." He squeezed Elle's shoulder and she grinned at him; then she turned to Mae. "Well," she said, "want to try some?"

She was so embarrassed that her appetite had vanished. "Thanks, but later. I'm not really hungry right now."

Elle frowned. "Suit yourself. I knew you wouldn't say yes."

Mae had a sudden and intense craving to be alone, but

she owed Elle some sort of explanation. There'd been so many secrets lately, and for once she could be honest. "Sorry I looked in on you. I was just wondering what you were doing."

"All you had to do was ask," Elle said. She shifted her weight. She seemed flustered like the old Elle for a moment, and Mae could tell she was upset.

"Well, I, for one, am flattered," Lance said.

"Hey!" Fern scrunched her nose. "What's with your hair, Elle?"

Elle stepped forward and grabbed Fern's finger. "It's rude to point," she told her. "And it's past your bedtime. I'll fix you a plate to take home to your mom." She glanced toward Mae with an unreadable look on her face before walking off around the side of the hedge. Mae's neck felt like it was on fire, and she couldn't believe she'd been caught.

"I'm taking you home," Lance said, giving Fern a playful shove. "After you apologize for pointing at Elle."

"How about this for pointing?" Fern stuck her middle finger up at him and then skipped away toward the truck and started singing. "*Somme-times the cat comes back, somme-times the . . .*"

Lance turned to Mae. "See you later," he said. "We might even have a surprise for you in a few days." He smiled as he said it, but then his jaw tightened and that crease in his brow appeared again.

"What sort of surprise?" Mae couldn't keep the suspicion out of her voice. Lance was full of surprises lately. And who was *we*: he and Fern, or he and Elle?

"Wait and see," he said. "I sure hope you will, anyway. It's for her anniversary."

Mae stiffened. "What are you talking about?" Her dad wouldn't want a reminder of Ro's death; he wouldn't want to mark the day. It was thoughtful if Lance had some memorial in mind, but he couldn't just spring it on them. Sonny hated surprises. So did Elle.

"You'll see. Trust me." He looked at her intently, his hazel eyes serious. "I want the best for you, Mae. For all of you."

"Lance, you can't just—" But he'd turned away and was jogging over to Elle, catching up with her and Fern in the side yard. Mae lingered at the corner of the hedge while they headed toward his truck, shadowy in the night. The engine started up, and Elle got in too, the door slamming behind her.

Mae was left alone, just like she'd wanted, only now she felt empty, as if something was missing. She dug into her bag, found the green book inside. The sight of it would get Cage to his feet, but she needed a moment to think first.

She walked over to the garden and sat in one of the chairs near the gift cherub's good eye. She blew out the candles on the table, watching the smoke fade away. A cloth napkin was draped over a bowl and she lifted it, revealing a pile of biscuits. She picked at one and then pulled the green book from her bag.

A nagging suspicion itched at the corner of her mind. Would she notice if Lance had ripped out any of the pages?

She flipped open the cover under the lantern light

from the hedge, breathed in the musky scent of the paper. Scrolling through the book, she checked to see if anything seemed different. Her eyes snagged on those strange words again, *Chana 4 chana*, written next to the note in the margin that she'd seen before, *RC = AC, J = E, H = GCI*. She moved past it, going faster now, skipping over the remedies and the section of rituals for curses and love. The raising ritual was at the end, and when she reached it she started going backward again, to find the page with Ro's writing, and then—

Something caught her eye and she stopped, the breath hollowing out of her lungs.

In front of her was a sketch of a ring. Three intricately detailed tear-shaped stones at the top. She gasped, held the page to the light. She would recognize it anywhere: it was the one she'd found in Ro's bedroom, the one from Cage. Written next to the band was tight cursive: *Your chana is my life.*

The handwriting didn't look like Ro's—though surely she'd been the one to draw the ring after Cage had given it to her? But that didn't make sense either. He'd asked her to marry him the day she died. . . .

Mae's neck tingled as she brought the page closer. Another sketch was beside the ring, done in the same style. It was of a thick, braided thread, with small objects scattered around it. A bone, some beads, a sand dollar, a lodestone. Cursive was in the margin.

For Lucky

It wasn't Ro's handwriting. Mae stared at the ring again, tracked its inky curves, the trio of tear-shaped rubies at the top. It was definitely identical to the one in Ro's room—Cage had given her his family ring, that was what he'd said.

But why was there a sketch of *his* family ring in the green book, if Ro couldn't have drawn it?

She felt a bead of sweat trickle down her face. The book fell from her hands, clattering to the table.

"Oh God," she breathed. Cage's ring was in the green book, which only meant one thing. Her heart was going faster now; it was hard to breathe. Cage was a Cole. Cage was related to them, to Ro. Had Ro known? The thought made her stomach turn. Of course she hadn't. The discovery was bursting in her chest—it was painful, sharp. So many questions were running through her head, and Ro's black door was shining in her mind like oil. Cage would be devastated if he knew. Ro would have been devastated.

Mae's stomach clenched again and she didn't know what to do. She had to tell someone, she had to know for sure. The metal chair she was sitting in scratched at her skin through the holes in her jeans, and she looked up along the wall of the house, all the way to the attic window. Her granddad would know what to do. He would help, somehow.

Mae got to her feet and unlocked the French doors behind her, running up the back steps. When she reached Ro's bedroom, she grabbed the jewelry box from the wardrobe. The ceramic ballerina was gone from the lid—

maybe it had fallen off—but what she needed was inside. She opened the box and grabbed the ring, feeling its inner rim for the engraving she knew would be there. YOUR CHANA IS MY LIFE. Her heart was beating so hard it hurt. She left everything else in place and then hurried up the attic stairs and threw open the door at the top. A vase of fresh lantanas rattled against the table.

"Granddad?"

He was sitting in his chair, staring out the window that looked over the garden and the bay beyond. His suit jacket was draped over the armrest, his cane was beside him, and his shirtsleeves were rolled up. The air-conditioning unit was pointed at him, and a tuft of his white hair was blowing up. It reminded her of dandelion seeds in the wind, the kind she made wishes on as a kid, but something about it seemed lonely.

She felt a stab of guilt. She'd neglected him lately—she'd been too worried about Cage to spend any time with him. And now what would her granddad say when she told him about the sketch? He'd be upset that she'd taken the green book against his wishes. He'd be upset about other things too, but she couldn't carry this on her own anymore.

"Granddad, I have to talk to you." She cleared her throat. "I'm glad you're sitting down."

She stepped forward, pressed the book against her chest. He was still gazing out the window. Maybe she was wrong about the family link. Her granddad would tell her what it meant. He'd say Cage wasn't a Cole.

"I'm sorry I haven't been up here lately, but I—I really need to talk to you."

He still didn't move, just kept looking out the window, his Bible on his lap. She waited, trying to be patient, even though worry was seeping from her every pore, she was trembling with it. She stared out the window, into the darkness of the woods. Overhead was the first of the night's stars and the moon. She thought of the barn where Cage was, still sweating out the fever he'd caught from getting soaked in the downpour. The book felt heavy, and the secret on her tongue felt heavier; a bad taste was in her mouth.

"Granddad, I—"

When she turned to him, she froze. His blue eyes were open, staring straight ahead.

She waved her hand in front of him. He didn't blink. A little smile was on his face. But it was empty. His eyes were empty.

Her stomach seized up and she panicked, shaking his shoulders. The smile stayed on his face. Someone cried out and she realized it was her.

"Granddad, no." She reached for his hand and squeezed as hard as she could. "Please," she said, desperation rushing through her, "wake up, please," only there was nothing in him to wake, he wasn't moving. "You're okay," she begged, "you're okay, just breathe," and then his mouth opened, but only because she was shaking him, because she'd clamped down on his arm, she was hurting him. She gasped and let go and saw the bruising she'd left—no, no, it was darker than that, so much darker—and she sank to her knees. His skin was streaked with soot where she'd touched him, and he looked wrong, it wasn't really him, it couldn't be. There was too much stillness and too little of everything else and he wasn't supposed to leave her like this, she wasn't ready.

"Granddad, I'm here," she said, grabbing his hand again, trying to warm it by rubbing it. His fingers opened, just a little, and something fell from them.

She looked down, blinking in shock, staring at the wooden floor underneath her knees. Her granddad's notepad was on the ground now; he'd been holding it. She blinked again, her eyes stinging—her whole body felt like it was floating away from him, from everything. His shaky writing was on the notepad, far below her. Her name was at the top of the paper, followed by lines and lines of ink.

Dearest little Mae, it started, *there is something you should know.*

CHAPTER 23

BLUE GATE, 1860

GRADY DOESN'T HEAR US, EVEN though he should. It's easier for us to get through at certain times. The moment before death, for example. At night, in the breath between sleeping and waking. And at the threshold of day, right before the sun has risen, when the eyelids start to flutter. *Listen*, we tell him. *Listen, Grady. Look.* But he doesn't wake up, he doesn't hear our whispers, not until the sun is high and hot. His eyes are finally opening now, wide and blinking at the blue ceiling.

Grady is startled awake and he's not sure why, because he doesn't know to listen. He doesn't know to take just one moment of quiet. No, Grady is young and he sits up fast.

Sunlight is dappling across the floor and he stares at it incredulously. He must have done the impossible and fallen asleep. He hurries to get out of bed and grins when he sees himself in the mirror. He's still dressed from last night. His hair is matted down from the pillow and his hat is smashed sideways and his shirt is buttoned all wrong. It's stained with blood.

Lucky was born in the middle of the night. Pearl helped deliver him, and Hanna's brother stood watch. No lights came on at the house, not one; his father slept through everything. And Hanna was fine; Pearl said it was an easy birth. Afterward, Grady gave Hanna his gift—she hadn't even known he'd taken her apron for it. Then Pearl sent him back home, just in case. Hanna kissed him first, then let him kiss Lucky. He still can't believe he's a father.

"Lucky," Grady says aloud, and his heart lifts as he says it. Maybe the little token Hanna made is working after all. That red thread tied around the baby's wrist with his family ring, along with a sand dollar and a lodestone for good luck. Grady reckons they'll need some luck. He'll tell his father today—he'll ask for his blessing.

But Hanna's angry at him for waiting this long. She said she didn't care about a blessing. Said she only cared about their son. She swore she'd give her life for him, for her children's children. But there's no reason to say things like that. His father will be fine with it, everything will be fine. And they'll be a family together.

There's a whistling sound, and Grady turns toward the bright window. The curtains are still, but with a sudden breeze they rustle just a bit. And then he smells it in the air. Smoke.

In an instant he's at the glass, looking out. Smoke is rising above the treetops, somewhere near the cabin. No. *No!* In another breath Grady's down the stairs and out of the house, leaping off the porch. He's running barefoot across the yard, past the corral, past his father, who yells out his name, past Jacob, who's sobbing, saying, *Why did you do it, Papa, why?* He's running into the woods now, along the dirt trail, faster, winding through the trees, all the way to the—

The cabin's not there. It's not where it should be.

The only thing left is the small fireplace. Beside it, the ground is blackened. Ash is everywhere.

Grady doesn't believe what he's seeing. It's not possible. He stumbles forward, collapses to his knees. He crawls over the dirt, the charred wood. A cast-iron pot. Shards of something, and—

Bones. There are bones where her bed was. It's burned down to nothing. No. *Comebackcomebackcomeback.* He's screaming, his voice is raw. He doesn't know that we can hear him, that we're all around him, trying to help. If he would just listen, if he would just clear his eyes and really look, he'd see she's right here with us too. But instead, through the trees, he sees something else.

It's resting on the tree stump past the well. Beside it is a bolt of red on the ground—her apron. And next to that are lines in the dirt, deep grooves that seem to be pointing, leading him ahead.

He gets to his feet and lurches forward, the ash all over

him, the soot smeared on his hands, in his throat. He takes a deep breath and his lungs burn as he stumbles toward the tree stump. His eyes are stinging and everything's blurry, but there it is. The book. And on the ground beneath it is the ax.

CHAPTER 24

A NUMBNESS SETTLED OVER MAE and she still couldn't believe what she'd found in her granddad's hand. Now that the house was empty she could read it again.

She pulled the Bible from the shelf and curled up in the dining room's window seat. Right now the sun was trapped behind passing clouds and the yard was as dark as her heart felt. She was meant to be choosing readings for the burial service, but all she could think of was the letter.

She pulled it from her bag, where she'd tucked it into the green book, and then carefully unfolded it. It was long, and written in his shaky handwriting. It would have taken him hours to write it, maybe days.

Dearest little Mae,
  There is something you should know. When you found the book and brought it to me in the attic, I behaved irrationally. I knew it was my duty to pass it

*on, yet again, but I was frightened of what I might do
with it.*

Mae paused, looked out of the window. She remembered the terror on her granddad's face that day. His paleness, that stammering as he tried to speak. The letter trembled in her hand and she smoothed it flat.

*The book of rituals is not to be underestimated. Your
sister knew this, yet I didn't anticipate the lengths she
would go to use it.*

Ro had laughed at almost everything in life, except for the book. Mae knew that from the first and only time Ro had shown it to her, her breath laced with red velvet cake, her voice hushed, reverent.

*When Roxanne was a child, she found the book in the
attic and attempted to bring your mother back to life.*

Anxiety clamped down on Mae's chest and she closed her eyes. For a moment she was a little girl again, watching Ro carry an Easter basket. Watching her in secret, following her to the woods. Her sister had bent over the basket in her white dress, her hands busy in front of her, and when she turned, her dress had been a different color. . . . Dark, dark red, streaked with blood.

Mae's eyes shot open. She stared through the window at the woods where she'd hidden so long ago. Ro's black door creaked open in her mind, and the woods spilled into the room, the smell of pine needles and dampness, the promise of hidden sweets, the giddiness of watching her older sister in secret. She'd wanted to jump out from behind the tree and surprise Ro that day, but the shock of the red dress had scared her. And then her granddad had appeared, yelling Ro's name, swooping in to grab her basket, her knife, and the fat book that was lying on the ground. But hadn't someone else shouted Ro's name too?

Mae shook her head, trying to remember. She stared out at the trees from the window seat, left with the sense that someone else was there that day, but the thought was hazy, like a dream. She looked down at the letter again.

At that time she did not know—how could she?—that the raising ritual only holds its power over life within a year of death.

Within a year of death. That hot anxiousness gripped her again, right in the ribs. The anniversary of Ro's death was tomorrow, the day of her granddad's burial. This letter was proof that he believed in the ritual's power, thought it could work. Was he telling her to perform it, or warning her?

Whatever you decide to do with the book—for it now belongs to you—I only ask that you leave me in peace; let me rest where I belong.

Mae's mouth felt dry and it hurt to swallow. She squeezed her eyes shut and thought of the last time she'd seen her granddad alive, standing at the attic window, waving to her. He'd died alone because she'd put off checking on him.

The ink swam in front of her and she wiped her eyes. Then there was the creak of hinges, the sound of the front door swinging open. Startled, she shoved the letter into her bag next to the book as heavy footsteps clomped down the hallway.

"Dad?"

Sonny appeared in the archway of the dining room wearing the same jeans and shirt he'd left the house in last night. One of his pant legs was shredded, and he had a gash along his forearm and a bruise on his cheek. "Time to go," he told her.

"Time to go where?" she asked. "Are you okay?"

He ignored her. "Get in the truck." His eyes were bloodshot as he stared at her from under his hat. "Go on."

"But I'm choosing verses for the burial," she said, picking up the Bible. "They need it by toda—"

"Don't make me say it again, Mae Eliza."

She shut her mouth, tamping down her frustration. She put the Bible in her bag and followed him out the door, the bolt scraping behind them as he locked it.

Outside, Elle was already standing beside the blue truck. She didn't meet Mae's eye. Her sister had sworn she wasn't angry about the whole breakfast-for-dinner spying episode, but she'd been distant since then.

"Hurry up," Sonny said.

A knot began to form in the pit of Mae's stomach. She climbed into the middle, the seat scalding her skin. Elle got in after her, smashing her knees against the gearshift.

"Where are we going?" Mae asked, but neither of them answered. She glanced at the gash on her dad's arm. The blood had dried to a blackish color and was bright red in the middle where it hadn't scabbed over. "What happened?"

He didn't say anything, just switched off the radio to hot silence. The knot in her stomach tightened as the truck jostled onto the dirt access road that ran through their property. Branches scraped across the windshield as Mae turned to Elle and raised her eyebrows, silently asking her to explain.

Elle shook her head—quick, like she didn't want their dad to see—and then went back to staring out the window. Mae glanced over at Sonny. His ponytail was greasier than usual, grayish-brown strands were sticking out of a twisted rubber band, and the bruise on his cheek looked painful. He smelled of liquor; the whole truck stank.

"I can drive," she offered, but he glared at her.

She was nervous, sweating now. Sunlight filtered through the branches and fell over the truck's battered hood. Mae glanced down at her bag and tried not to think of her granddad, or the last part of his letter, but it was seared into her mind, as hot as the sun that sent her eyelids red when she shut them.

And remember, when the night is at its darkest, that the answers you seek can be found in King James.

And remember this too. You are quiet yet brave, Mae, which is why I have chosen you. You make me proud; you have always done so. I am blessed to have you in my life.

Your loving grandfather,
Grady Deacon Cole VI

The truck rocked over a pothole, and Mae opened her eyes and squinted at the sunlight. The bag felt sweaty on her lap; everything felt wrong. The letter was hidden under the canvas with the green book and the Bible. *The answers you seek can be found in King James.* She knew her granddad had been trying to comfort her, thinking she'd find some sort of peace by reading the Bible like he had, but he was wrong. Nothing could make this better. It wasn't fair that he'd died alone, and it wasn't fair that Ro had too and that everyone thought Cage had done it. It was an accident—she'd fallen off the boat and hit her head, drowning before she could be saved. Cage had dragged her to shore and done all he could, but no one would trust his word. Too much added up against him. He'd asked Ro to marry him and she'd said no; Lance had seen him running away from her body. She could forgive him for that, for running, even if he couldn't forgive himself. And now he wanted the green book to bring her back, to make all the pain go away.

She wanted it to go away too. But if she brought him the book, he'd see the sketch of the ring. He'd figure out what it meant, just like she had. Would it make him feel even worse than he did now? There was a shrillness inside her head, the start of a headache coming on. She gripped the bag strap and closed her eyes.

After everything that had happened, she'd only been able to visit him twice in the past few days. He was still sick, but his fever seemed better. He hadn't eaten anything she'd left for him in the barn, though. Only one piece of bread had been touched—its crusts peeled off and cast aside. When she'd held his hand, he felt hot, but his face was peaceful, even with that cut on his forehead. She liked how when he wasn't sleeping his eyes would steal all the beauty, pale blue cutouts from the very sky itself. She hoped he'd be awake later today when she checked on him. No matter how painful it was, she had to tell him about the ring. She owed him the truth.

Sonny passed the highway turnoff. He was holding the wheel like he might be strangling it, his eyes intent on the dirt road. They should be getting on the highway, not going straight—this way would only take them to the dock or the barn. All of a sudden Mae's heart felt like it was in her throat, and she forced herself to breathe.

"Dad?"

He didn't answer. She looked at Elle for help, but her sister turned away, and all she caught was the back of her head, a sheen of sweat on her neck. Sonny was still bearing down on the wheel, his hands clenched tight.

"Where are we going?"

He glared at her again, and Elle kept staring out the window. "I think you know," he said.

Mae's heartbeat ratcheted up. She had to concentrate on getting air, on filling her lungs. He couldn't be going to the barn.

Sonny pressed his foot down on the accelerator, and the truck picked up speed. The trees were blurring past now, and Mae held her bag tight and glanced at Elle again. Why was she so quiet? Then it hit her—Elle had told him about Cage. Sonny was going to confront him. In the rearview mirror she could see her dad's gun rack, the rifles mounted on it, and she felt a surge of fear. Maybe she could stop him before he got them unloaded, but if he had his pistol in reach she'd be useless.

She leaned forward and popped open the glove compartment, peering inside. A whiskey bottle, tobacco, cigarette papers. That was it—no pistol. But she knew he sometimes kept it by the driver's-side door.

She felt shaky, ramped up with adrenaline. Maybe she should just come clean, try to talk him down. "Dad, I—"

He turned, and the look on his face silenced her. His knuckles were white over the wheel. "It's gone on for too long, Mae." His voice was raw as the truck shot forward.

"Slow down," she begged, but he wasn't listening. She steeled herself for the accusation: she'd been helping Cage, and he'd never forgive her. Trees were whipping past them, the shocks bouncing over the dirt. They veered to the right of the fork, heading uphill toward the barn. Mae's heart was in her throat; they'd be there any moment. Panic welled inside her, she felt like crying. "Dad, please slow down."

The truck lurched over another set of potholes and her mind flashed to Cage, sprawled on the raft in the barn. He was too weak to run, to defend himself.

"Elle!" she called out, too sharp, but her sister shook her head again, staying out of it. The barn was less than a half mile ahead. "You're going too fast, Dad."

He clenched the wheel tighter and she scanned the woods. There was movement ahead, but instead of Cage's dark hair and lean height, she saw a glint of blond. Fern was standing at the side of the road, close to the edge. Sonny wasn't slowing down, and then Mae realized he didn't see her, he wasn't going to—

"Stop!" she shouted, and she did the only thing she could: she yanked the wheel. She felt the sharp pain of slamming into the dash as Sonny hit the brakes and the rear wheels locked. Elle screamed as their whole world started turning, the truck spinning past Fern, impossibly close, the tires screeching as they finally jerked to a stop near a tree.

"What happened?" Elle asked, her eyes wide. "Is that Fern?"

"Goddammit," Sonny swore, his eyes on her as she ran off into the woods. "Kid came out of nowhere."

He opened his door, got out, and then walked to the front of the truck and kicked at the fender. Mae jumped out after him, found him bent over the hood.

"Please talk to me," she said softly. If they could just talk . . . She braced herself, ready for his anger.

Her dad turned away, pulled his hat down. He fumbled for his pack of cigarettes. "Wanted the boat," he muttered, and it took her a moment to catch up. "Wanted to do something as a family. Take you girls fishing like I used to."

Mae leaned against the truck as it all sank in. Sonny hadn't been going to the barn for Cage, he'd been going for the boat, and she'd almost confessed everything.

"Being at the house . . ." Sonny trailed off as he struck his lighter. "Jesus. I can't even make it to the water anymore." He took off his hat and ran his hand through his ponytail. "Fishing reminds me too much of her. Everything does. My mind's messed up."

"It's okay," Elle said, coming around the other side of the truck, "it's okay, Dad."

But Mae knew he wasn't able to shut the pain behind a door in his head to mute it, and even then it built and built, always threatening to come out. She could feel the heaviness in the air. It was never going to be okay unless Ro was here again, alive and grinning.

Heat thrummed off the car, hit her in waves. She put her hand on the hood of the truck, felt the warmth travel up her fingers. She wanted to fix this, fix her dad, but she didn't know how.

"Your grandpa, I should have taken him out more." Sonny's voice broke, his hand shaking as he inhaled. "He loved fishing. Taught me everything I know. But did I help him this year? Spend time with him when he was sick? No, course I didn't." He shook his head, almost dropped his cigarette. He was upset, agitated; she'd never seen him like this before.

"He was happy being at home," Mae said, wanting him to feel better. "He liked being around us. You did the best you could, Dad."

Sonny inhaled again, his hand with the cigarette still shaking. "No, I didn't. Your grandpa, now, he was a good father, especially after what I put him through. Didn't ever want to do a thing he asked, laughed at his ideas, told him he was an ignorant old man. He adopted me when no one else would, and I treated him like shit."

Mae felt the air leave her chest. Adopted? She glanced at Elle and saw the shock on her face too. "What did you say?" Mae asked, her gaze darting back to her dad.

"He took me in." He exhaled, his eyes far away, staring into the distance.

"You mean—" Elle started, and then gave up and just looked at him, waiting.

He'd gone silent, but after a minute he shrugged. "I was four or five then. My mom worked near the Childers place, helped out with the stables, did some cleaning around town, that sort of thing. She got sick and didn't make it, and your granddad took me in."

"We had no idea," Elle said. She sounded as dazed as Mae felt. *Adopted.* He'd never said a word about it . . . but it explained a lot: Why he never talked about his childhood. Why he'd never wanted his portrait added to the family collection. Why he didn't mind selling Blue Gate. Maybe part of him had always felt the way she did—like she didn't quite belong anywhere, didn't fit.

"Probably should've let you girls know." Sonny stubbed

out his cigarette and lit another. "Just didn't want to talk about it. Besides, it was a long time ago." He let out a bitter laugh. "Too long. Figured it didn't matter anyway."

But it did matter. All the worry Mae had over telling Cage about the ring slipped away. He was more a Cole than they were.

"You could have told us," she said. "You can tell us anything, Dad." Then her throat clenched tight as she thought of the lies she'd stacked up lately. Maybe they'd all been doing the same thing this past year. The three of them, full of secrets.

Sonny's eyes settled on Elle. "I know you want that hotel thing," he said. "But we need to move. Nothing good ever happens here. Can't take much more." He wiped his face with the back of his sleeve.

"Dad, we're here for you." Elle put her arms around him. "We'll always be here."

Mae wanted to hug him too, she wanted to tell him that she loved him, but what would he think of her helping Cage? She flinched inside, felt shame run all the way down to her toes.

"You okay to go home?" Elle asked, and after a minute he nodded.

"Yeah," he said, watching the ash from his cigarette float down to the dirt. "Yeah, I'll be okay. We all will."

Mae squeezed his hand and he managed a half smile. He was far from fine; it was all over his face—he needed some good news to shake him out of his grief. They all did.

"Come on," Elle said, "let's go home."

Sonny's eyes narrowed on the trees, in the direction of the barn, and Mae felt her heart skip. "Hey, Fern!" he called. "Get on over here!"

"Hey, Mr. Cole." Fern was running toward them now, her Invisible Man T-shirt tucked into her dirty shorts, her curls falling across her eyes. "What are y'all doing besides almost hitting me?"

Sonny scratched at his ponytail again. "We're gonna go eat some lunch," he said, his voice gruff.

"I'm pretty hungry," Fern said, dancing from leg to leg.

"Thought you were. Fern and Mae in the back. Elle's driving."

Mae almost smiled. He was trying, he really was. She was still worried, but this was like the tiniest sliver of hope. Sonny tossed the keys to Elle as Mae got up on the bumper, holding out a hand to Fern.

"That was a pretty close call," Fern said. The truck engine revved over her voice. "Also, you're not a very good liar."

The gun rack was digging into her back, and Mae tried to scoot over. "And I suppose you are."

"Well, I can keep a secret," Fern said. "I've kept *yours*, you know. And Lance's too, since he needs my help."

Mae tensed. "What secret?"

Fern poked Mae's ribs. "Wouldn't be one if I said it out loud."

So she was bluffing. Mae relaxed, leaned back against the truck, trying not to look too interested. They were closer to the house now, farther away from the barn. She needed some quiet to think, a slender paintbrush in her hand, but after a few minutes she felt sticky fingers grab her elbow.

"Here's another secret, Mayday. It starts with *I*." Fern edged closer, breathing into her ear. "*Initiation.*"

It was so unexpected that Mae couldn't hide her shock. She fumbled her words, the question catching in her throat. "What do you mean?" she choked out. "Where did you hear that?"

Fern smiled. "I know another one too," she said, "and it's gonna come true tomorrow. On the beach."

The truck rocked onto the driveway, nearing Blue Gate, the spire on the roof jutting up through the trees. Tomorrow her granddad would be buried. Tomorrow was the anniversary of Ro's death. Mae's eyes welled up, and she couldn't help but ask. "What?"

Fern held a finger to her lips and shook her head. "Shh," she whispered, "he'll hear us."

"Tell me," Mae said, sounding harsher than she meant to. "Tell me what you know."

Fern smirked as the truck pulled in front of the house, wrenching to a stop as Elle parked and shut off the engine.

"Fern!" Mae hissed, but the girl only laughed as Sonny and Elle got out, slammed their doors. Mae knew she'd been played, and Fern knew it too. She couldn't risk asking her anything more if they weren't alone.

"You'll see," Fern whispered. "Tomorrow will be here sooner than you think."

CHAPTER 25

A WHISPERING NOISE WOKE HIM. He felt like he'd been sleeping for years. He opened his eyes and found he was lying on a blown-up raft in the barn. A gallon of water was beside him, some bread and saltine crackers. His stomach rumbled, and he tore open the package and ate half of the crackers in a minute, sucking on the beady grains of salt. Mae wasn't in the barn, and the whispering noise was gone—maybe it'd been a dream.

He glanced up at the skylight and saw the haziness of almost-dusk and wondered how long he'd slept. He inhaled the rest of the crackers, liking their flaky weight in his empty stomach as he stood, unsteady on his feet. The boat was covered by the white tarp and he leaned against it, caught his bearings. He felt better. He felt, for the first time in a long time, hungry. It was a good feeling. The feeling of being alive.

I didn't kill her. He knew that now, no matter what they said. The memory of the dream with Ro ripped through him and he held on to the boat. He hadn't killed her. It'd been an accident. Probably no one would ever believe him, no one except Mae, but at least he knew the truth.

There was a bucket near the raft—Mae must have put it there in case he got sick again—and next to it was a blanket and a twisted rope of sheets. He remembered falling in and out of sleep with fever dreams so vivid he might have lived them. How many days had passed since he'd been sick, stuck in the barn? Mae had been here, taking care of him, and Ro had too, somehow. He'd been with Ro, and—

A smell hit him. He sniffed under his sleeves, got the foul stench of sweat. He peeled off the T-shirt, took it over to the sink near the fridge. Mae's pocketknife was there, along with a bar of soap. The tap was working, so he scrubbed his face, his neck, under his arms—he'd gotten thinner. He glanced over at the door and then dropped his shorts and splashed water everywhere, running the soap along his body, dripping suds onto the concrete. Christ, it felt good to be clean. It felt like he'd died and come to life again. Hell, maybe he had. He didn't know what to believe, the dreams were mixing into things, clouding his head, but he was alive and now he knew what had happened with Ro that day. He hadn't lost his temper, hadn't hurt her. It didn't matter that she'd said no about marrying him. He'd only loved her, and he loved her now, and that was the truth.

He started washing the shirt he'd taken off, and his shorts too. He wrung them out as dry as he could and then slipped them back on, cool and damp. A creak came behind him and he grabbed the knife as the barn door swung open. A second later his grip relaxed. There she was, five foot and not much more, with that thick hair of hers and that pixie face he was glad to see. Mae was wearing cutoffs and a thin T-shirt, and the start of a smile was on her mouth.

"You're awake." Her feet were quiet across the cement and then she was in front of him, her bag strap slung across her shoulder, her brown eyes peering up at him with concern, like she was his Florence Nightingale or something, his guardian angel. He felt embarrassed. She must've seen him sick—throwing up, ranting with fever.

"I feel better," he said, not sure what to say, not sure what she'd been witness to. Come to think of it, he didn't recognize the shorts he was wearing. He cleared his throat, feeling jittery, like he'd just chugged a Coke. "Much better," he said, "thanks to you."

A corner of her mouth turned up. "It was nothing."

"Are we . . . still safe here?" Was *he* still safe in the barn—that was what he really meant, because he was the one who shouldn't be here.

She nodded. "I've seen Fern around, but no one else," she said. "And my dad's out hunting right now, trying to keep his mind off things." She crossed her arms over her chest. "Probably it's fine."

"Probably," he repeated, and he guessed that had to be good enough. ·

And then Mae's hand was on his shoulder—so gentle. It was her touch that made him really look at her, and he found himself staring. Her brown eyes were distant sometimes, lost in thought, but when she glanced his way it was like the sun on a boat after being caught in a storm.

He looked down, remembering the garden. The night he'd gotten sick. He forced himself to examine the dust on the floor, and then the sink, the wet bar of soap. He could feel her standing beside him; the air was charged with her so close.

"How long was I out?" he asked.

"A few days." She searched in her bag and then pulled out a package wrapped in tinfoil. "I would've made more but didn't expect to find you awake."

He opened it. Three homemade chicken sandwiches with the crusts cut off. His mouth watered just looking at them.

"Thanks," he said. "I never eat the crusts."

A hint of a smile on her lips again, and it warmed him to see it. Her face was smaller than Ro's, and he liked the way it looked. No makeup, no earrings. She was just herself, and though she didn't talk too much she had a presence to her, a quiet that made him wonder what she was thinking.

"I know you took care of me," he said. "Don't remember too much else." Except the dreams; he remembered them.

"You scared me." Mae ran her hand over his discarded shirt on the counter. She touched it tenderly, same way she'd done to him when he was sick. It was all coming back now, how she'd taken care of him. She'd brought him water, and painkillers, made him sit up to swallow them.

"You wouldn't go to the hospital." She was still holding his shirt and he looked away, not wanting to stare.

After a moment she reached up and tilted his chin so he was facing her. He let her—unsure of what she was going to do. Her fingertips were soft and she held his gaze as she reached up with her other hand.

There was the lightest brush against his forehead. "You feel normal. Not as hot." She leaned in again. "Stand still," she said, and then she was dabbing near his temple with a tissue. He winced as red blossoms spread across the whiteness.

"Your cut's bleeding again. Did you scratch it?"

"Must have." He steadied himself on the counter as she wiped at his head.

"I'm glad you're better." The tissue was wet with his blood, and she looked worried. "Do you remember what I told you? When you were sick?"

That was when he saw her worry for what it was: she was hurting too. The pain of it was all over her face, her narrow shoulders. A heavy sadness underneath her skin. And then he remembered the thing she'd told him— what, an hour ago, a day? He'd been lying on the raft; she'd been holding a cold washcloth to his forehead. And she'd told him her grandfather had passed.

Christ, it wasn't fair. Some people had to deal with so much death and others only their own. His heart ached for the girl in front of him. Mae Cole was something special. She didn't deserve all this pain. No one did.

"Hey." He grabbed her hand. "I'm sorry. About your grandfather."

The light in the barn was fading fast, but he could still see her eyes flood before she spoke. "It's okay," she said. "The doctor told us he went fast, that he wouldn't have felt much. The funeral's tomorrow."

He didn't know what to tell her. What he wanted to do was just hold her, but that didn't seem right either. "You want to talk about it?"

She shook her head. Tucked a lock of hair behind her ear. "Do you remember what else I told you? When you were sick?" She reached into her bag and pulled out the green book. "I got it back. We have everything we need."

He thought he'd be excited to see it, but instead a wariness filled him. He stared at the coffins on its cover, wondered if the ritual could do what Ro had sworn it could.

"Only I need to show you something first." She nodded at the ribbon. It was marking a place toward the back and he turned to it, and then nearly dropped the book.

The drawing looked so real, like the ring might just slide off the page. The cut of the stones, the shape of them, the detail—it matched the one he'd given Ro, he knew that for sure. The worry snake slithered in his gut.

"Ro couldn't have drawn this," he said. "I gave her—"

"I know," Mae cut in. "Your ring came from the same place as this book." Her eyes moved between him and the sketch. "Which means . . ." She let out a nervous laugh.

"We're related," he said, then shook his head. "No. We

can't be. No way." He felt nauseous, like he might be sick again. Ro had seen the ring and thought they were family. His hands were shaking, and then Mae touched his elbow. He tore his eyes from the page to look at her.

"My dad was adopted," she said softly. "I just found out. . . . I don't think Ro knew."

He took a step back, all of it sinking in, flooding over him. If only she were here right now. If only he could tell her.

"So actually," Mae said, "you're the true Cole."

He stared down at the sketch of the ring, hardly believing it. But it was his, all right. Back when Ro had first told him about her family book it reminded him of what his mother used to tease him about. *I suppose you're like your daddy, thinking you got magic in your blood. Thinking you're special.* He'd chalked up Ro's book as coincidence—there were plenty of stories of old magic in the South, that was what he'd told himself—ignoring all the signs that it could be something more. That his mother could have been talking about the same sort of thing. But his dad had left them when he was a little kid, and she'd hated those stories ever since.

"Did you know you had roots here?" Mae asked. Before he could answer, she pressed on. "Is that why you came?"

"My uncle offered me a job in Gulf Shores." He'd moved over this way for work, but Ro was the one who'd brought him to Blue Gate. "I stayed because I met your sister." And meeting her had felt like home. Funny, he kind of felt the same way around Mae now. If he was being honest.

"I never expected this . . . ," Mae said, trailing off. She got that distant look again.

"Never would've expected any of this, Mae." It was strange as hell that he'd ended up at Blue Gate, back where his family was from—but that didn't really matter, not now, at least. What mattered now was the book. "You got this off Lance after you said you couldn't. Ro'd be proud."

Mae shrugged; there was a flush over her neck. "You're a Cole," she said. "So the way I see it, it's yours."

"Only one reason why I want it." He looked into her eyes to ask permission, holding back the urge to touch her cheek. "Are we going to try this or what?"

She searched his face, maybe to see if he meant it. The start of a smile came to her lips, as if she was satisfied with what she saw. "Okay," she said. "Let's go."

In the woods there was a hush in the air—but Cage felt stronger, hopeful even, and it was because of Mae. She was moving fast and quiet through the dark like it was second nature, and then they were finally breaking out from under the trees.

Ahead the cemetery was lit by moonlight. She climbed up the iron gate with her heavy bag over her shoulder and dropped to the other side, and he followed her.

Together they passed the statue of the angel, then went all the way back to the blackened tree and her grave. They stood there for a minute, staring at each other, until Mae pulled the book from her bag and opened it.

"I brought what we need," she said. "At least I think so."

"Tell me what to do." He wasn't sure of anything, just that they had to try it.

He glanced up at the sky, the scatter of stars overhead, the moon, and when he looked back at Mae she was sitting down. He sat too, the grass damp and cool. The green book was on her lap and her legs were folded underneath her the way a kid would sit. Behind her was the spindly old tree that'd been split by lightning, and the headstone, the etching of Ro's name.

"Are you sure you're okay?"

It was like Mae knew things about him before he did, because now he could feel his head throbbing, his insides still hot. "Better than I look." It was painful to be here by Ro's grave, to think about raising her, but he didn't want to change his mind. "Let's just get this over with."

"I don't like it either," she said, seeing straight through him again, all the way to his soul, but she opened the green book anyway. Watery moonlight fell over its pages.

"Do you want to do it?" he asked.

Mae paused, holding a flashlight over the last page. "This is it. I think you should read. I'll help."

She leaned forward and handed him the book, and when he took it his heart hurled against his ribs. Then she set a crumpled piece of notebook paper beside it and he blinked, realizing what he was staring at. He'd dug it up near the cherub.

"First we should think of how we love her," Mae said. "Hold her in our minds and our hearts."

Touching the book was weird; it was warm and humming under his fingers, or maybe he was shaking. He glanced up, saw Mae's hands balled tight—she was nervous too. She was whispering something, it sounded like *Good deeds for good*, and then she was saying Ro's name over and over.

Think of Ro. Cage imagined her. Her green eyes with that gold coming through around the irises. The gap between her front teeth. The way she laughed so loud, like it was shooting all the way up her spine, bursting from her entire body.

He looked over at the choppy dirt and grass, the pair of graves. What would his mother think about what they were trying, what would Ro's dad? His head started to throb again as Mae grabbed her bag. She reached for his hand and turned it up, and then dropped Ro's gold locket into his palm. He made a fist, felt the cool metal against his skin.

"Keep holding it," she whispered. She dug into the canvas again and placed a shoe box in front of him, and then a bundle wrapped in a red sweatshirt, a paper bag that looked greasy at the bottom, and a jar with something dark floating inside it. He did a double take. It was a hoof, a horse's hoof.

He turned to Mae, found he was speechless.

"I didn't kill them," Mae said. "They were . . . already dead."

"You didn't kill them," he repeated slowly. His head was hurting even more now; it felt like someone was pressing down with pliers.

"Are you ready?" She flicked on her flashlight and the page in front of him glowed. She glanced over her shoulder, looking toward the cemetery gate, the narrow path. "I think we should start."

"Okay." He stared down at the book, and the ink went sideways. There was a smell in the air, a stinking sweetness, and now it felt like the pliers were digging into his eyeballs. He blinked.

On the page was the heading *A Ritual for a Raising*. Below it were words in clumsy writing. Down at the bottom of the page was the smeared thumbprint. He knew he was stalling, but he wasn't sure why.

"Okay," he said again, louder now, and then read the first line. "'Harbor love in your heart, while in your hand hold the loved one's belongings.'" His voice sounded jerky to his ears. "'Then begin the offerings. For death feeds life as blood feeds the ritual.'" His tongue felt mangled, almost like he'd been hit in the mouth. "'And little creatures show the way.'"

He didn't dare look at Mae, didn't dare slow down. *Keep going, keep going.* "'A cat for nine,'" he said as Mae pushed the red sweatshirt in front of him. He stared at her as she unrolled it. Inside was the little black stray. His stomach heaved, but he had to keep reading.

"'A bird for vision,'" he said, onto Ro's copy now, that pink pen over the notebook page. Mae slid the shoe box on the grass in front of him, the blackbird inside half eaten by ants. The smell rose and clung to his nostrils. He guessed what was coming next and forced himself to look back at the book.

"'A horse for the passage,'" he said, dreading each word. Mae set down the jar, a single hoof inside it. Hell, this had better be worth it.

"'A snake for new skin.'" There went the paper bag, the snake dropping onto the grass as she shook it out. It was a dark olive color, a cottonmouth with its head chopped off.

"'Laid out in a row of four, only this will open the door.'" The night around them was quiet, not even a breeze, and he felt drowned by the heat. His sweat was dropping onto the paper, onto his hands, which were covered in something black and dusty.

Mae was whispering again—*"Roxanne Elizabeth Cole, Roxanne Elizabeth Cole"*—her voice burrowing into his brain as the letters on the page blurred. But he kept on.

"'Then save the most brutal for last.'" He paused, stumbling over the next word. "'Chana for a life, since all should be equal. Do these tasks and see the return,'" he read, "'except if the earth has traveled the sun.'"

He'd reached the end of the ritual; there was nothing more to do. He looked up, and a coldness hit him right in the chest. Across from him on the ground, Mae was sitting with her back straight. Her hands were gripping her knees and she wasn't moving, was hardly breathing. The worry snake slithered up his throat, and he thought he might gag. He could feel someone's breath, right in his ear. It had to be Mae.

"I can feel her," she whispered.

The blackened tree behind Ro's grave started swaying. Everything else was still—the woods were quiet, unmoving, the cemetery silent. The angel statue was a gray ghost in the night, and there were the spikes of cut flowers beside the graves and the shadowy hunch of the empty caretaker hut. Nothing else moved, not a leaf. All was quiet and still. Except for the tree, which was slanting beside them.

Mae's eyes were squeezed shut and the branches behind her were wavering.

"Do you see it?" Cage asked. "Do you . . . ?"

She opened her eyes and in them he saw fear and he felt it himself, it crawled up his spine, up to his heart, all the way up to his skull.

He could hear something now, faint. Almost like a voice—only it wasn't coming from outside, not from the cemetery or the night air—it was coming from inside him. He shut his eyes and felt his ears hollow out like he was underwater and then his insides went panicky and he couldn't move, he couldn't breathe, it was like he was dead. He was so tense he felt himself separating from his body, or growing out from his body, and then he wasn't just his skin and blood and bone but also the earth around him and the little stones and the grass in the cemetery and the dark sky above—he was all those things at once, he was either dead or all of life itself. When he opened his eyes, time slowed and lengthened and he looked down and saw he was standing now, that he and Mae both were, and now they were turning, stepping toward the gate because they could hear the creak of hinges and it was her—he knew it was her, she'd found her way back, she'd come home to them and his head was splitting like he was being broken apart and the air was cold, so cold, and the gate swung open, and . . . it was not Roxanne—it was *not* Roxanne.

The thing stuck its head through the gate. Mae let out a rush of breath beside him and the deer turned and sprinted off, its hooves fast against the dirt.

He could breathe again. He took a step toward Mae, felt for her hand, and gripped it tight. Her face was wet, she'd been crying. She looked stricken; she'd lost her sister all over again.

The book was on the ground next to Ro's grave, but it seemed wrong. He wasn't sure what he'd expected to see—Ro coming through the gate? Ro, alive, like none of it had ever happened?

He was still holding Mae's hand and her thumb was circling his palm and he watched the small movement, it was the tiniest whirlpool, and then he remembered his dream—how strong Ro was, how she always knew what to go after in life. Maybe it'd just been his imagination, or maybe she'd really come to him in his sleep, but he knew suddenly that he was in this cemetery not for her but for him. He was the one who wouldn't let her go. He felt himself sweating all over, the fever was back, rolling over him like a wave, and then Mae pulled her hand away from his.

She sank to the ground, knelt as if praying. He looked down at her small shoulders and thought of Ro, how he would've done anything to save her. But she wouldn't want this, not this way. Ro had never needed saving her whole life and didn't need it now.

He replayed the memory of her over and over again. He wanted a wormhole, he wanted to stretch out the past, go back to that very moment when she was still alive on the boat, so he could tell her goodbye one last time. But it wouldn't have changed things and now she was gone, and the only person beside him was Mae.

He knelt down next to her. "Are you okay?"

She nodded, still mute.

"I'm sorry," he said.

"I thought it would work." She turned to him. "The sacrifices, the ritual. We did everything right," she said. "I thought, I almost thought . . ."

He shook his head. He'd read everything in the book, exactly how it was written. He hadn't missed a thing. The grief in Mae's eyes cut into him. It was his own pain too, like looking at himself in a shard of glass. He got a flash of green kudzu, those vines covering him, wrapping around his bones so tight. Maybe they'd messed up the ritual, or maybe they *had* done it—and it just took time to work. Or maybe they were both in a bad way, so confused they didn't know what was real anymore. But he wouldn't say a thing because he didn't want to see Mae upset again.

She sniffled, wiped at her eyes. "The worst thing is, a part of me was scared that it was her."

"Why?"

She looked down at her hands and something twisted inside him. "Don't get upset if I tell you."

CHAPTER 26

BLUE GATE, 1860

HIS BROTHER BEGS HIM NOT to go inside, but Grady doesn't listen. He tells Jacob to wait in the woods, makes him swear to stay away from the house. Then Grady finds his father in the dining room, lighting his pipe. It reeks of sweetness, and the smoke makes his eyes water.

Grady stops at the archway of the room, keeps the ax at his side. His throat tightens and he wants to cry, but he can't in front of this man. He's afraid he won't be able to say what he needs to.

His father speaks first. "I did you a favor. Do you know how people would talk?"

Grady's mouth won't open. Through the pipe's trickle of smoke he doesn't see the dining room, the window seat, or the sleek wooden cabinet. Instead he sees the burned-out cabin and glowing embers. He sees bones in ash.

"Jacob was there. He saw everything." Finally the

words come, and Grady's surprised by how calm he sounds. "I know it wasn't an accident."

"I warned you the first time," his father says. "I told you never to go there again."

Grady knows what he means. He means to the witch's cabin. He means Pearl and Hanna. "You killed the woman I loved."

His father sweeps flecks of tobacco off the table with his handkerchief. "What do you know of love?" His blue eyes narrow. "You disgrace yourself," he says. "You disgrace this family."

This is all Grady needs to hear. Even though his mother asked them to be kind to each other. Even though. His grip tightens on the ax.

His father laughs. It's a bitter sound that hangs in the air. "You wouldn't dare."

Grady steps toward him, stopping at the table. "This is to fix what you've done."

His father loved his mother, Rose, but now she is dead. With her gone, there's no goodness left in him.

Grady steps closer. His father takes the pipe out of his mouth and glares.

"I refuse to fight you," he says, but the challenge is in his eyes. It's always been there. The ax trembles in Grady's hand.

"You will put that down and apologize." His father glances at his pocket watch. "Don't make me say it again." His mouth is hard, pressed tight with conviction.

Hanna, Hanna, Hanna, Grady thinks. *God, our son too.* Hanna, Lucky—they're all he can think of, always. He knows what he's doing is wrong, but his father killed them. He killed them and he's not sorry and there's no other way. Grady's jaw bears down and his heart feels like it's exploding in his chest and he can't live without her, he can't, and he won't. Then he moves so fast that it's all a blur.

The first thud makes his ears ring, and they're still ringing as he drags his father's body from the house. He sees Jacob watching from the trees and calls for him to help. There's another small bird in his brother's shirt pocket and his cheeks are wet.

"I'm making things right," Grady says. "Don't you understand?" Jacob stares at him with teary eyes and shakes his head. "Help me anyway," Grady tells him.

His brother's eyes well up again but he takes their father by the ankles while Grady holds under his shoulders as they limp into the woods. After they reach the burned ground where the cabin once stood, he yells at Jacob to leave. When he doesn't listen, Grady shoves him, and only then does his brother turn and run. Watching him go makes Grady feel like he's choking on ash. He feels like his lungs are going black, his heart too. But there's no stopping now.

"I did it," he says.

In front of him, Pearl is standing near what used to be the fireplace. A barn cat is in her arms, along with the book, half hidden by her long white hair. At her feet are two woven baskets. The baskets are moving.

"I'm ready," he tells her, setting his father's body on the ash. The chest wound is seeping; his mouth is half open. Even though he's dead, Grady's afraid of him.

"This is his doing," he says to Pearl, hardening his voice so she can't see how scared he is.

"Yes. This is his night." Pearl's jaw tightens and she shuts her eyes like she's praying. Her hair lifts around her in the breezeless air. When she nods, he knows it's time.

Grady opens the book, sees his fast handwriting down the page, the ink just dry. It's the ritual he needs—the one Pearl recited to him before he took the ax to the house.

Now there's nothing left to do but go through with it; there's nothing left for him if he can't bring her back. He starts to read from the book and all sense of time disappears and then suddenly he's at the end and it's finished, it's finally over, and he's covered in blood. He collapses to the ground, his knees hitting the earth, the book falling from his hands.

Pearl touches Grady's shoulder and all her fierceness leaves her. She is crying, and she never cries. She is crying because she was too late to save her daughter—she was away when Grady's father came. She doesn't know Hanna heard him in the woods and gave the baby to her brother, telling him to run. Hanna stayed behind in the cabin, believing love was stronger than the darkness that was coming. But sometimes terrible things come to pass, and they can never be undone. They can't be fixed or re-versed. They can only be made anew.

Like right now. The old witch wipes her eyes when she realizes who's watching them. She knows who's listening when Grady shouts Hanna's name, begging her to rise. But only Pearl sees the return as shadows swirl in the air, swirl and settle overhead.

A moment later, the new Hanna takes a breath as she looks at Grady from the edge of the trees. Her body smells of smoke and ash and earth. In time it will begin to hurt—the headaches will come first, and then the chest pain, the bruising—but for now she feels strong. She almost feels like her old self. Almost.

She is Hanna, but not quite. She is different now.

This new girl turns and walks deeper into the woods, alone, away from the blood that's soaking into the dirt, the blood that she didn't ask for. Her heart is searching for her child, who escaped. Her feet are taking her far from Blue Gate.

And so begins a new life.

CHAPTER 27

CAGE FELT ON EDGE. HE kept looking over his shoulder, but there was nothing behind him except shadows. The moon lit up the ground enough to see by, his boots crushing over twigs and dead leaves. Even now, he could still feel Mae's warm hand holding his. Her brown eyes, that thick hair of hers twisted back. She'd said in the cemetery that she felt close to him, more than anyone else. And as much as he'd wanted to hear it, and admit that she was the only real friend he had, he knew what she was saying came from missing Ro. The truth was, everything that had happened was bigger than them both.

Cage ducked under a branch, kept heading toward the barn. The smell of rain was in the air, another summer storm on its way. Behind him, the cemetery had been swallowed by trees, and the woods seemed to buckle and pitch with the wind. He hunched his shoulders and went straight into it, the way a sailboat couldn't.

He'd promised to meet her tomorrow but it'd be better

for them both if he didn't. He didn't belong here, not really. He felt aimless—nowhere seemed right, especially not Blue Gate. And then, just like that, he jumped ship, veering off the path to the barn. He charged past leaves and brambles that tore at his skin, dug into his elbows. He could hear his mother, see her pointing at him, saying, *Just like your daddy. When you ever gonna finish what you start?*

But Mae deserved better than this. Ro was dead and she wasn't coming back, and they thought he'd done it. He didn't have the money for a good lawyer, so it'd be Lance's word against his. No one would believe him over the cop's son. Hell, not even his own mother trusted him. He needed to start over somewhere, find work fishing out in Alaska, where the land was so big there'd be room for a new life. Or he'd go down to Mexico—he could get there with no passport. Either way he wouldn't ask his uncle for help again. Probably best if he and his mother thought him dead like Ro was. Buried in those green leaves, that kudzu weed.

There was a rightness to it—that they should both be dead to the world. Cage Lucky Shaw and Roxanne Elizabeth Cole, gone together. She'd tell him to go far from here, to stand on his own two feet. He just had to get out of Blue Gate first. The place was tearing his logic to shit. Blue Gate, with all its mossy trees and graves and memories—it was like some drug, making him believe in things that shouldn't be possible.

Cage got to the tree line and jumped over the ditch to the dirt road. He'd made his choice. Maybe he'd never had one, just like Ro had known what she was looking at when he'd given her the ring. He wiped the sweat from his forehead and followed the tire tracks toward the highway. A few minutes later he saw a clearing. A truck was parked there, a big FOR SALE sign taped to its window. It felt like Mexico was calling to him. The truck would take him there.

He halted, staring at it. He wasn't close enough to see in the cab, and someone might be in it. He couldn't let his guard down now, not when he was on his way out. That was when it always happened—when you thought you were out clean.

He stepped off the dirt road and into the woods, wanting cover as he went around the windshield for a better look. It was slow going. The undergrowth was thick, full of thorns that came up to his knees, and he had to walk around a large tree trunk that'd probably been growing for a hundred years and would shade the earth for a hundred more. When he finally passed the truck, his shoulders relaxed.

It was empty.

Finding it here felt like a shred of luck, like Ro was showing him the way out. The money he'd stolen at the hospital was rolled up in his boot. He could leave it under a rock for the owner and take the truck; it couldn't be worth much. Throw some mud on the plates, spark the starter wire, and go. Simple.

A blowfly buzzed past his face. Then he saw a few more gathering around the truck bed. In the back was a heavy white cloth, spread out over something bulky. There was the scent of something metallic—*blood?*

He took a quick look around. Nothing in sight but the curve in the road and the moonlit trees. He was drawn to the bed, the lumpy shape underneath the cloth, the smell of it. He reached toward the edge of the cloth and tugged.

The first thing he saw were scales.

He yanked away the rest of the cover as the stench hit him. The alligator was canted to the side, a smear of dark blood on its body. Next to it was a long black rat snake that he thought was alive before he saw the mangled head. Another blowfly flew at his face and Cage swatted it away, all thoughts of Mexico gone.

He touched the alligator and its claws scraped the side of the truck—its belly was still warm. Someone had been hunting, just dropped off the kill. He had to get out of here. *Now.* He was pulling up the cloth when a light swept across him.

"Hey!"

Cage whirled, shielded his face to block the brightness. A boot thudded nearby, and then another. "What's this?" a voice drawled.

Cage's throat closed up and he stepped away from the truck. It was that cop—he could tell from how tall he was. The flashlight was pointed at him, scathing his eyes. His hands pressed into fists and he forced himself to stay calm.

"I'm talking to you, kid," Childers said, bouncing the flashlight from his face to his chest.

Say something. But his throat was still clamped up, so he nodded, hoped it looked like a greeting. His mind was scrambling for a way out. *Think, Cage, think.* He could bolt. Or make up some story about his car breaking down. Or . . .

Now that the flashlight wasn't on his face he could see Childers was wearing camouflage and holding a dog on a chain. It was a big muscly thing, some sort of bulldog mix, and it was showing teeth. He didn't see a gun on Childers, but swearwords alone hadn't killed that gator. He needed to talk his way free, get going. *Now.*

"I was just gator hunting," Cage told him. "Can you point me to the highway? Supposed to meet a friend there."

"You're on private property," Childers said.

"Sorry, sir." Cage took another step away, his hands going up, almost automatic. If Childers recognized him, he might just get shot—he knew how it worked.

"If you were hunting, where's your gun?"

Cage didn't answer, just took another step. He was unarmed, alone, no way to protect himself. They were in the middle of nowhere, and it was dark. Accidents happened. He could die out here and no one would know, not even Mae. If he ran now like he wanted to, he'd get shot for sure.

"I asked you a question," Childers said. The dog growled.

"It's in the truck with my friend," Cage told him. "Can you point me to the highway or not?"

"Haven't decided yet," Childers said.

Cage's whole body went stiff, and he felt a swell of anger rising. Then came the jingle of keys, and—

"Hey! Who you talking to?" The shout belonged to Lance, and then Cage heard the spike of a laugh. When he realized it was Sonny, the last bit of hope inside him vanished.

There were flashlights through the trees, half a football field away. Two minutes, tops, before they saw him. He was pinned in a bad way—a cop and a dog in front, the truck in back, Sonny and Lance heading at him. Nearby some bushes rustled, but he didn't turn to look, didn't dare take his eyes from Childers, who was stepping forward. "What's your name, anyway?"

Hell—he was in hell. It felt like someone was sitting on his chest. The flashlight was searing his eyes again, and he struggled to hold back his temper. *One. Two. Three.* If Sonny saw him, he'd be locked away forever or shot here and now. He braced himself, knowing what was coming. He could taste the fight in his mouth. His fists tightened, ready to swing, to maul. His entire body craved it, had been craving it his whole life—

And then a voice rang out, high and loud. "Over here!"

Cage whirled, glimpsed a flash of skin in the brush. Was it Mae? His heart picked up, and a split second later he saw her. That neighbor girl, disappearing around a tree trunk, screaming loud.

"Help me!"

Childers bolted toward her, the dog whining, as someone—either Sonny or Lance—shouted out her name, and then there was the sound of them running, crashing through the undergrowth. Cage saw his opening and tore off in the opposite direction, sprinting over rocks and fallen branches as fast as he could go.

A shout came from behind him and he forced his legs harder, his arms pumping, his chest tight, leaves scraping at his skin as he barreled under branches, dodging tree trunks, running blindly now, deeper and deeper into the woods. He knocked into a tree stump and spun and kept going, ignoring the sting at his shin. His chest was tight and burning, but he kept running until he couldn't breathe, until he couldn't feel his legs, and then he stopped and looked back, his lungs heaving for shreds of air.

There was nothing. No footsteps. Nothing.

Cage doubled over, tried to catch his breath. He thought he'd heard them behind him, but now he wasn't sure. Could be they hadn't noticed he'd gone until it was too late.

He paced in a circle, needing to slow his breath so he wasn't gasping so loud. Why had the girl called out like that? She'd done it on purpose. Either that or it was a damn lucky coincidence, had to be. She'd distracted her uncle, Sonny, Lance—she'd saved him.

His legs felt like putty, and one of his eyes was swollen, scratched by a branch. It stung, his whole body did. From somewhere far off, he heard a peal of laughter. It came again: this time sounding more like a wail, a baby's cry. It did his head in—it was a warning.

The sweat on the back of his neck went cold. Up through the dark canopy he saw the broken moon and its icy light shining overhead, and the trees closing him in, corralling him where he didn't belong.

Then he heard footsteps tramping through the woods and he knew to run.

CHAPTER 28

MAE WISHED SHE WAS IN a dream. She stared down at the walnut casket and then shut her eyes so tight there were bursts of color under her lids.

When she opened them, Sonny had his fists welded together as if praying hard enough to hurt. He'd stayed out all night again, showing up at the house just before the burial. Elle stood next to him, her blond streaks swept back, her chin held high and firm.

Watching her sister and her dad fight off tears was easier than looking at the casket, or thinking about what she'd tried with Cage in this very place, or remembering what she'd found afterward. Fern's whisper had been trailing her, haunting her. *Initiation*, she'd said in the truck. Mae had stayed up all night reading the green book, and that was when she found it—that single, incriminating line.

More of Ro's handwriting, next to a sketch of Blue Gate's woods. That single line had felt like a barb as she read it.

*Initiated Lance on his sixteenth, as declared
here. Vow of silence undertaken.*
—RC.

Mae had stared at it for what seemed like an hour, trying to shake off her jealousy. Ro had chosen Lance over everyone—her and Elle and Cage, and even their granddad, who'd wanted the book kept a secret. It felt like a betrayal. And Lance had deceived her too, he'd let her believe that he was kindhearted when really he was a liar. He'd known what the green book was all along. She could only guess what else he'd lied about.

All of it felt worse today, and she didn't want to think about why she was at the cemetery again, so she shut her eyes and thought of that Easter long ago, when she'd followed Ro into the woods. She knew now what Ro had been doing that day—but just before their granddad caught her, someone else had yelled from the trees. Someone else had been there with Ro.

She drew in a sharp breath, the memory taking shape, Ro's black door bursting open.

Lance. It was Lance.

Mae dug her fingernails into her palms and glanced at Childers, standing solemn beside her dad. Even with his head bowed he loomed over everyone, his big hands folded in front of him. He'd said that one of his foals had gone missing that morning, that Lance was coming to the cemetery with Fern after he checked the fences. Mae dug her nails deeper, the pain helping her focus. If Lance showed his face here, she'd confront him. She wasn't nervous anymore, she was hungry for it. She wanted him to show up like he was supposed to; she wanted answers.

"See that?" Childers mumbled to her dad.

Sonny turned his head, staring off at the woods. Mae's heart sped up and she scanned the trees past the fence. Was it Cage?

Beside her, Childers was whispering to Sonny, and her dad's jaw clenched as he looked back at the casket. Mae followed his gaze, the pastor's voice like a tide at her ears. The words she'd heard before, at her sister's funeral, came back. "He that believeth in me, though he were dead, yet shall he live."

Elle mouthed along, reading from the program they'd put together, and Mae felt her fingers twitch. She should paint the burial later, preserve every detail. She should focus on her granddad—this moment, before it slipped by—except her mind was veering out of control, her thoughts wild.

Lance should be here by now, but he wasn't the only one missing.

She lifted her eyes past the casket and searched the woods again. All she saw were trees and the darkening sky. Everything had gotten away from her, yanked out of reach. Cage should have met her at the barn this morning. He hadn't shown, probably because of what she'd said to him. Life was too short to stay quiet, she knew that now. So she'd done it—she'd told him how she felt, that she didn't want him to leave—but it was just one more thing that had gone wrong. She hadn't been able to fix anything. She didn't have a truth about Ro that her dad would believe, and the anniversary of her death was today, which meant she was never coming back. And Mae had been so wrapped up in the green book that she'd let her granddad die alone. She kept playing it out in her mind: How he'd waved to her from the window, wanting her to come up and see him. How she'd ignored him, thinking she could do it later. That was the thing about life—people always assumed there'd be more time. More time to say *hello*, more time to say *I love you*. More time to say *I'm sorry*. Until there wasn't. Now he was shut inside the casket, his freckled hands across his chest, his cane beside him. She stared at the headstones, the lightning tree, the scattered clouds at the horizon. Anywhere except the casket.

A warm breeze was in the air, but she shivered. She squinted at the pastor, who was saying how Grady Deacon Cole VI was the last of his name, a legacy that began over a hundred years ago on this very land. The clouds were darker now, and the pastor kept glancing overhead, as if praying it wouldn't rain. Or maybe he was imagining the upward path of the soul, since no one could say for sure what happened when someone died. Were all thoughts extinguished at the moment of death, or did a person's memories, feelings, all their dreams, continue to roam the world? Maybe those closest to the dead inherited their desires—like a hand-me-down sweatshirt, an old red car, a ring, a book, a lover.

The pastor raised his hands. "Grant unto him eternal rest," he boomed.

"And let perpetual light shine upon him." Elle's voice was loud and fast as she read the response, and Mae glanced down at the program again. The cover had a photo of her granddad as a young man, his blond hair and pale blue eyes shaded by a hat, a little twitch at his mouth like he was trying not to smile. Inside was the passage her dad had picked—"Requiem," a Stevenson poem he said was her granddad's favorite.

> *Under the wide and starry sky*
> *Dig the grave and let me lie:*
> *Glad did I live and gladly die,*
> *And I laid me down with a will.*

He must have taught it to Ro, since she'd recite part of it every time she saw Cage. She could see her sister now, a thumb hooked into her pocket as she leaned against the porch, one long leg bent at the knee, foot resting on opposite shin, flamingo-style, that grin as Cage walked up the drive.

> *This be the verse you 'grave for me:*
> *"Here he lies where he longed to be;*
> *Home is the sailor, home from sea,*
> *And the hunter home from the hill."*

Here he lies where he longed to be. It reminded Mae of what her granddad had written in his letter—to let him rest. Her chest was aching. The coffin lurched on its ropes and her dad stepped forward, his hand raised.

"Now hold up just a minute."

Mae turned toward him. The pastor kept his face composed, but Elle and Childers looked as shocked as she was.

"I brought something," Sonny continued. He stepped to the edge of the plot and grabbed the memory drawer in the lid of the casket. It creaked on its rails as he slid it open. "His Bible," he said. "He never goes anywhere without it." He pulled it out from his suit pocket.

Mae's breath caught and she stepped forward without thinking. His Bible. The one always by his side. The one that'd been on his lap when she'd found him in the attic, the letter clutched in his hand. *The answers you seek can be found in King James.*

She touched her dad's elbow and his face flashed with surprise. She caught the scent of whiskey, it was coming off him in waves.

"May I keep it instead?" she asked, loud enough that he wouldn't be able to ignore her. She could see Elle tense up beside Childers, probably worried Sonny would lose his temper, but she had to know for sure if this was the Bible her granddad meant. "To remember him by," she added. She couldn't think of the last time she'd asked her dad for anything, and she had no idea what he'd do.

For a long moment it seemed like everyone was holding their breath. Her dad was looking at her with confusion in his eyes, Elle's mouth was open just a little, and Childers had his head down, embarrassed for the both of them. The pastor stared at the casket politely, a peaceful expression on his face.

Mae could hardly swallow she was so nervous. She needed that Bible. If her dad refused her, then she'd never know for sure. The answers might be buried with her granddad.

"Well . . ." Sonny cleared his throat. "You always did take care of him, Mae." Her heart lifted, but he set the King James in the drawer and pushed it shut. "I just think it belongs here."

And then the words were out of her mouth and she didn't want to stop them. "I told you I'd like it," she said firmly. "It's important to me."

Before he could protest, she reached into the drawer and pulled out the Bible. Pressing it to her chest, she turned, expecting her dad to yell as she stepped back from the casket. But Sonny only looked at her with raised eyebrows and nodded. "All right," he said. There was a hint of a smile on his face. "He'd like that."

Mae felt a swell of gratitude, her eyes flooding as the coffin lurched again and began to lower. This time there were no protests and no one called out, even though she wanted to with all her heart. She imagined her granddad squeezing her hand, imagined hearing his cane through the hallways when they got home: tap *tap*, tap *tap*. Her eyes felt hot, and when she opened them again the pastor was walking away.

Childers grimaced as he set some flowers by the grave. After he stepped back, Mae heard him whispering into the two-way radio he wore at his hip. There was the sound of a car door slamming, an engine firing up. The burial was over.

"Almost ready," Sonny said to Childers. He lit a cigarette. "You girls doing okay?" His speech slurred, running together, and he swayed closer to them, reeking of smoke. "Let's say our goodbyes and go."

Elle nodded, and Mae remembered the bundle of pink lantanas she'd brought. She took them out of her bag and bent down next to her granddad's grave. When she looked up, she glimpsed movement at the edge of the trees.

A shadow. Someone was crouched behind a nearby bush.

She waited, holding still. It was Cage, it had to be. He'd finally come to say goodbye. She stayed kneeling, her legs going watery. Her granddad's Bible was still in her hand, but she couldn't look at it yet, not here. Her palms felt sweaty and cold at the same time.

Sonny nodded toward the grave and then walked a few paces away, stopping next to Childers. "Find out who it was last night?" she heard him ask. "And Fern," he said, stomping out his cigarette and lighting up another one, "what was that all about?"

Mae scrambled to her feet, didn't risk glancing toward the trees again.

"Just crying wolf." Childers let out a sigh as the radio on his belt crackled. "If it was him last night like Lance thought, we'll get him."

Mae's stomach tensed. If Cage had almost been caught by Childers and Lance, then—

"Get who?" Elle asked, lowering the phone she'd been using as a mirror.

Both men turned to her. The knot in Mae's stomach twisted tighter. Fern had said she knew secrets, so maybe she knew about Cage too. And now she wasn't here, and neither was Lance.

Sonny shook his head. "Don't worry about it," he said gruffly. "You two ride with us to the house."

"But I've got my car here." Elle gave him a pointed look. "Are you going to tell us what's going on?"

"Later, if there's something worth telling." He ground out his cigarette slowly, like he was thinking. "Drive back with Mae, but go straight home."

Elle was already heading toward the parking lot. "Fine," she huffed. Mae had no choice but to follow her. It had to be Cage she'd seen in the woods, watching them. Surely he knew to keep his distance right now. Her granddad's Bible nearly slipped from her hands and she wiped her palms on her shirt and then got into the car.

It was warm inside, the air thick, pooling like stagnant water. Mae rolled down the window, took in a breath. Out of the corner of her eye she saw Elle fiddling with her phone. "I've got a bar," she said, staring at the screen. "Give me a minute."

Ahead, their dad's truck shot off down the road, fishtailing and sending up dust, Childers's dog tied up in the back. Mae turned away from Elle and opened the Bible.

Genesis stared back at her. *In the beginning, God created the heaven and the earth.*

No, no, no. She needed it to be something more. She didn't know what she was looking for, but it wasn't this. She slammed the book shut and then stifled a gasp. Just past the opening section were a series of yellowed pages, the gilding on the edge stripped away. Her pulse quickened as she flipped to that section. Instead of print, there was handwriting.

She stared at the pages, her heart skidding in her chest. It was the missing part of the green book. Her granddad had sewn it into the spine of his King James.

She glanced over at Elle. Her phone was pressed to her ear, her fingers drumming against the steering wheel as a number rang. Mae looked back at the hidden section in the Bible. *January 1860* was written on the page she'd turned to. It seemed like a journal; each entry was dated. She scanned the writing, faster now, but there were only the entries—no rituals—so she turned all the way back to the beginning. To the page she'd missed a moment ago. The page directly after Genesis.

Chana 4 chana, it said at the top. Her heart leaped into her throat. *Chana*. The word she'd seen everywhere—in the house, on the ring, in the ritual, and now in this hidden part of the book.

Right below the phrase was a sketch she recognized. It resembled the one in the attic tunnel, only it was slightly different this time. A transparent woman in a dress was rising toward the moon. She was hovering over the ground where another figure stood, this one darker, more solid, alive. And next to this figure was someone else, someone who hadn't been part of the drawing in the tunnel. It was a third woman, only she was lying on the ground, like she was sleeping or—

The car engine revved up, startling Mae. Hot air blew out of the vents and she coughed and slid the Bible to her side so her sister wouldn't see it.

"I know what you're doing," Elle said as she pulled away. Mae eyed her warily; she didn't know what to say. "You're never around anymore," her sister accused, glaring out the windshield. The iron gate was behind them, the dirt road winding into the trees ahead. "You're keeping things from me."

Mae didn't want to lie, but she couldn't tell the truth either. "Is that why you've been distant lately?" she asked, stalling.

"I've been distant?" Elle asked. "*I've* been distant? I don't believe this." She shook her head. "No, I've been mad. Because *you've* been distant."

Mae knew she should explain, but now wasn't the time. "It's going to rain," she said instead. "Looks like a sto—"

A shadow leaped in front of the car and Elle shrieked, swerving and hitting the brakes all at once. There was a loud crack and the sound of metal crumpling as something dark swung up onto the hood with a force. Mae pitched forward, the belt searing her waist as the windshield smashed in, spraying glass. A black hoof came right at her face, barely missing her head.

The car rocked to a stop and the deer fell forward, sliding off the hood to the ground. For a moment there was silence, both of them staring in shock, and then Mae's breath was back and she could move—her hands were fumbling with her seat belt.

"Is it? Did I . . . ?" Elle started. She was rigid in her seat, looking at the broken windshield and the smear of blood. There were small scratches across her cheeks and forehead, but otherwise she seemed fine.

Mae threw open the door and ran around the car. She knelt down beside the deer, taking its head in her hands, watching its lungs going fast as it panted, a shard of glass in its neck. Its heartbeat thudded against her, echoed inside her, fainter and fainter.

"Mae?" It was Elle, her hand was on Mae's shoulder. "Is it dead?"

The deer was warm and heavy and trembling, and Mae couldn't move. Part of her wanted to shut everything away behind the black door in her mind, keep the pain at bay, but that wouldn't stop the deer from dying. The clouds threw shadows over the blood on the ground and she felt a thrumming in her body, a tingling down her neck that told her to look closer. She remembered touching Ro's body when Lance had carried her to the house. That brief moment of hope when she thought she was only asleep in his arms. But Ro's hair had been wet, the water running in rivulets—in blood-red ribbons down her back. And now this animal was bleeding, the life seeping out of it. It looked like the deer in the cemetery last night, the one that had appeared after the ritual. The same deer she'd almost thought was Ro . . .

"Did I kill it?" Elle asked.

Mae didn't answer. This was the deer that she'd thought was Ro—she'd mistaken it for her sister, raised from the dead. Somehow, that was important. She thought of the shrine with the four animals in the pantry, that phrase scrawled on the floor. *Chana 4 Chana.* The same phrase had been written in the book, next to a row of equivalents. $RC = AC, J = E, H = GCI.$

Her mind was racing. They were initials, maybe? RC could stand for Rose Cole, except she didn't know who AC was. But GCI, that could be Grady Cole I, and H could stand for Hanna. Grady Cole I equals Hanna? The answer evaded her, swirling in her head like smoke and dissipating, and she thought of the engraving on the ring. *Your chana is my life.* Her heart was going fast now, she felt like she might faint. She heard Elle calling her name, but she sounded far away.

Mae looked into the deer's dark eye and thought of the sketch in King James. The ghost rising up toward the moon, and the two women below it. One of them standing, one of them lying on the ground. Her arms tightened around the deer. When she'd first seen the charcoal sketch in the tunnel, she'd thought the figure that was floating was the one being raised, but maybe the ghostly woman was coming down, entering a body again. *The answers you seek can be found in King James.* The ghost was forming into flesh, while another body bled out on the ground.

Mae sucked in a breath. That was why the ritual hadn't worked last night. She squeezed her eyes shut, trying to remember everything Cage had recited. *Then save the most brutal for last: chana for a life, since all should be equal.*

She hadn't known what it meant. That word—*chana*—that was the missing piece. *Chana 4 chana.* A woman alive, a woman dead and bleeding. Human life for human life.

The deer's blood was slick in her hands and she stared at the shard of glass in its neck. That was why her grand-dad had split the green book in two. He knew, when Ro inherited the book, that she'd be suspicious if the raising ritual wasn't in it. He knew she'd remember it from when she'd stolen the book as a child. He hadn't wanted her to try it again, not in its entirety—so he'd halved the book and halved the ritual, rendering it harmless. Except Ro and Lance had remembered it anyway, her sister hiding a copy under the gift cherub. Mae could see it all unfolding, all of the grisly colors interweaving, all of the things her granddad had been afraid of.

She gently set the deer's head on the ground as Elle hovered, her phone out. "Why won't you get up, Mae? What should we do with it?" Her sister crouched down and grabbed her shoulders. "You're in shock, aren't you? You're all covered in blood." And then Mae thought of Lance, how Ro had initiated him. He'd always followed Ro around, did everything she did, hung on her every word. He'd do anything to have her back, but he'd need a human life. He'd need—

Fern.

Fern had said that Lance's secret would come true today on the beach. The day of Ro's anniversary. The last day to bring her back.

Mae's heart seized. If Lance knew the ritual, he wouldn't give up. He'd tried it before, she was certain now. But his earlier rituals had been powerless because he hadn't known what *chana* meant. Maybe he'd finally figured it out, just like she had. Lance, the initiate. Lance, who was in love with Ro—who'd do anything for her. He'd said so himself.

And then Mae could move and she scrambled to her feet, wiping her palms on her jeans. "Elle, hand me that." Her sister glanced down at the deer, and when she did Mae tugged away the phone. "I'll meet you back at the house," she said, and then turned and started sprinting.

"Hey!" Elle called out. "Where are you going? Dad wants us home; we've got to—"

But there wasn't time to fill her in, not now, so Mae kept running into the woods, heading toward the beach. Her ears were ringing, and all around her the leaves seemed to flutter in the wind so that everything had a green shine to it, a blurry green shine as she ran. The back of her neck was tingling and she felt cold, a chill was all through her, and she knew she had to hurry. Fern was in danger.

Then, just ahead, there he was—stepping out from behind a tree.

CHAPTER 29

THE WIND FLOGGED CAGE'S EARS as he sprinted through the woods with Mae. As soon as she'd told him about Fern and Lance, he'd known where to go. The dock. The *dock*. Lance would take the girl to the place on the beach where Ro died, he was sure of it. Adrenaline spurred him forward and he heard Mae right behind him, trying to keep up.

It'll be okay, that was what he wanted to tell her, but how did you ever know? He hadn't known he'd be too scared to meet her this morning after almost getting caught last night. But he hadn't been able to leave Blue Gate without seeing her either, so he'd watched the burial from a distance. And when he saw her running his way, he knew he'd stayed for a reason.

He picked up speed, heading toward the dock. The wind funneled through the trees with a moan, a drawn-out cry. A gust swirled around them, thrashing them, and he pushed himself harder. Christ, what was Lance going to do?

One, two, three, Cage chanted as he ran, *four, five, almost there, six, seven, almost there*—and just as he made it to the beach, cold pellets of rain began to fall. The bay was choppier than he'd ever seen it. No seagulls, no boats, no people, no girl.

He ran out onto the sand, launched himself over the dunes, Mae right behind him. The summer storm was in full force now, the rain pouring down on them, onto the waves—pockmarking the water and swirling it into whitewash. Where were they, *where?*

Then, ahead, something hunched on the dock. Something dark. Mae saw it too and gasped, and then they were both sprinting faster, running out onto the planks, and the dark hunch was Lance. He was twisting, looking over his shoulder, and in his arms was something limp—*Fern?*

Mae yelled, and he threw the girl over the edge as Cage lunged forward, his fist already rearing back on instinct. It slammed into Lance's head and down he went, crumpling to the dock.

"There she is!" Mae shouted.

He turned, scanned the waves, only whitewash and dark water and rain. She'd drown if they didn't find her, it could already be too late, and then he saw something gold—*there!*—and he dived in. The water was a shock, and he kicked out hard. When he broke the surface, there was something ahead.

It was her.

He swam as fast as he could, swallowed a mouthful of ocean, and spit it out and kept going. There she was again, her blond hair in the choppy water, sinking down, down. He sped up his stroke and his shoulders burned and the rain stung and just as he almost reached her, her body jerked away. His first thought was *current*—she'd gotten caught in a current.

Cage took a huge breath and went under, looking for her, reaching for her, but the water was dark and churning. Then, just ahead, another glint of gold hair and he grabbed it and felt nothing but water. He kicked forward and reached out again and suddenly remembered Ro, the blood he hadn't wanted to see, and then his screaming lungs drew him out of the memory, his ribs about to burst, his legs kicking up just as something fleshy moved past him—*the girl!* It was her, Fern, and her eyes were closed and he needed to breathe. He reached out with the last of his strength, flinging his hand toward her in one desperate grasp, everything inside him needing air, and then his fingers tangled in hair and he grabbed hold and kicked.

He broke the surface and gasped in a deep breath, yanking her up. He had her now, but her eyes were still shut and her lips had gone blue and he hurried to lift her against his side. With his arm tucked underneath her, he craned his neck, tried to gauge how far he was from shore. Mae was still standing on the dock, Lance lying beside her. Cage kicked harder, faster, choking in the whitewash, the swell from the storm lifting him up and spitting him out. His ribs smacked hard against the pilings as he grabbed the edge of a plank with his free hand and hoisted the girl up. He went under and then managed to grab the dock again and pull himself after her.

His knees hit the planks and a cough racked his body and then he turned. Mae was bent over Fern, rolling her onto her back and starting chest compressions—*one two three four*—and next to them was Lance, still passed out, one of his arms hanging over the edge of the dock. Cage felt like kicking him into the water, but first there was Fern.

Mae worked fast, pinching the girl's nose, breathing into her mouth, and then waiting. *Live*, Cage thought, desperate to see her chest rise. There was nothing, and he knew they were too late, but he didn't want to believe it.

"Live!" he shouted as Mae leaned down to breathe into the girl's mouth again, and suddenly Fern began to cough. Now her chest was rising and falling on its own, but her eyes stayed shut—something else was wrong.

Mae stood, pulled a phone from her pocket. "There's no signal," she said, her voice lost in the wind as she pounded at the screen, huddling over it to keep the rain out.

Cage's body tensed but there was no choice, no time to think—they needed help and they had to get away from Lance.

"The house." He bent down, heaved Fern into his arms, and started forward, half stumbling over the wet planks, Mae behind him. They hit the woods, just a little farther now.

"Fern," Cage said, looking down at her as he ran. "Fern?" She coughed up more water, but her eyes stayed

337

shut. He kept on, the extra weight slowing him down, the weakness still from when he'd gotten sick. "It'll be okay," he said, because he wanted it to be true. "It'll be okay."

His legs were burning and the girl was heavy, and he looked down and saw *her*; he was carrying Ro, her body in his arms, the sticky wetness of her hair.

"It's okay," someone whispered, "it's okay," and then Cage blinked and he was holding the girl. He ran forward, branches scratching against his face, the wind and rain flaying him. All of a sudden he remembered that day on the boat, and he could see it now, how Ro was standing across from him, on the other side of the deck, and how there was a jingling sound, like glass breaking, or like . . . *keys?* Then she was stepping back and slipping, and—

"Cage!"

It was Mae, she was ahead of him now, she'd passed him in the yard. Behind her the tall house rose up like some bluish thing in the sky, and everything inside him shrank back.

"No," Fern moaned in his arms, but her eyes were still shut, so he kept going forward, straight for the house, for Mae, for help. He ran faster and the wind pushed against him, and then he heard footsteps behind him, something jingling, but there was no time to see what it was because Mae was running inside the house now and he had to follow her. He stumbled and looked down at Fern, at her little round face, and she was enough to propel him through the yard, past the fountain and the beech trees flailing in the rain and Sonny's blue truck in the driveway.

He could feel the girl's chest rising and falling, quick and shallow, and then he remembered holding Ro on the beach and the last thing she'd said to him. A breath came out of her mouth that she never got to finish, a long drawn-out *Caaaaaaaaaaa* . . . and that was it. He'd pulled her against him, but she was already gone—

"Dad, stop!"

Cage jerked his head up and saw Mae standing by the open door. He hesitated a split second, and then time snapped back full speed and his legs wrenched into motion as he charged onto the porch and burst through the doorway.

Her dad was there, pointing a rifle at him, and Mae stepped in front of it, just like she'd done before. "Get out of the way!" Sonny shouted, but she wasn't moving and neither was Cage.

He heard the sound of dripping and realized it was him—the rain was running down his clothes and onto the wooden floor, the water puddling under his feet, and he could feel it everywhere, in his bones, his head, his mouth, but now he had to talk, he had to.

He held out Fern. "She needs help, sir."

Sonny's rifle was still trained his way, Mae blocking its path. "Give her to Mae."

"Dad, put the gun down!" she yelled. "He didn't do it!"

"Give her to Mae," Sonny repeated. "*Now.*"

Mae shook her head. "I called the ambulance, it's on the way. Set the gun down."

"Move!" Sonny shouted. Cage could tell he was losing it, and had to do something.

"Here," Cage said, holding out the girl. "She's breathing fine, just hasn't woken up."

Mae stepped toward him, her arms open. He handed Fern over and then raised his hands. Sonny's trigger finger tightened.

"But Cage saved her," Mae pleaded, trying to step in front of the gun again. "Lance was—"

A gust of air hit Cage's back as the door swung open behind him. Someone was standing just out of sight. He couldn't turn to look, not with Sonny staring down a rifle at him. Cage tried to keep calm, but his heart felt like it was emptying rounds in his chest and he knew he was trapped.

Mae was shaking her head, tears in her eyes. "Dad, he—"

"He did it, Mr. Cole." A lower voice now, interrupting Mae. "He killed Ro, and he tried to hurt Fern too."

It was Lance behind him; he must have followed them back to the house. There was no time to explain now, no chance of being heard. He was cornered, no way out.

"Dad, please listen to me!" Mae begged. "Lance did this!"

Sonny kept the rifle raised. "Don't move," he said. "Either of you."

"Mr. Cole," Lance started again. Cage heard the creak

of a floorboard as he closed in on his back. "Whatever he tol—"

"You got to help her," Cage said, his fists tightening. He glanced at Mae's arms. Fern seemed to be asleep on her shoulder, her ribs stuttering under her thin T-shirt.

"He's dangerous, Mr. Cole," Lance said, sounding so sure of himself.

"No, Dad," Mae said, "he's—"

"But I *saw* it." An edge in Lance's voice now. "I saw what he did to Ro."

Anger was welling up in Cage, threatening to escape. He wanted to spin around and flatten Lance, pound his lying mouth, show him what to be afraid of. He sucked in a deep breath, let it out. *One, two, three, four,* and then on five it hit him.

"Sir, it's true," Cage said, "he *did* see it." Mae sucked in a breath beside him, but he kept going. Sonny's face hardened, and he aimed the barrel at his chest.

"Lance was there, watching her from the trees, like he always was." As he said it, it all clicked into place. The jingle of keys the moment before Ro fell, the sound of *Lance's* keys. He'd been there all along. "He *saw* that I didn't kill her, that it was an accident."

"Liar," Lance said, taking another step forward. "You *ran.*"

"Hold still, both of you!" Sonny's grip strained around the rifle.

"Listen to Cage, Dad," Mae pleaded. "He's innocent, I know it."

341

"You're just confused, Mae," Lance said. "He's tricked you. Just like he tricked Ro into falling for him. This is all his fault."

"*Enough*," Sonny said, his dark gaze boring into Cage. "Now talk. *You*."

"I know it was wrong to run," Cage said, looking Sonny in the eye, his teeth clenched to keep from shouting, "but I got scared and—"

The screech of sirens drowned him out. Doors slammed in the driveway, and then footsteps were pounding up the stairs. Sonny kept the gun on him as the shove came at his back, knocking him to his knees. Next came a pull on his wrists, the snap of flex cuffs. Someone behind him hauled him to his feet and pushed him through the open door.

Cage shut his eyes. Rain hit his face, wind whipped against him—it was slow going toward the cruiser in the driveway. Every muscle in his body ached and the wind tunneled around his ears. He was thrown into a cop car, the door slamming shut, the lock clicking. He turned and watched Childers hustle back to the porch, where the ambulance crew had Fern on a stretcher.

Behind her, red lights flashed across the windows of the house, across its painted walls. Rain thrashed down on it, water ran down its sides, and it looked to Cage like a sinking ship. This house that maybe—way back when—one of his ancestors had come from, and now he wasn't welcome here. Not before, not ever.

A shadow fell across the window, and he glanced over. It was Lance, leaning against the vehicle, rain soaking him. Cage snapped up straight in his seat. The adrenaline was back, and he strained against the cuffs, the hard plastic digging into his skin.

"You know the truth."

"Some of it," Lance drawled out, his voice muffled through the glass and the rain. His gaze was on the ambulance loading up, the cops talking to Sonny and Mae on the porch. There was the sound of a bolt clicking as Lance opened the driver's-side door.

"I know it's your fault," Lance said, and Cage could hear him clearly now. "She's dead because you couldn't save her."

"Come back here." The rage was hot inside him, and Cage kicked the seats, jolting them forward. "Come back here and settle this."

Lance shook his head. "She would have been safer with me," he said, turning away and jogging over to the ambulance.

Cage yelled when he saw him get into the back. He threw himself against the door and the grate and yelled again, but no one turned to look at him. No one saw Lance get in behind Fern, no one was watching but him.

Ro, help her, he thought, shouting out again as the ambulance drove away. And then the side door was opening, and the wind hit him in the face. Mae was reaching for him, dragging him across the wet seat and out of the car, into the rain, his wrists still cuffed behind his back.

"You've got to go," she said, grabbing his elbow, shoving a small knife in his hand. "*Go!*"

He spun toward the house, but the porch was empty. The door was wide open, but no one was there, like some magic veil had been pulled down, like Ro had played one final trick. Mae tugged at his arm, but he shook his head, his legs locking up.

"Lance went with Fern," he said, but she didn't hear him, she was still yanking him away from the house, begging him to run, and then came the blast that thundered in his ears and he was falling, the gravel rising up in front of him, and Mae was falling too.

EPILOGUE

MAE'S ARM WAS SWEATY IN its sling as she turned away from the headstone. Sonny and Elle were already past the gate and making their way home. Her sister spun around, her lipstick bright enough to see, her hair chopped short, all the blond growing out. "You coming or what?"

Mae waved with her good arm, the one she hadn't landed on when her dad had shot Cage and they'd fallen together, hand in hand. "Right behind you," she called out.

Elle strode forward, catching up to Sonny, his neck sunburned from their fishing trip. Their first and last before the school year started, but they'd already planned another one—Elle beat them three fish to zero, and she wanted to win again. There was time for fishing now, since the reporters had finally lost interest in Blue Gate. In all the publicity over Fern's near death, someone from the city council had come to the house and declared it a historical landmark. It'd been something good in the news instead of all the stories about Lance.

Lance had surprised Mae as much as anyone else. He eventually told his dad that he'd gotten in the back of the ambulance to make sure Fern stayed quiet for good. But she woke up from the pills he'd given her—the ones he got from her mother's supply—and he realized he couldn't do it. Not when she was blinking up at him, asking questions. It had been easier when she'd been asleep at the dock, he said. When his dad had pressed him, he claimed that something had made him try to drown her. Said he didn't believe in ghosts, but that when he took her down to the water, he thought he was doing it for Ro. That he loved Roxanne Cole more than anyone and always would.

Mae knew the last part had gotten to her dad the most, though he was trying not to hold it against Childers, who came over every day to apologize for his son. Because Fern had told everyone her cousin's secret when she woke up. That Lance had asked if she wanted to go to sleep and see Ro again. He hadn't denied much; he'd even mentioned the green book—something he described as an old book of rituals that belonged to Ro. By talking of magic, Lance probably hoped to get a psychiatric examination instead of spending the rest of high school in jail. Either way, he wouldn't be around Blue Gate next year.

Mae touched Ro's grave and then turned and started down the path. The iron gate creaked as she pushed it open, its metal wet because it had rained again that morning. A humid dampness was rising in the woods, the smell of rotting leaves and new green shoots, that sharp stench of life and decay. When her arm healed, she might paint this: the moment after a storm, the little muddy path leading out of the cemetery.

She ducked past a low branch and shivered, shoved her good hand deeper into her thin pocket. Her Cons squelched in the mud, but she kept going, ignoring the tingle at her neck. It felt like someone was watching her, but it wasn't Lance, and it wasn't Cage. It couldn't be him. She looked over her shoulder and then stepped off the trail and headed deeper into the woods. There was one last place she needed to go today, one last thing to be done. She would do it for him—she had to.

Mae walked until she heard the creek. Soon enough the trees opened into a clearing, the one with the stretch of kudzu and the old cement dome. The graves it shaded were still covered by vines, except for where the edge of a stone peeked out from the carpet of green.

Mae strode forward, careful not to trip this time. When she got to Hanna's grave, she opened her bag and pulled out a bundle of wildflowers, setting it down by the small headstone. Hanna had given her life for her child, for her children's children. For Cage. Everything she had was taken from her, her grave hidden by the very earth itself. But soon the historical society would find out—they'd dig into Hanna's history, into the Cage Shaw family link, as they should. Until then she'd keep the secret. Keep this place green and wild and quiet, just the way it was now.

Mae looked over her shoulder again but didn't see anyone. The sharp tingling at her neck was still there as she knelt down and used the trowel she'd brought to dig away the vines. After a few minutes, she'd cleared a small section of ground so there was only a round circle of earth at her feet. Then she pulled the book from her bag and untied the ribbon, fighting off the ache in her chest.

For a moment she closed her eyes and stood there, with the weight of the book in her hands and the necklace hanging over her heart. On a thin chain was Ro's gold locket and Cage's family ring—he'd asked her to keep it safe until he came back. She thought of what he'd told her, right before he left: that she was going to do something big one day, something people would remember. That he would always remember what she did for him. But unless he'd read the green book to the end, the half that her granddad had hidden away, he didn't know there was one last thing remaining.

She glanced over at the cement dome, wanting to see him standing there. His dark hair, the tiny cut near his temple, his pale eyes. He'd already left the state, gone to visit his mom. He said she was sick and he hadn't been to see her in a while. By this time he should have gotten to her house, should already be on his way back like he'd promised.

Mae stared down at the green book she was holding, at the etching on its leather cover. Two coffins, side by side, so the dead would never be lonely. There'd be no more raising anyone, no more enduring eternally on earth. And there'd be no more suffering for those who'd been raised, she'd make sure of it.

Because she had to. She'd read the book from cover

348

to cover, the first part and the last, and she knew what needed to be done. She'd read Grady's account of his life with Hanna and all he'd learned from watching her, all the rituals he'd written down with good intentions, to make the magic his. He'd seen the impossible happen at Blue Gate, and he'd tried to re-create it. Hanna had raised his mother when his day-old sister, Amelia, died. She'd raised his brother Jacob too, on the night Miss Etta died of a cold. But Hanna had never intended for the ritual to be passed on to those who didn't understand its power. Both Grady's mother and Jacob had suffered from walking between worlds, and they'd wished for nothing but peace, to go home.

Mae let out a deep breath and forced herself to open the book. A sudden breeze caught its pages and they fluttered and then settled, landing right where she needed them to. She stared down at them and felt her throat tighten. She wanted to go back to Blue Gate without doing it, she wanted to see him again. How was making things right so hard? But this was the only way to set him free, she knew that now. He deserved this much. She fumbled in her bag, found the beads and the bundle of herbs wrapped in muslin. She lit the dried sage like the ritual instructed, inhaling its smoke.

"Putting to rest," she started, and then swallowed down the knot in her throat. She wiped at her face, surprised to find it wet. She looked down at the page again, at the drops of tears staining it. "Putting to rest the raised," she said, louder this time, and she thought of him. She thought of Cage and her sister, and her granddad, and Hanna too, and Pearl and Grady, and her mother. They were all swirling in her mind and her eyes were hot and stinging, but she made herself read the next line, her fingers working over the beads with every breath. She kept going, faster now, so fast she wouldn't stop, the words tumbling into each other, all the way down to the end of the page. When she finished, she dropped the book; she was shaking.

Before she could change her mind, she pulled the tinder from her bag and placed it on the ground to make the firebed. Then she struck a match and held it beside the book, watching the flame lick the paper. It crackled and spit, and heat rose from it.

She stared at the fire as it took hold next to Hanna's grave, and then she turned away, the brightness behind her. She could feel the power of it, calling her back. But Grady's obsession with raising the dead would end with her; it wouldn't be passed down to anyone else.

Mae didn't want to look at the book burning, so we watched for her—just as we watch her now on the path back to Blue Gate. She's wiping the soot from her hands and she has a sudden longing for her paints and canvas, to create something. She'll start with Cage on the sailboat with Ro. Her granddad holding the stray black cat. And then it all seems too much—it feels as though her heart has been torn in two. But the heart is resilient and can grow back over time, stronger than before. Mae will find solace in her paints and her family; they're waiting for her on the porch, they're looking toward the woods and calling her name. She has almost found her way home, and she hopes Cage has too.

Right now he's on the highway, going west, a paper map spread on the seat beside him. He's late to visit his mother because his headache got so bad he had to pull over. Now he's on his way again, heading to her apartment in New Orleans, and it's one of the hardest things he's ever done. He doesn't want to smell the cat shit, see the dishes overflowing in the sink, or meet her new boyfriend, but what he really doesn't want to see are those pill bottles of hers, the way they make her angry. She's angry that she's sick, always has been. The sickness has made her mean, but he's been mean too. He gave up on her, even though she's still alive, battling through her pain like she battles everything in life, never believing in even a shred of magic. He won't say he's sorry for moving out, because he's not, but he can at least say hello, tell her she doesn't have to worry about him anymore. He'll start with hello and see what happens. Trace his steps home.

Cage yanks down the visor and squints into the sunlight. Next gas station he sees, he'll pick up a pair of sunglasses. He'll take another round of painkillers too, because his head is hurting again in a bad way and so is his shoulder. He lifts a hand from the ratty wheel and feels the bandage. It's dry but still tender.

The road curves, and when it straightens again an exit sign comes into view, a side road heading off into the trees. Tempting, but he'll wait till the needle's low. Part of him wants to turn off, head south toward Mexico, work as a fisherman down there for a while. Save up some money to pay back the people he owes and then some.

The tires hum over the pavement and he lets himself think of Mexico, how no one will know him. They won't know where he comes from, won't know about his family, about his record, about the things that have been said and unsaid about him. But Mexico doesn't hold a candle to Mae. Maybe he can work for his uncle in Gulf Shores instead, finish up his last year of high school and visit her now and again. Her dad even apologized to him for getting it wrong. Can't blame him, not really, though he didn't have to shoot him in the driveway. Lucky Sonny's more a fisherman than a hunter, because the shot went wide, just got him in the shoulder. Another scar, but that's okay with him.

Earlier this week, when they released him from the hospital and he told Mae he needed to go home, she and Elle let him borrow their car. He didn't want to take it, but they asked him to. Sonny's exact words were *Don't make me shoot you again, son.* Followed by maybe his first smile, ever. Thinking about it now makes Cage grin, and so does thinking about Mae. He remembers how she hugged him before he left. Her not-quite-blond hair, her brown eyes looking up at him. The softness of her lips on his cheek as she stood on her tiptoes to kiss him goodbye.

His head starts aching again, and he lifts a hand to rub his temples. He picks up his water bottle and pours the last of it over himself. The coolness hits his neck and wets his shirt, but the pain doesn't go away. He squints at the sun and sees splotches of light across the road. It comes over him all at once, and he shoves on his blinker and pulls onto the gravel shoulder. The ballerina hanging from the rearview mirror jostles as he stops.

Breathe, breathe. He squeezes his eyes shut and hunches over the wheel, wanting the pain to pass. But it's worse now—a tire-iron sort of headache, all the way into his spine. Fresh air, that's what he needs. He pushes open the door and staggers to the side of the road, steps over the guardrail. Throws up on the gravel, onto the grassy slope beyond. Throws up again, clutching the hot metal rail. The pain feels like it's splitting his skull, and behind him is the beep of the open car door. Maybe he just needs to sleep it off. He can get into the backseat, close his eyes. *One, two, three. Breathe.* Get back to the car.

He tries to straighten, but another wave of sickness rushes him and his knees buckle, hitting the gravel, and when he stands back up he loses his balance and then the world tips and he's sliding down the grass. He shuts his eyes, feels branches snapping past him and small bushes that he grabs at and a rock hits his shoulder and he yells out and then the ground levels and he tumbles to a stop.

He groans and rolls onto his knees, opens his eyes. His arms and legs seem to be moving, so he hasn't broken anything, but his shoulder bandage is torn off and he's bleeding. He forces himself to look around, get his bearings. Tree trunks swirl above him and sunlight cuts through green leaves and he shuts his eyes, collapses back onto the dirt. He'll lie here for a minute. Just a quick minute. But sometimes in life, minutes have a way of turning into hours, and then days, and then . . .

"Cage," he hears, and his eyes snap open. The green canopy churns above him, far, far above him.

"Cage."

Is someone saying his name?

His mouth is dry, and he tries to lick his lips. Starts to get up but can't. He feels heavy, his limbs like sludge, and when a shadow falls across him he stares up at it, trying to focus.

His heart nearly stops. Actually, it's already stopped, but he doesn't know that yet.

"Cage," she says, and her smile gets him in the chest. Her hair dangles down, blocking some of the light, so it's easy to keep his eyes open, straight on her. He won't look away, even if the pain kills him, but he won't be feeling any of that anymore.

She holds out her hand. He thinks he must be dreaming, he must, because they all think that at first. He reaches up to touch her hand and his headache disappears all at once—it goes away and his pain goes away and the memories rush from him too, into something vaster, a bay emptying into an ocean, into endless water, and for a moment, this one long moment, the only thing he can feel is her.

This time it's easier, much easier, to take him home.

ACKNOWLEDGMENTS

Writing a novel is a lot like holding up a match in the dark, hoping you'll find a path. And the path of this book was lit by some extraordinary people along the way.

Catherine Drayton, thank you for your belief in my work, and for your wisdom, advice, and persistence. I am so grateful to have you and everyone at InkWell Management in my corner.

Many heartfelt thanks to my brilliant editor, Krista Marino. *The Breathless* wouldn't be the same without your insight, guidance, and enthusiasm at all the perfect moments. I must have done something right in my life to be working with you.

To the entire team at Random House Children's Books—Beverly Horowitz, Monica Jean, Jen Prior, Colleen Fellingham, Alison Kolani, Alison Impey—thank you for your support and amazingness.

My deepest gratitude to early readers of *The Breathless*, especially Mark Harding, Lucas Southworth, Peter

Durston, Nancy Winifred Pullin, Paul Shirley, David Irwin, Tim Croft, Brian Buckbee, Candace and Tod Evans, and my family.

Countless thanks to my writing soul mates for the encouragement and attentive eyes and ears. Caroline Graham, I will always want to be your conjoined twin. Here's to singing (badly) on the road from Darwin to Kununurra, where it all started. You, my friend, are a gift in so many ways. Shady Cosgrove, thank you for the Red Door retreats, endless conversations about writing that inevitably led to dancing, and for all the very "serious" fun.

Merlinda Bobis, thank you for your solidarity and sharpness on the page. Steve Pett, you're one of the best; I will always remember your class. Page Buck, for teaching me that hard work is worth more than talent. William Pierce and Sven Birkerts, *AGNI* was the first to publish one of my stories, which gave me hope. Michael Martone, Kate Bernheimer, Wendy Rawlings, Catherine Cole, Joshua Lobb, thank you. And to the University of Alabama, the University of Wollongong, and Varuna, The Writers' House, for allowing me the time and space to write.

Many thanks to my friends, past and present, for your encouragement over the years and across the continents. You all know who you are.

Special thanks to Hank Spangler, my oldest friend; Courtney Parker, Kristin Irwin, and Katie O'Neill, my musketeers; Joel Naoum, Sophie Hamley, Anna Valdinger,

Emma Rafferty, for showing me Sydney publishing; Christine Lindon, for your faith in me; Sean Ottley, for making me laugh; Rosemary Lewey, Paula Sue Burnum Hayes, for your stories about Alabama; Jane Sandor, Lauren Choplin, Nick Parker, Danielle Evans, for your magic; Kerry Kletter, Heather Lazare, Shelly King, for welcoming me into the book crowd in California; Katherine Kendall, for the impromptu author photo; and to my Momentum friends and fellow writers in the 2017 Debuts, and every author I've admired since reading my first book. You all inspire me in ways you probably don't even realize.

Thank you to my entire family, for putting up with me, and for reading, and reading some more. Somehow I scored the best parents and brothers in the world. Thanks also to the Lenths, Porrases, Witczaks, Kiffs, Stumps, Lords, Krauses, Smiths, Lindseys, and Goedjens. And all of my heart to Jack, for being my champion, and to our daughter, Cora. I am blessed in so many ways to have you in my life.

Lastly, many thanks to my readers. This book wouldn't exist without you.

ABOUT THE AUTHOR

Tara Goedjen grew up in the South and has a Master of Fine Arts from the University of Alabama. *The Breathless* is her debut novel. To find out more about Tara and her novel, follow @TaraGoedjen on Twitter.